THE BLACK SPRING
CURATED BY EDITOR LUCA VESTE

Praised and endorsed by some of the biggest names in Crime Fiction...

'Time to strap yourself in.' - **IAN RANKIN**

'I love, love, love great new crime fiction. How do I find it? Usually I ask my friend Luca Veste. I owe him hundreds of hours of great reading. Now he's doing it for real, not just for me - he's working with Black Spring Press, which means they're going to have a crime list that everyone will get excited about. Luca Veste is our genre's best talent spotter - Black Spring Press will be one to watch.' - **LEE CHILD**

'I know nobody with their finger more acutely on the pulse of crime fiction. I value his recommendations; they show a great eye for what's worth my reading time.' - **VAL MCDERMID**

'Nobody knows more about the world of crime fiction than Luca Veste. Most importantly of all, he knows a great crime novel when he sees one.' - **MARK BILLINGHAM**

CAST NO SHADOW

CAST NO SHADOW
A YAZ MOY NOVEL

NICK QUANTRILL

This edition published in 2025
By The Black Spring Crime Series
Black Spring Press
An imprint of Eyewear Publishing Ltd.
The Black Spring Press Group
London, United Kingdom

Cover design by Juan Padrón
Typeset by Subash Raghu
Printed and bound by Short Run Press Ltd, Exeter EX2 7LW

All rights reserved
© 2025 Nick Quantrill

ISBN 978-1-915406-90-3

The right of Nick Quantrill to be identified as author of this work has been asserted in accordance with section 77 of the Copyright, Designs and Patents Act 1988.

This book is a work of fiction. The characters, incidents, and dialogue are drawn from the author's imagination and are not to be construed as real. Any resemblance to actual events or persons, living or dead, is entirely coincidental.

www.blackspringpressgroup.com

For Alice, as always. You're probably old enough to read this one…

ONE

Yaz heard the floorboard behind her creak and stopped what she was doing. She'd made a mistake. The farmhouse was abandoned, but not empty. Unsure of what her next move should be, she stood still for a moment. Maybe her mind was playing tricks on her. The floorboard creaked again, this time louder and closer to her. Turning around on instinct, there was no time to set herself as the figure lunged forwards, closing the gap between them. An arm came out and landed a strike, pain shooting down the side of her body. Another blow, this time to the head, the room spinning as she fell to the floor.

Rolling over and pushing her back against the nearest wall, ready for another attack, this time she'd be ready and would kick out. Nothing happened. Listening, all she could hear was her own breathing. Swallowing down the fear she was feeling before shuffling up into a sitting position, her vision settled. She was alone. It meant she had to move quickly. Pushing herself up, hands going to the wall as she steadied herself, she gave herself a moment before heading from the hallway to the open door at the rear of the farmhouse. Stepping outside in the hope of hearing something that would give a fix on the direction her attacker had headed in, there was nothing. There were too many potential escape routes. It was hopeless. Whoever had attacked her was gone.

The email had dropped into her junk folder, no name or mobile number to contact, just the address of the building she was inside of. *You should investigate the murder of Jake Shaw for your next podcast.* No reply when she'd responded. No way she could ignore it, either.

Moving to the front of the farmhouse, the wooden fence was sinking into the earth, the land around the cottage overgrown and out of control. Looking back down the road leading to the nearby village, it was in darkness and asleep for the night, populated with holiday lets that would turn over every couple of days.

Heading back to the rear of the farmhouse, she looked over at the outhouse she'd seen when first arriving. Walking over to it, the building was actually a garage, but had lost its door. Using the torch app on her phone, she slowly walked inside and swept the beam around the space. It was empty and smelled of damp. Bending down, she swept her hand around feeling for a sign it had been recently used by a vehicle. There was nothing. There was no oil on her hand and she hadn't felt any warmth.

Pocketing her mobile and moving back outside, an overgrown greenhouse and dilapidated shed stood in the corner. Heading across to them, the grass underfoot slippery and dense, she quickly checked them out. Nature had reclaimed them, nothing of interest to see. Beyond that, patchwork fields made up the Yorkshire Wolds.

Circling back to the farmhouse, sheet metal tacked over the back door flapped gently in the wind, not fully secure. Yaz let her eyes to adjust to the gloom again, standing in what had once been a kitchen. A handful of discarded units and cupboards remained in place, spaces where white goods would have once been installed. The walls had been taken back to bare brick in areas, crumbling plaster elsewhere. Mould was everywhere, an earthy smell quickly entered her nose from years of grime and neglect.

Moving carefully to avoid the rotten floorboards underfoot, she took her mobile back out and filmed the scene as best she could before adding some photographs. Walking further into the farmhouse, stone and broken glass crunched underfoot. A small pile of rubbish she hadn't initially spotted on top of one of the units caught her eye. A half-eaten tin of beans with a spoon had been pushed to the back, an empty supermarket sandwich wrapper next to it. Picking up the wrapper, the food was still in date.

Stepping out of the kitchen, the farmhouse grew darker. Looking at the staircase, several steps were missing. The walls in the hallway had been stripped back like in the kitchen. Turning and heading into the front room, it was similarly rundown with exposed floorboards, cold from the lack of heating. Looking down at the floor there were more discarded food wrappers, this time chocolate bars and empty cans of lager. A sleeping bag had been bundled up and thrown into the corner. It wasn't a huge leap to conclude that dossing down in such a place didn't make much sense unless you were determined to be off the grid.

Taking out the small surveillance camera she'd packed, Yaz walked back to the kitchen and placed it on top of one of the high units in the kitchen. There was no Wi-Fi to connect it to, but it would record any movement and could be collected later. Looking around one last time, it was where the story had sent her, a siren song that couldn't be ignored.

TWO

The night air pinched and pulled at Yaz's face, head still throbbing from the blow she'd received at the farmhouse. She pressed the buzzer to the apartment and stepped back. Talking to Kerri Lewis, the journalist who'd originally covered the murder of Jake Shaw, was a gamble. Stories were to be kept close, not for sharing, but she needed the inside track.

The entrance door clicked open. Heading up the stairs, Yaz could see light escaping from the bottom of a door. She knocked, the shout saying that she should come inside. The main living space was small, lined with bookcases and vinyl. The trinkets and ornaments on display suggested someone who was well-travelled.

Kerri Lewis pushed the laptop she was working on to one side. 'I got sidetracked with writing, but I'm just about to eat. Do you want something?'

'I'm not hungry.' There was the smell of curry coming from the kitchen.

'It's been a while since anyone wanted to talk about Jake Shaw's murder.' Lewis cleared the chair in the corner under the window of the stacks of paperwork balanced on it, gestured to it. 'Sit down.'

Yaz hesitated before taking a seat.

Lewis picked up the bottle of wine she was drinking from. 'Fancy a glass?'

'I don't drink.'

'Very wise.' Lewis topped her own glass up before placing it down next to herself on the carpet. 'Full disclosure, I checked you out. I'm a fan of what you're doing.'

'You don't need to flatter me.'

'It's meant genuinely.' Lewis offered a smile. 'I assume you're starting work on a podcast about Jake Shaw's murder?'

Yaz didn't want to answer the question directly. She'd worked through the day scoping out what had happened to the man, still plenty to unpick. 'I'm thinking about it.'

Lewis turned back to her wine, not pressing the point. 'Tell me about yourself?'

'I didn't come here for a job interview.' She wasn't in the mood after what had happened at the farmhouse. 'You covered the Jake Shaw story yourself, back in the day?'

'I did.'

Lewis's contemporary reports in relation to Jake Shaw's murder were online and had proved useful pieces of background reading. Despite trying to read between the lines, there was little to be gleaned. The conclusion was that following Shaw's murder, the police would learn lessons from what had happened. Procedures would be reviewed about how their detectives worked and corruption wouldn't be tolerated, the usual drill; best practice would be determined and shared. No one was to blame. It felt counter-intuitive. *No one was to blame.*

'You left Hull shortly after Shaw's murder?' Yaz asked.

'I had to so I could further my career. Different times back then.'

'I want out of Hull. There's nothing for me here.'

'I felt the same when I was younger. A place like this is either the start or the end of the line, right?'

'So why did you come back?'

'I did London for a bit and was a staffer at some decent places, but things changed.'

'Right.'

'Truth be told, the game changed. I got the chance to write books, so I didn't need to be there in the same way. Add in some personal stuff and it was the right time to come home.' She offered a shrug. 'It's not all bad, is it?'

'It's shit.'

'You want to make some noise and rattle some cages? I get it. You're impressive and you've got balls, but you want more, right? If you reveal the truth about Shaw, you think it might be your route out of the city?'

'It's my story.' Lewis wasn't stupid and had read her intentions all too easily.

Lewis picked up her wine. 'Cards on the table, then. You know I spoke to a lot of people back then, but it's not on my radar now. I'm scripting documentaries and working on books, but if you want my help, I'm happy to give it.'

'Why?'

'Call it sending the elevator back down.' Lewis toyed with her glass. 'Like it or not, we all work with people. The trick is in choosing who you work with and whose aims align with your own.'

'That's not an answer.'

'It's the best you're getting.' Lewis sipped her wine before speaking again. 'I have to quickly form judgments in my line of work, Yaz, and the vast majority of times, I'd say I'm correct. You're the right person at the right time to tell this story.'

Lewis was fucking with her, and she didn't like it. 'Maybe there's nothing more to it than Jake Shaw was corrupt and took the easy money on offer?' It was a case of playing devil's advocate, seeing how much she could shake free. 'Maybe there's no story here at all?'

'There's more to it than you know.'

'How can you be so sure?'

'How are you so sure when it comes to any story you tell? You just know, right? Call it intuition, call it experience, but there's a point when you recognise it for what it is.'

'What's that?'

'The truth. These things didn't happen in isolation. There's a pattern of behaviour, but it was absent here.'

'The police said he was a lone wolf, a rogue bad apple.'

'They would do, wouldn't they?'

'Why are you so invested? What's in it for you?' Cynical thinking or not, there was something Lewis wanted from the story. Everything in the world came with a price tag.

'You put the shout out on social media, remember? You started this, not me.' Lewis stood up and headed out of the room, saying she had something for her to look at.

Yaz walked over to the patio doors at the end of the room, opening them onto a small balcony space. Taking in the view over the rooftops, the city's illuminated skeleton sprawled outwards. It was a once industrial northern city struggling to find a new identity. The rundown warehouses directly beneath had been converted into funky restaurants and boutique shops, urban living for those who could afford it. Bullshit of the worst kind. It was a city she needed to leave behind before it suffocated her.

She needed the break for herself if she wasn't going to spend her mid-twenties going nowhere.

Lewis called her back inside, holding out a box file to her. She looked at it, the sticker on the front carrying Shaw's name. 'Your records?'

'Have a look whilst I finish off in the kitchen. Maybe we can help each other out here? When you've figured it out, give me a shout.'

Yaz looked at the box file again, feeling its weight before placing it down, waiting for Kerri Lewis to leave the room. Once she was alone and the door was closed, she went to work. Glancing at the contents, it was a record of not only the contemporary newspaper reports Lewis had written, but also her own notes. Lewis had been a teenager, a trainee reporter at the time. Her first job. Taking out a photograph of Jake Shaw, she turned it over, seeing it was dated a month before he'd died. Flipping it back over, she stared hard at his face and the young child sitting next to him. The colour had faded and lacked vibrancy, but it showed them sitting against a tree in some woods, smiling at the camera. Shaw's dark hair was cut short, swept to one side. She thought he looked relaxed, a man without a care in the world. He would have been approaching thirty at the time of his murder, but definitely looked younger than his years.

Putting the photograph to one side and working quickly, Yaz's first job was to sift the information into two piles. The first pile was the publicly available records, of little initial interest. It was information she could piece together easily enough. The official record was clear. Jake Shaw had been murdered by Mikey Birch at one of the raves the man promoted. The raves were put on in partnership with Dale Harker, working under the name

Bliss, and took place out in the vast swathe of flat fields in Holderness out towards the North Sea. The second pile was notes containing Lewis's thoughts and off the record work. Her thinking was to photograph as much of it as she could with her mobile. The door opened, Kerri Lewis walking back into the room. Her eyes went straight to the piles Yaz had arranged.

Yaz's camera app on her mobile was open, the screen lit up. She held Lewis's stare, jutted her chin out, daring her to say something.

Lewis folded her arms and leaned against the doorframe. 'I'd do the same in your position.'

Yaz felt her face burn, knowing she'd been caught out. She picked up the batch of handwritten notes made by Lewis herself. 'The knife that killed Shaw was found in Birch's flat?'

Lewis nodded. 'He returned to his flat and left it behind as he fled.'

Yaz knew what had happened next. Birch had disappeared in the aftermath of Shaw's murder. His finger had been found in an empty flat with links to organised crime the following day, along with blood and personal items. Forensic tests had confirmed the findings, but as the investigation stalled, the story simply faded away in the news cycle. Intelligence reports confirmed off the record that Birch had been murdered, his body disposed of. The most likely conclusion was that he'd been fed to pigs on a remote farm, but no definitive proof had been offered.

'And evidence of Jake Shaw's corruption was found? Money and drugs were found in a garage he rented?'

'That's what the record shows.'

Yaz waited for more, knowing the dispassionate answers were inviting her to read between the lines, but it didn't come. Instead of pushing things, she changed direction. 'Did you speak to the detective who investigated Jake Shaw's murder?' Yaz flicked through the notes she'd been given access to. The investigation had been led by a detective shipped in from South Yorkshire Police.

'She played things with a straight bat,' Lewis said.

'And no arrests were made?'

'No.'

'What was your conclusion?'

Lewis itched at her arm. 'I didn't find any evidence that challenged the official record.'

Yaz placed everything back into the box and closed the lid before turning to face Lewis. 'You're not telling me everything.'

Lewis headed back into the kitchen without answering. Yaz followed, instinct telling her that these things didn't happen in a bubble. She was choosing her words carefully, testing things out. 'Shaw can't have acted alone?'

Lewis turned back to face her. 'You mean his colleagues and friends?'

'Did you speak to them about his murder?'

'They weren't keen to help, on or off the record. A corrupt officer is a corrupt officer. I went through everything before I was stopped and there was nothing out of place; no debts, or money issues. Jake Shaw was considered to be a decent detective going places, but who would want to be tainted by association?'

'We both know there are other reasons for corruption, though,' Yaz said, cutting to the chase. 'It's not always about money. Maybe he'd been put under pressure to do certain things? Maybe it was personal in some way for him?' Everyone had secrets and some were more dangerous than others. 'How was he behaving before he died?'

'His wife said he was on edge about something. That's the best way she could describe it. The deal they had was that he wouldn't bring his work home or talk about it. It suited them, I guess, but there was something heavier weighing on him.'

Yaz walked back into the front room. Glancing at the box of cuttings and notes, things were starting to come into focus. Both the official record and what wasn't being said.

Lewis followed with a bowl of food steaming in her hand and sat down. 'Can you smell the bullshit yet, Yaz?'

Yaz started at her, hearing Lewis's words again. *Maybe we can help each other out.* 'He wasn't corrupt, was he?'

Lewis placed the bowl down. 'So what was he doing at the rave?'

Yaz knew it in her bones. Only one thing made sense. 'He was working undercover.'

THREE

Heading out of the city, the urban sprawl gave way to market towns and then to desolate countryside. Unable to stop thinking about Jake Shaw, Yaz had lots of questions to ask Lewis about the undercover operation. More than anything, she had to come to her own conclusions, not the ones Lewis wanted her to come to. Yaz asked her first question. 'If he was working undercover, why isn't it public knowledge? Why is the story about Shaw being corrupt? It sounds like he was the victim.'

'Because you need proof if you're going to challenge the narrative. Otherwise it's just gossip you can't print or publish. That's the whole point. No one official will confirm it for you, so the challenge is to crack it open yourself.' Lewis slowed the car as they approached a junction.

Yaz hesitated for a moment, but thought, fuck it. It was no time to be pulling any punches. 'I want a shot at doing this properly.' Being from the North and having no connections wasn't going to hold her back from getting into the industry and telling important stories, but she wasn't going to open herself up to someone she didn't know.

'Newspapers?'
'Why not?'
'They're on the way out, Yaz.'
'Not all of them.'

Lewis accelerated again. 'The world's changing and they're less important than they've ever been. You click on social media and everything's already there for you. No one even needs to go behind the paywall. Games up for them as it stands. The old days of being able to work your way from the local newspaper to the nationals has gone too. There are different opportunities out there now for people like you.'

'I'm not naive.'

'I agree. You're definitely not naive, but you still need a story to grab people's attention, give yourself some options, right?'

That much was true, but she didn't want to talk about herself and changed the subject. 'There was no question Mikey Birch was the target of the undercover investigation?'

'Absolutely. He wasn't exactly what you'd call a major player at that point, more what you'd call a gateway. The large-scale movement of drugs goes much higher than someone like that. Don't get me wrong, he was a sizeable scalp for the police, but he wouldn't have been the major prize they wanted.'

'They wanted to leverage him?'

'It's common practice. Think of it as a ladder. If charges against Birch were proved, he'd receive a prison sentence, but that doesn't get you the people supplying him and the guys doing it on an industrial level. You always look to the next rung on the ladder, weigh up whether you can get your catch to give them up. Maybe the investigation had grander aims, but that's me speculating. Sometimes investigations plateau and everyone's happy to draw a line in the sand.'

Slowing down, Holderness was bleak and desolate, its small hamlets and villages pinpricks on the landscape. It was a collection of fields and hills, the coastline eroding and slowly crumbling away. Pulling off the main road, they soon became the only vehicle around. The road narrowed with overhanging trees and overgrown bushes, no streetlights. Bumping along the uneven surface, the car's headlights picked out a fox darting across the road, a wooden road sign pointing the way to the nearest village.

Finding the track she was looking for, a *For Sale* sign at the entrance, Lewis edged the car along it, trying to avoid the potholes. The private road opened up into a small yard. Pulling on the handbrake and killing the engine, she left the headlights on to illuminate the space. Yaz looked at the scene. The farm had been abandoned and left to rot.

'The farmer's son had been keeping it going until a couple of years ago,' Lewis said, 'but it's up for sale now.'

'Not much demand for farmland these days?'

'It's a mug's game after Brexit.'

'Everything is.' Yaz opened the door and got out of the car. She'd watched the contemporary news reports on YouTube, a helicopter flying over the farmland as the police had worked. Not much had changed. The farmhouse to her right was in darkness. To her left, various outbuildings were dotted around haphazardly, forming a loose horseshoe shape around the yard. Looking beyond them, she picked out the barn standing isolated from everything else.

The files she'd read in Lewis's flat had laid it out. The farmer had hired the facilities out to Mikey Birch, the deal cash-in-hand. The farmer had taken the money and disappeared for the weekend with his family.

Using her mobile as a makeshift torch, Yaz walked across the field towards the barn. The old wooden door wasn't locked. Yanking it open, she headed inside before closing it behind her. The engrained smell of animals and machinery in her nostrils, she stepped further inside, her Doc Martens echoing off the concrete floor as she moved forward. Running the torch light around to get a feel for the size and scope of the place, there was a pile of rubbish on the floor. It looked like some kids unlucky enough to live in the middle of nowhere had set up their own party.

Setting her mobile to record, she wanted to capture her thoughts as she looked around. With the addition of a sound system, a light show and a DJ, the barn must have felt like the most exciting place on earth. Add in smoke and strobes, and it must have been a huge rush for those lucky enough to be there. Yaz pictured hundreds of young people dancing, loving and making the world revolve around themselves for a few hours before it all went wrong.

The door behind her rattled open, another torchlight sweeping around the barn. Yaz turned and lowered hers, her other hand instinctively going to her eyes.

'I spoke to the farmer's son,' Lewis said, walking deeper inside. 'He reckons it ruined his father.' She lowered her torch. 'He called me a parasite and accused me of ruining lives and spreading lies.'

'Is he still alive?'

'Neither of them are, but why do you think a farmer has to rent his space out for a rave?'

'Tell me.'

'Because they're always skint.'

Yaz chewed the thought over. The risks will have been weighed up against the rewards, actions always having consequences. 'How old was his son back then?'

'Early-to-mid twenties.'

'Was he the one who met Mikey Birch?'

'Why's that important?'

She didn't answer, feeling Lewis was fucking with her. The farmer's son would have been roughly the same age as Mikey Birch. It wouldn't have hurt negotiations.

'According to the farmer's son, Birch was polite and quiet,' Lewis said. 'The one with him, Dale Harker, needed taking down a peg or two.'

The way Kerri Lewis was drip-feeding pieces of information was starting to get annoying. 'Why are you doing this?'

'Doing what?'

'This should be your story.'

'It's no more my story than anyone else's.'

'It's unfinished business for you.'

'Doesn't mean I have to be the one who finishes it. I'm not a podcaster like you, but I can see the potential of your medium. A well-placed story will give you the spotlight and then you can lay the full thing out, do it right once you know how it ends. That way people will have to listen.'

'I need more.' Some people would always be happy to talk; some would need more incentive to speak to her. 'Otherwise I'm wasting my time.'

Lewis weighed the request up. 'I wasn't sure if I should show you this or not.' She pulled up a photograph on her phone, quickly pressed some buttons. 'I've sent you it.'

Yaz's mobile vibrated and lit up. Downloading the attachment, it showed a photograph of a photograph, the original image creased in the corner. Two men stared at the camera smiling, another one looking away. They were huddled around a pub table, empty glasses piled up between them. They looked confident in themselves, not yet old enough that life had beaten them down. Still masters of their own destiny. She got it. It was the undercover team. She immediately recognised Jake Shaw. Focusing on the man she didn't know, Kerri Lewis gave her the name of a serving police detective, saying he was now working cold cases. But it was the slightly older man, positioned slightly apart from the pair, that she couldn't take her eyes off. Conrad Knott was now a high-flying Member of Parliament, someone she religiously followed in the media. Reports had him marked down for an imminent promotion, on course for a place in the Cabinet. He would soon be sitting at the top table, one of the most senior politicians in the country.

'I tried to speak to them, but as you can imagine, I didn't make a lot of progress. No one was prepared to talk, but maybe that's changed now? Loyalties always shift and time makes people feel differently about things.' Lewis stared at her. 'Maybe if you do that, it'll give me something for a documentary, who knows?'

There it was. Lewis had laid the price of her help on the table. Nothing came for free.

'Do you get it now?' Lewis started to walk towards the barn door. 'Do you get the implications? Taking it on won't be easy, but if you think this story is your ticket out of here, you've got to grasp the opportunity and run with it.'

Yaz looked at the photograph again, zeroing in on the face she knew. Taking things further would have consequences for her.

Following Lewis out of the barn and back towards her car, what she wasn't going to share was the fact Conrad Knott was her father.

PODCAST EXTRACT – EPISODE ONE

NOT YET UPLOADED

Welcome to 'CrimeTime', a podcast series filling in the gaps between the headlines and the clickbait, taking us into the dark heart of crimes and exploring those stories we think of as being told and settled ...

This new podcast examines a crime committed over thirty-five years ago, a story we think we have all the answers to ... but not every story is suitable for the mainstream media, as they inevitably look for neat answers, their job done and time to move on to the next one ... some stories demand an in-depth exploration from a fresh perspective, taking the time and effort to hear from people who haven't previously been heard ... everyone's voice is important as crime isn't just about the criminal ... it's about victims and the wider networks around them, communities and their worlds ... it's how we tell the full story ...

The official findings around the murder of Detective Constable Jake Shaw in the summer of 1989 are well documented ... my website contains scans of the contemporary newspaper reports and YouTube links to television reports ... the suggestion he was corrupt has been vigorously denied by his family and colleagues ... there are many more questions surrounding this and the illegal rave scene of the time ... what started as a celebration soured when money started to taint the vibe, things souring very quickly ...

It's clear the response in 1989 to Shaw's murder was one of embarrassment for the police ... they didn't want what they described as being a rogue officer reflecting poorly on the rest of the organisation, and that's probably a reasonable position to take if you accept that Shaw was corrupt ... however, what if you don't accept Shaw was corrupt? Well, that opens up a whole raft of questions ...

If Shaw was corrupt, why hadn't his colleagues blown the whistle themselves and made sure he was stopped? Why was the situation allowed to develop as it did? ... there's no way at this stage of knowing what happened at that rave, but it's increasingly clear there are many more questions that require answering ...

The full story behind Jake Shaw's murder has remained untold ... but such stories never completely fade ... it's a story of young men which ends in the most violent of ways, but one which still demands closure ... this podcast doesn't profess to have all the answers, it's not the intention ... but what this podcast can do is re-examine and challenge earlier findings ... questions remain, and truth still needs speaking to power ...

FOUR

Yaz shielded her eyes against the low sun and kneeled down to look at the gravestone and read the details –

*** Jake Shaw***
04.11.1960 to 08.07.1989
A loving father, husband, son and friend
Taken from us far too soon.

It was all too easy to lose sight of the fact it wasn't just a story. It was about a human being, a life being lived and then snatched away.

Yaz hadn't slept, too busy turning it over in her head. The knowledge Jake Shaw had been an undercover detective turned everything on it head and opened up a whole raft of questions and possibilities. Top of the list was asking herself who would benefit from it resurfacing, and why? Who would want it to remain buried? And that was before she factored in her father's involvement. Peeling back the truth would add a personal element to things, something that would need strength to confront. The truth was the end game, but this felt different the moment she'd looked at the faces of the men in the photograph. It was a test she had to face up to.

Hearing the sound of twigs snapping underfoot, Yaz turned and stood back up. Sarah Shaw would be closing in on forty, but looked older. She wore no make-up and was folding in on herself, the lines on her face speaking of a hard life. Her online research had confirmed she was the only surviving relative who it made sense to reach out to. 'Thanks for speaking to me,' Yaz said. 'I'm working on a podcast about your father's death.'

'His murder.'

Yaz nodded, accepting the difference in meaning between the words. 'Sorry, his murder.' They lapsed into silence, both looking around at the empty graveyard. Some graves looked better tended than others, every one of them an individual story.

'I spend a lot of time here. It probably sounds weird, but I find it comforting. It made me feel close to my father. It maybe doesn't make a lot of sense, but if you're remembered, it means you did something right.'

'It makes sense.' She'd tracked the woman down via social media, sending a message over Facebook. Sometimes it worked, sometimes it didn't. For all the toughness the woman wanted to portray, she'd answered and agreed to meet. It meant she wanted to talk.

'It's like a scab I can't stop picking at.'

'It's tough when you lose a parent.' Yaz didn't want to make eye contact. 'I was sorry to hear your mother died too.' The details were online, a short news story in the local media. Even in death, she was the widow of a corrupt detective.

'That's the worst of it. She died without my father's name being cleared, and my father wasn't corrupt.'

'I've spoken to Kerri Lewis about it.'

'She lost interest when she moved to London.'

There was no missing the venom in the words. 'I've seen her files and spoken to her.'

'What do you think?'

'I don't believe your father was corrupt.' It was the question she'd spent the night agonising over. Her gut screamed at her that Kerri Lewis had told her the truth. There was no evidence that Jake Shaw had been corrupt, no smoking gun. Yaz took her time, searching the woman's face. Time had definitely taken its toll. It had weighed her down. 'It fucked up your life?' It was a trite question.

'I was seven when my father was murdered. Any idea how much that fucks you up? I can't remember him, but I can remember him. I've got the photographs my mother gave me, but it's like he's a constant shadow in my memory. I remember bits, but there's no face and he's always just out of reach. This might be a story to you, but it's my life and it still hurts more than you can know. How do you think kids reacted when I went back to school? Their parents had told them everything. My life was made a misery, but we didn't really talk about mental health back then. They pushed me to the brink, if I'm honest, especially once I went to high school. I was never allowed to forget what they thought my father was.' She kicked out at a stone underfoot. 'It's something that never leaves you.'

'You had professional help to get through it?'

Shaw took a packet of cigarettes out and shook her head. 'I had to self-medicate.'

Yaz understood. It hadn't been hard to piece together the background. It had been alcohol and substance misuse, and inevitably, trouble with the police and a close shave with the justice system. She'd read the horrendous headlines in the media, dragging up the woman's past. The perceived sins of the father had become hers. It would be enough to break anyone. 'Are you getting help now?'

'Some.' A small shrug. 'Not enough.'

'Were you ever tempted to move away and start again?'

'Why should I?' She toyed with the cigarette in her hand, not bothering to light it. 'It's a small city, though. You can never really hide from things here, can you?'

'I know the feeling.'

'You know nothing.'

'I know more than you think.'

Shaw lit the cigarette and inhaled. 'This is my life.'

'I get that.' Yaz watched her toy with the cigarette, the background hum of traffic growing louder as the city geared up for another day. She wasn't wrong about the city. You could never hide. It was too small, too insular for that. 'I want you to speak to me for my podcast.' She watched the woman pace in small circles, head back in the air as she puffed clouds of smoke upwards.

Shaw tossed the remains of the cigarette to the ground and stared at her. 'What good can a podcast do?'

Yaz walked back over to Jake Shaw's grave and stared at the words on the headstone again. 'What good has the media ever done your father?' It was a crude way of putting it, but she wasn't about to apologise for it. By the time she turned around, Sarah Shaw was heading towards the exit. 'I can't do it without your help,' she said to the woman's back.

FIVE

Stepping back and moving to the side, Yaz lined up her position with the photograph on her phone. Looking up the hill at the abandoned farmhouse, she was in the exact spot the image she'd been sent via email had been taken from, its isolation and dilapidation even more apparent in the daytime. Returning to the farmhouse was the obvious thing to do, but it hadn't offered anything new, any sign of life inside of it cleaned out. She'd collected her spy camera back up, placing it safely in her bag before quickly leaving. Circling the property, there was still nothing of note. The outhouses were still empty, no sign of life. The conversation with Jake Shaw's daughter was weighing on her mind, the knowledge she hadn't handled it well. There were other angles she could take, but Sarah Shaw was closer than anyone to the story. Yaz needed her viewpoint, but wanted her approval. It was only right.

Heading into the village, the man behind the counter in the local shop shrugged with nothing to offer, and with the pub not yet open for the day, suggested she speak to the woman running an exhibition in the village hall. Thanking the man, she agreed it was the best option available to her.

Standing outside of the hall, Yaz pulled up the exhibition's website. "Resist and Don't Comply" showcased a series of images taken by Nell Heard over several decades. They started with images of New Age Travellers and moved through to the modern-day environmental protesters she recognised and admired, like Extinction Rebellion taking over the streets of London, plus images from more recent protests against draconian police powers.

Pushing open the door and shouting out a greeting, no one responded. A radio played somewhere in the back of the building, a dog barking. Yaz shouted out again, moving further into the photography exhibition. Maybe Heard would know something about the farmhouse, details only a local would have. It would be a starting point. Taking her mobile out, she snapped a series of the images, wanting to look at them again when she had time. The woman who appeared from the back of the hall was maybe in her mid-thirties and certainly heavily pregnant.

'You're not Nell Heard,' Yaz said, putting her mobile away.

'Bella,' she replied. 'I'm covering for my mum.'

'Right.' Yaz stared at the bump. 'Boy or a girl?'

'It's going to be a surprise.'

'Sounds like the best way.' Yaz picked up a leaflet. 'This is an unusual place to hold an exhibition?'

'It's a preview event before it moves to a proper exhibition space. It's my mum's way of giving a bit back to the local community, even if they're not particularly keen on what she's got to say.'

Yaz smiled at the thought. 'If you're controversial, people will always have an opinion.' The images were confrontational, and she knew full well that people didn't necessarily want to face the truth, or be forced to ask themselves difficult questions. That cut across all manner of things. She glanced down at the leaflet. The quoted reviews from the left-leaning press were as good as she'd expect for something that was so decisively anti-establishment. Turning her attention back to Bella, she wanted to get down to business. 'I was hoping to speak about the farmhouse at the top of the hill?'

'It's stood empty since I moved here a few months back.' Bella pointed to her bump. 'I moved in with my mum. Suspect I'm going to need her help a bit.'

'Must be a close-knit community around here?'

'Without doubt, but that doesn't mean everyone wants to be part of it.'

Reading between the lines, Yaz knew she was being asked to make a connection.

'Someone's living up there?'

'It's officially stood empty since I moved here a few months back.'

'How about unofficially?'

'That's a different story. There's a man sleeping up there.'

'Have you got a name?'

'No.'

The initial excitement of what she thought was going to be progress drained away. 'What do you know about him?'

'Not a lot, to be honest.'

'Can you describe him?' The description Bella gave was too vague to be of any real use. It could be anyone.

'He sometimes drinks in the pub I work in, I know that much. He just sits quietly in the corner with his book.' She shrugged. 'Not a crime, is it?'

'I suppose not.'

'The assumption is he's doing up the farmhouse, maybe getting ready to put it on Airbnb for the next summer season. It's what most people around here do these days.'

It made sense. The village felt sleepy, a place where very little happened. It was somewhere for ramblers and those looking to spend time exploring nature would stay for a night or two. A staging post.

'Have you ever spoken to him?'

'No.'

'No friends or family in the area?'

'Not that I know of.'

'Does he talk to anyone in particular?'

Bella shook her head. 'He would sometimes drop in and have a drink, but he didn't really speak to people.'

'No friends or family?'

'Not that I know of.'

Yaz thought about that, how it didn't sit right. Maybe some people went to the pub for solitude, but why make the effort to come down the hill to sit in the corner? If you were dossing down in such a rundown and remote property, it said something about your character. How you led your life.

Bella spoke again. 'Can't say I particularly like him, to be honest. He stares, you know what I mean? I guess some older men are just that way, aren't they?'

'You shouldn't accept it.' Yaz moderated her tone, wanting to keep her talking. 'Did you speak to anyone about it?'

'Maybe I should have, but you get a vibe off people, don't you? To be fair, I've barely heard him speak beyond asking for a drink, so I left it. The pub can't afford to be losing any more customers, so it's easier to ignore him.'

It didn't sit right, but Yaz knew she couldn't fight everyone's battles, however much she wanted to. 'Did he ever speak to any of your regulars? Maybe they'll know more?'

Bella shook her head. 'People talk, but there's not that many of us around here. Most of the people you see come and go. Today's customers will be back home tomorrow and then it'll be another batch after that. Don't get me wrong. Their money is as good as anyone else's, but it doesn't do much for a community feel. Plus, I don't really remember faces all that well.'

Bella fell silent. Yaz didn't push it, even though she knew nothing would escape the notice of the locals in such a place. The man in the farmhouse would have been noticed and discussed in great detail. Instead, she turned her attention to the photographs on the wall, the most recent showed some taken on the streets of a European city she didn't recognise, others showed school-age children protesting against climate change in support of Greta Thunberg. Another recent image had been taken in South America. Comparing them to the earlier images she could see, they were more reportage in style. Maybe everyone knew how to act these days when an image was only ever a click away on a mobile phone.

Bella pointed to the early section of images. 'My mum used to like photographing them, back in the day.' She pointed to one showing a group of half a dozen New Age Travellers smiling for the camera, more in the background oblivious to Nell Heard taking the shot. The main group split down into four men and two women. The men were all topless – the sun shining to suggest it had been taken at the height of summer.

'She's brilliant.' Yaz took her mobile out and pulled up the photograph of Kerri Lewis she'd download.

'Do you know this woman?' She held it out for Bella to inspect. 'Have a look.'

Bella shook her head. 'No.'

'Maybe you've seen her around in the village?'

'I don't think so.'

It felt like an honest answer. She put her mobile away. 'Fair enough.'

The door to the hall opened and a woman Yaz instantly recognised as Nell Heard walked in. She was in her mid-fifties, skin prematurely weathered from smoking, a red bandana pulling back her dark hair. Her clothes were well-worn, faded jeans and scuffed boots. 'Bella was talking me through the exhibition.'

'That's very kind of her.' Heard turned to her daughter. 'Be a love and put the kettle on for our visitor, please?'

Bella smiled and moved away slowly, rubbing her stomach as she walked. Yaz held Nell Heard's stare before gesturing to the photographs on the wall. 'Good of you to give something back to the community.'

'I think the community see me more as an irritant.'

'If you're controversial, people will always have an opinion.' Yaz glanced at an image on the leaflet she'd picked up. 'I was looking at your website. I'm a fan.'

'Kind of you to say so.'

'We share a home city too?' It was laid out in the biography section. Heard had started her career by taking black and white photographs of Hull and they'd become shorthand for the decaying North in the late 1980s, images that signalled her talent to the world. Yaz pointed to the board showing one. 'It's not that difficult to still see these places.'

'I got out and saw some of the world.' Heard pointed to the image they were standing in front of, changing the subject. 'People say protesters are lazy, you know? That we were a hassle to ordinary people going about their lawful business. That we were stupid. Maybe I can change some minds? Who wants to be ordinary?' She pointed to the photo of the New Age Travellers. 'People only saw the dreadlocks and the rags for clothes and didn't want to understand the lifestyle, but you couldn't say there was ever a lack of conviction.'

'And you've carried that forward?'

'As best I can.' Heard pointed to the numerous pin badges on Yaz's own denim jacket highlighting various social justice causes. 'I'm guessing you know the score, too?'

'I do what I can.'

'You can do more. We all can.' Heard paused. 'So what brings you here?'

'What does that mean?'

'No one really passes through here without good reason and you don't look like a bird watcher or a hiker to me.'

'You think I've got a reason to be here?'

'I do.'

Yaz smiled, liking Heard's directness. There was no point lying. Heard was the sort of woman who'd sniff it a mile off. 'I'm a podcaster.'

'A journalist?'

'No.'

Heard nodded. 'Good, because that's nothing to shout about these days. The industry's a cesspit.' She straightened a pile of leaflets on the table next to them. 'Doesn't explain why you're here, though?'

Yaz made sure she was looking Nell Heard in the eye. 'I'm interested in the man in the farmhouse.'

'There's a thing.'

'Is that so?'

'I asked Bella about him. Seems he's the local weirdo? Might have been some dossing down going on, but there was no sign of life in the place when I looked.'

'I wouldn't know about that.'

Yaz rolled the dice. 'I was up there last night.' She explained what had happened, making reference to Jake Shaw and his murder thirty-five years ago. She took out the photograph of him she'd found online of the man. 'Mean anything to you?'

Heard stared back at her, barely glancing at the photograph. 'No.'

'Have another look, please.'

Heard studied the image before handing it back, saying she still didn't recognise him. 'Sounds like someone's fucking with you.'

SIX

The conversation with Nell Heard had ended in stalemate, but Yaz had made her point and knew someone was dossing down in the farmhouse. It was enough for now. Leaving the village behind, she needed to speak to people connected to Mikey Birch and Jake Shaw. By hook or by crook, she was going to get to them. Asking permission would wait until later.

Dale Harker was heading towards his mid-fifties and dressed in ripped jeans and a plain white t-shirt. His closely-shaven head and dark-rimmed glasses knocked ten years off him. The office next to his recording studio was like any other; paperwork piled up, a laptop idling on the desk, a mobile phone plugged in and recharging. It was hidden away on the edge of the city centre, an anonymous looking light industrial unit. His neighbours were a small plumbing trade supplier and a printer. With no signage over the door, it was anonymous and low-key.

Yaz took out the spare mobile she used for its voice recorder app and placed it down between them, wanting to keep all her interviews in one place and separate. 'Mind if I record?'

'You didn't tell me this is about Mikey Birch.'

She held Harker's stare, not backing down. 'It's all part of your story, right?'

'I hope we're going to talk about my new record,' he said. 'I was told this was a profile piece about it.'

'We'll be doing that, too.' She'd knocked on the door, telling him she'd been commissioned to write a piece ahead of his album release. Dropping his publicist's name she'd found online had sealed the deal. Her lie could easily be checked out, but his ego had gotten the better of him. 'You and Mikey took different paths?'

'The raves were only ever going to be something that burned brightly for a short period. Nature of the beast.'

'You went legit?'

'You've done your homework.'

'I read your Wiki page.' After *Bliss*, Harker had established the club that made his name, a place attracting punters from around the North for his nights. 'You obviously did well remixing tracks for bands in the 1990s and now you have the new album ready to go.' He'd also done some reality television, putting himself back in front of an audience again. It was so transparent and cynical, a chance to present the image he wanted the world to see. It wouldn't be a good time for a story about his former partner to resurface. 'You and Mikey really did something back then.'

Harker reached for the bottle of water on his desk, unscrewed the cap and drank a mouthful before putting it back down. 'As you said, we took different paths.'

She nodded, knowing that his explanation was an understatement. 'You met through the raves?'

Harker smiled and agreed, tilted his head back. 'Different times, but good memories. We did what was necessary to make them happen.' He flipped forward again. 'Definitely more fun back then, though. I can't deny that.'

'Even though it was illegal?'

He glanced at her mobile next to him on the desk before deciding to speak. 'That's where the fun was.' He looked at her. 'I didn't have you down as being easily offended?'

'I'm not.' Reading up on Harker, the man had always been smart in playing along with things in the media over the years, not directly answering questions about his involvement. It created the edgy credibility he was happy to trade off. 'How did it work between you? You were the main DJ, I assume?'

'You flatter me, though it was more my thing. I'd share the decks with Carolyn, his girlfriend back then, but music has always been my life. I was learning to play the guitar when raves broke, you know? Completely changed things for me.' He shrugged. 'Mikey got more of a buzz from organising things and bringing people together, I guess.'

Yaz made a mental note to speak to Birch's then girlfriend. There'd be a way to track her down, get her on the podcast. 'Plenty of legal grey areas back then, too?'

Harker laughed. 'If you're trying to make me feel old, you're succeeding.'

'You fell out with Mikey?' She held his stare, knowing she was moving towards more dangerous territory. He'd given her some background, but she was close to asking questions which might see him clam up.

'Let's say it was artistic differences,' he settled on. 'Who wants to speak ill of the dead?'

'What does that mean?'

'We had different visions for the future, that's all.'

'You moved on to Blaggers?' It was in her notes, a city centre night club that had thrived for a period before clubs went out of fashion.

'It was fun whilst it lasted.'

Yaz listened to him outline the details, the vibe of the place until he closed its doors as Britpop started to hit and guitars came back. Leaning in, the man would either answer her next question or shut her down. 'Drugs got in the way with Mikey? He was involved with bad people?' The official record had Birch marked down as a drug dealer, tied to bigger and darker forces following his death. Harker had walked away without a mark on him. She was trying to find the gaps and contradictions in the narrative to push things forward.

'That's a bold statement to make.' Harker rubbed his face. 'You don't mess around, do you?'

'I'm not judging.'

Harker sat back again in his chair, scanning the room as he thought through his answer. 'It was part of the scene back then.'

'Sure.' Yaz followed his gaze, standing up as her eyes locked on a framed photograph. She walked over to it and plucked it off the top of the filing cabinet. The colour had faded, but it showed two young, arms around each other, behind a DJ deck with a large crowd in front of them. Harker on the left, Birch on the right. Both were laughing, both having the time of their lives. She continued to look at it, trying to feel the euphoria it hinted at, chemically induced or not. 'You look like brothers?' she said, turning back to Harker.

'Brothers from another mother back then.'

'You still DJ?'

'Rarely.'

'I'm surprised you've stayed in the area.'

'You thought I'd head for London?' He laughed. 'You haven't done much research, have you? I've travelled all over the world with my record collection; America, Asia, Europe, even a few nights in London,' he said with a smile, 'but there's no way I'm moving. You want the truth? I like it here too much. That maybe sounds a bit ridiculous, but you can do your work quietly in a small city like this. Nobody bothers me, nobody cares who I am. You go to a place like London, and it eats you up. Why would you want to do that to yourself?'

Yaz swallowed his words down, feeling the exact opposite. Instead, she changed the subject. 'Mikey's death must have hit you hard?'

'It did.'

'But I guess you were growing apart?' She let the suggestion hang there for a moment. 'You went legit afterwards with the club? Mikey wouldn't have done that?'

Harker was momentarily knocked silent by the question. 'You're really quite confrontational, you know that?'

Yaz ignored the barb. 'We're both busy. I just wanted to put it out there. It was all peace and love to start with, right?'

'All good things eventually get hijacked and become something else entirely.' Harker leaned forward and pointed to her mobile. 'And you're well off-topic.'

Yaz made a show of stopping the recording. 'Mikey obviously had enemies and took a different path to you.'

'He got into some heavy shit because it's easy to do. It's as simple as that.'

'Did he ever come to you for help?'

Harker held her stare. 'No.' He drank another mouthful of water. 'What could I have done? If you get involved in that kind of thing, you're stepping on people's toes. Serious people. That's the reality.'

'Whose toes did he stand on?'

'The police seem pretty certain they know what happened. I'd leave it at that.'

'Other drug dealers?'

Harker took out his own mobile and toyed with it before speaking again. 'That kind of scene was nothing to do with me. Wasn't into it at all.' He pointed to the photograph of himself with Birch. 'We had different ambitions back then. He wanted money and he wanted it fast. It was tempting and everything back then felt easy. We thought we were untouchable, but there's always a price to pay. There isn't a story there, not really. It's the past now.'

Yaz smiled back at him, knowing that wasn't true. 'Mikey murdering an undercover detective, though? That must have been scary shit?'

'I'm not prepared to talk about it.'

'It must have been terrifying?' she said, not willing to let it drop. 'That's the kind of thing that stays with you, right? It must have turned your life upside down in many ways?'

Harker leaned back, arms folded, picked his words carefully. 'If you want to talk about all that stuff, it's the police you should be talking to, not me.'

Harker's mobile sounded. He glanced at the screen and said he needed to take the call. Yaz watched him leave the office, taking the time and opportunity to glance around. She looked at the photographs on the wall properly. Most of them showed Harker with various musicians and celebrity friends, or enjoying himself in glamorous locations around the world. One made her pause. It showed him backstage at festival, arm around a young man. His son? The resemblance was obvious looking at them side by side. She'd seen the face before, though. It took a moment to make sense of where and why it was familiar. Taking out her mobile, she pulled up the image she'd looked at of Conrad Knott's son in his new bar. Her brother. The faces matched. His business partner was Dale Harker's son. Knott and Harker had once been on opposite sides of the law, but that had changed.

SEVEN

The large clock on the wall ticked close to the hour, the sound of the newsreader bringing the latest bulletin to a close. As the broadcast switched to the traffic news, the audience clapped enthusiastically as Conrad Knott took his seat, an appreciation he returned with a smile and wave. Yaz had made sure to sit on the front row, eyeballing her father. Gunning for him would have implications. The look on his face said he didn't have a care world, something she was going to change.

A pull-up banner on the edge of the stage showcased an image of her father. She stared at what was undoubtedly a carefully considered stance, airbrushed sufficiently to knock a few years off his age and make look nearer to fifty than sixty. If the aim was to present him as a man you could trust and warm to, it was as pathetic as it was transparent. His politics were reactionary and reductive, not remotely the kind of politics she wanted to be represented by.

The interview underway, Knott comfortably batted away questions about national politics, saying he was there to focus on local issues. His insincere words washed over her, a PR show. It was an effort to keep thoughts of what he'd done to her mother to one side, trying to keep them locked away at the back of her mind. She had no relationship with him and nor did she want one.

Taking out her mobile and setting it to silent, she looked up his website. The expectation was that he was about to become a Minister of State for Regional Growth. The reports were littered with phrases about the North and levelling up, aspiration and ambition. His diary for the day detailed his next media stop being at the opening of a new factory on the docks, little more than another photo opportunity. He was applying another sticking plaster when the city was suffering from an open wound which needed stemming.

Turning to Instagram and using one of her empty shell accounts that couldn't be traced back to her, her finger hovered over the profile of Conrad Knott's son, the half-brother she didn't know and had never met. It showed him with his arm draped around a young woman. Clicking on it, she read the details – *With my besties at the opening of our new bar. Come and have a drink and check us out!* She knew that bar was part-owned with Dale Harker's son. It was a dangerous connection she needed to think about. Clicking through the photographs attached to her brother's profile, the bar was already carving out a reputation as a buzzy place. The place to be seen. They didn't even know each other existed.

Looking back up, the interview session came to an end, more warm applause from the audience. Knott paused for a series of photographs, a handful of selfies. People started to collect up their coats and drift away. Knott continued to thank people for their well-wishes. Yaz edged closer, wanting him to see her. Taking another step to the side, she was in his eyeline. It took a moment for him to recognise her, but he paused his conversation before straightening up and taking a breath. His eyes locked on hers. Gesturing to the corner of the room, he headed towards the door, a member of staff opening it and standing aside.

Yaz followed, the low buzz of the public space deadening and replaced by the sterile sound of the studio in the next room broadcasting live. Some things had to be faced up to, however raw and uncomfortable they were. It was her story, her ticket out of the city.

He led her into an empty office space, the door automatically closing behind them. She waited for him to speak, arms folded.

'This is a surprise,' he said, a smile on his face. 'I didn't expect to see you here at such an event. I didn't think it'd be your style for a start.'

'It isn't.'

'I don't recall seeing your name on the media list, either.'

'It wasn't.'

'I must slap some wrists in that case.' He laughed before turning his attention back to her. 'What did you make of the interview?'

'I wasn't paying that much attention. Adverts either grab me or they don't.'

'That's a good answer, Yaz, but I hoped you'd at least want to disagree with me? Politics is about feeling something, right?'

'I'm hoping to get the chance to vote for a better society soon.'

'Aren't we all?' He perched on the edge of a desk and relaxed. 'It's good to see you.'

'Bullshit.' Her mother had told her the truth before she'd died. It had been a one-night stand, no question in her mind. It hadn't required a paternity test. Yaz had turned up at his office and told him exactly what she thought of him. He'd listened, stony-faced, before denying he even knew who her mother was. So she'd laid it out for him. How he'd taken advantage of her when he'd employed her as a cleaner for his family home in the comfortable suburbs of the city. How he'd made the move on her mother, how he'd pursued her. He'd denied everything, told her to leave and not return.

'I'm trying to be cordial.'

'There's no need.'

'There's every need. We've no need to be enemies, right?'

Yaz kept a lid on what she really wanted to say to him. 'Let's talk about the murder of Jake Shaw by Mikey Birch, shall we? I'm exploring it for my new podcast series.'

'Happy to talk further if we can set up an appointment.'

'So you can stall me and cover up your own involvement?'

He folded his arms, a quick scratch at the side of his nose. 'You'll have to explain that to me, I'm afraid. The record speaks for itself. Mikey Birch was a criminal whose choices caught up with him.' A pause and a pained look on his face. 'Same goes for Jake Shaw.'

'I don't need you to tell me the official account.'

'You're barking up the wrong tree if you're looking for a story.'

'Kerri Lewis doesn't think so.'

Knott laughed loudly. 'If you'd said you were working with her, you could have saved us both a lot of time.' He walked towards the door. 'I'm really not trying to patronise you, but she's someone who's traded off conspiracy theories for her entire career. I'm sure she makes a very good living by poking holes in stories where they don't exist, but don't confuse that with something it's not.'

'She speaks truth to power.'

'Ask yourself this; does she do any good? I think if you study her hard enough, you'll see she doesn't. At best, you'd say she was misguided, at worst you'd say she has an agenda. All she's interested in is her own career. It's about profile for her books and TV work.'

Yaz took her spare phone out. 'You'll say that on the record?'

'Don't embarrass yourself here. Kerri Lewis isn't your friend.' He gestured to the phone. 'Switch that off.'

He stepped towards her, so she raised the handset into the air. 'Keep the fuck away from me.' She waited for him to back off before putting it away.

Knott stared at her, his face unmoving. 'You're not so different, you know? Don't kid yourself on that score. Lewis was desperate for the story to go somewhere for her own reasons. She just wanted to sensationalise things. Jake Shaw's death was just another story to her.'

Yaz didn't blink. 'My podcast is different. I don't owe anyone.' Stepping away, she needed to think clearly for a moment. Rightly or wrongly, it was the inevitable consequence of the thrust of the story being about police corruption. It contained all the titillation the mainstream media required.

'If you want to make an official inquiry, I'll personally make sure it's looked at,' Knott said. 'That's procedure and the best I can do for.'

'You want justice for your friend, surely? My podcast is interested in making sure that happens.'

Knott stepped back, styling it out. 'You're making a lot of assumptions here.'

'I don't think I am.'

He took out a business card and placed it down, shaking his head as he headed for the door. 'I haven't got time for this.' His mobile sounded. Staring at the display, he hesitated for a moment before rejecting the call, letting it go to voicemail. 'We're done here.'

She followed him out into the busy foyer area, shouting after him. 'We're nowhere near done.'

EIGHT

The pub door opened slowly, a gust of cold air working its way inside. Ian Stonegrave ignored it as he hunched over the bar, the last handful of clues in the newspaper crossword just beyond his grasp. Kelly stared at him, the look on her face suggesting he should turn to look at who'd walked in.

Doing as his daughter wanted, he turned around. The hair was thinner than he remembered, definitely greyer, but Conrad Knott wasn't faring badly as he approached his mid-sixties. Stonegrave stood up, knowing it wasn't going to be a social visit.

'Can I get your guest a drink?'

Knott stared at him, but spoke to Kelly. 'Just an orange juice for me, please.'

Stonegrave picked up the glass of water in front of him and led Knott over to a table in the corner, out of earshot and careful to make sure he had his back to his daughter.

Knott made himself comfortable, unbuttoning his overcoat as he sat down on a stool. 'I'd say you looked well, but I'd be lying.'

'You're not the first person to say that recently.'

'I'd heard you're not well.'

Stonegrave took a tissue out of his pocket and wiped his mouth. 'Waiting on more test results.'

'Did you know I lost my wife to cancer a couple of years back?'

'Sorry to hear it.'

'It's a bastard and no mistake, but what can you do? You fight it with all you've got it, but sometimes it isn't enough. There's no logic to it, or any justice. It's life.'

Stonegrave watched Knott taking in the dated decor. The pub nestled against the brown sludge of the river that split the city in two. It was the small bunch of hardy regulars and remaining industrial workers in the area that kept the place ticking over. It didn't need to be said the pub was too quiet to remain a going concern. Kelly's after-work crowd has dwindled to next to nothing, people hunkering down and keeping whatever money they had in their pockets for now, waiting for better days to come.

'This is where you're living these days?' Knott asked.

'It is.' Knott would know that already. He wasn't a man who asked questions without already knowing the answers. 'It's temporary.'

'Must be tricky, given your daughter is the landlady? A kind of reversal of the parent and child dynamic?' Knott made a show of looking around again. 'Not everything changes, though? I like places like this. It's like it's resolutely out of place and time, all that chipped paint and peeling wallpaper, sticky carpets and toilets that smell of piss. That inescapable smell of a thousand smoked cigarettes.' He shrugged. 'Beggars can't be choosers, I guess, after your divorce?'

Stonegrave didn't dignify it with an answer, waiting for the man to get to the point. Bending over the table, a violent burst of coughing set his throat on fire. Struggling not to let it show, he fumbled for the glass of water and swallowed down a mouthful. He closed his eyes, telling himself to get a grip before taking a deep breath in a bid to regain some control over his body. Straightening up, another mouthful of water eased things. Kelly brought Knott's drink over, lingering for a moment and asking if he was ok before leaving them to it.

Knott smiled and picked his glass up, raising it into the air. 'To your good health.'

Stonegrave mirrored the move, looking again at Knott. 'You look like a politician.' He offered a weak smile, knowing what the man saw when he looked at him. Life had weathered him and taken its toll.

'We had some decent times together?' Knott said. 'We put some bad people away, did some good work together?'

'It was a long time ago.'

'Once a cop, always a cop.'

'You're not a cop. Not now. What do you want?'

Knott smiled and relaxed, taking his time. 'I want to help you.'

'I don't need helping.' His voice was hoarse, the words nowhere near as forceful as he'd wanted them to be.

Knott looked him up and down again. 'Sure about that?' His eyes bored into him. 'Your wife has moved on with her life and you're sleeping on your daughter's sofa? Look at you, you're an absolute mess.'

'And you're well-informed.' Stonegrave sensed the man was enjoying listing all his failings for him. 'It's also none of your business.'

'Must be a stressful time for you?'

'It's none of your business.'

'I'm just saying you could use some good news?'

'Who doesn't?'

'I've got a job for you.'

He should have known it from the moment Knott walked in. He didn't want to show it, working hard to maintain a neutral face, but his insides were churning more than usual. 'I don't need a job.'

'Let's call this finishing one off, then, tying up loose ends.' Knott took out a photograph and placed it between them on the table. 'You remember this one we worked together?'

Stonegrave glanced at the headshot and nodded. Detective Constable Jake Shaw. The man who bound them together whether he liked it or not.

'Kerri Lewis has been stirring it up again. Remember her?'

He nodded. Of course he did.

Knott took another photograph out of his pocket and laid it down between them. It showed a young woman in her mid-twenties, dark hair pulled back into a ponytail.

Stonegrave looked at it, taking his time. 'Should I know her?'

'Yaz Moy calls herself a true crime podcaster, but it seems she can't catch a break.' He shook his head sadly. 'What a world we live in. Doubt she's got any journalism qualifications or training, but what can you do?' Knott tapped the photograph. 'I'm not keen on her asking around and raking things back up. I assume we're on the same page here?'

Stonegrave didn't offer an answer, instead thinking of decisions made decades ago. How he'd always known they'd eventually create a tab that required paying.

Knott pushed the photograph across the table before sipping at his drink. 'How's the work with the Cold Case unit going?'

'We do good work.' He'd taken on a short-term contract with the police, one of several retired detectives drafted back in to review unsolved cases. It was undignified, embarrassing to admit it was where life had led, especially when Knott's career had gone in the other direction. But it was money that would tide him over a little longer and supplement his pension.

'I'm sure that's right.' Knott gestured around the pub. 'What's your plan? Get some money in the bank and get back on your feet, maybe help run this place?'

'Maybe.'

'You've put the years in, you deserve to sail off into the sunset.' Knott leaned in again. 'No one wants to see that go south.'

'Why would it?'

'Shit happens.' Knott sipped at his drink again. 'Who do you think is making sure your unit remains open and funded?'

There it was. Stonegrave chewed on the implications of the question, knowing where the questions were leading to. A good detective always knew what the subtext of a question was. What its real purpose was.

'What can they do? Let them investigate if they want, let this podcaster do her worst. There's nothing to hide.'

'Neither of us wants people poking around in the past, even if it wasn't our fault.'

'It would be embarrassing for a man in your position?'

Knott stayed as still as a statue for a moment before speaking, ignoring the question. 'We're talking about a long time ago, but you know what it's like. Everyone judges on today's standards, don't they? Once they start poking about, nothing's off the table.' Knott pushed his stool out and stood up before leaning back in. 'Get ahead of things for everyone's sake. Find out what Yaz Moy knows and shut her down before she does any more damage.'

NINE

Stonegrave sipped at the water in front of him, no real appetite for it, but Conrad Knott had finally gone. The message had been delivered loud and clear. Taking a breath before walking back over to the bar, he wanted Kelly's questioning to be over with. Placing the glass down in front of her, he asked for a whiskey, knowing what the answer was going to be. 'A man can't get a drink in a pub?'

She swiftly took his glass from him, topped it up with more water and passed it back. 'Thank me later.'

'I'm not so sure I will.'

'I didn't expect to see my MP popping in here for a drink and chat.'

'He's not a friend.'

'I gathered that much.'

There was no need to offer anything more. 'It was just a shock to see him,' he settled on.

Kelly leaned over the bar. 'So what's on your mind?'

It was a hell of a question. There were some things he wasn't going to share with his daughter. A problem shared wasn't necessarily a problem halved. Certainly not his problems. They were a complication she didn't need. Knott had zeroed in on him with laser precision, knowing exactly where to inflict the damage. 'We used to work together,' he said, choosing his words carefully.

'Something happened and maybe it wasn't all that I thought it was.'

Kelly considered what he'd said before giving a small shrug. 'Wouldn't be the first time?'

'I suppose not.' It was definitely the first time in over thirty years that Knott had felt compelled to talk to him. That meant something. He was scared of Yaz Moy.

'Sounds heavy.'

'It might be.'

'Something bad?'

'Without doubt.'

'How do you feel about it?'

'I don't know yet.' If he'd learned anything, it was that the truth was always complex. Knott had been absolutely correct about one thing, though. Looking around, the pub was going to shit, same as his life, but things could easily get worse.

'Sounds like you need to do some thinking, Dad.'

Stonegrave pushed the stool out and stood up, taking the point. 'Can I borrow your iPad?'

She nodded, telling him it was upstairs. 'Bring it down here if you like.'

Heading upstairs, he found it on the coffee table in the front room, but wasn't in the mood for more conversation. He took his reading glasses out and sat down. More than anything, he wanted a proper drink as he went to work.

The first question he needed to answer was in relation to Yaz Moy, figure out who she was. The world of podcasts wasn't something he was particularly aware of, not really his thing. Reading up on Moy's website, it was obvious they appealed to a new audience of people who hadn't lived through the crimes being discussed.

Everything was viewed through the luxury of hindsight. Anyone could call themselves a podcaster, there was no entrance barrier, but you needed the material if you wanted to be the real deal. If he wasn't so invested, he might even think they were a necessary development given the way the mainstream media had gone to shit.

Scanning the background on her most recent podcast, she'd looked at an infamous case, a young man charged with several murders in the city in the late-1970s. Kelly was a fan of true crime podcasts, devouring them as quickly as they were made available, and he knew she'd listened to this one. It had been before his time, but he'd heard stories passed down in police cars and canteens. It was hard to know where the truth was amongst a web of accusations about police brutality and accusations of mis-practice, how much was uninformed gossip, but Moy was shining a light into dark corners that many would prefer to leave in darkness. The story had been overshadowed in the press by the crimes of the Yorkshire Ripper and his reign of terror around the North, but the young man arrested had clearly been troubled, still detained and considered unfit for release. It was easily the kind of activity that could see the file land on the desk of the Cold Case unit.

Looking at Moy's website, he scribbled down the name of the detective she'd spoken to. A couple of calls later, he had the number for Paul Carter, the Detective Inspector who'd led the original investigation. Now retired, he was living a comfortable existence in an affluent village outside of the city's boundaries.

There was a moment's hesitation before he punched in the number, the call connecting and Carter willing to talk once he'd introduced himself. They made small talk, police gossip, until Carter got to the point.

'I assume this isn't a social call?'

Stonegrave agreed it wasn't. 'Yaz Moy, the podcaster.' He heard Carter sigh. 'What can you tell me about her?'

'That bitch?' A door closed before he continued to speak, a nervous laugh. 'We're off the record here?'

'Of course.'

'She needs bringing down a peg or two.'

'You spoke with her?'

'You're reopening the case?' Carter answered the question with a question. 'You'll be wasting your time. There's nothing there.'

'I'm scoping things out, that's all. Trying to get ahead of the story, so to speak.' Carter had made the assumption, he was happy to play along.

'I've got nothing to fear.'

'I'm sure that's correct.'

'Some things are best left where they are.'

'I agree.' Stonegrave paused for a moment. 'How did you find Yaz Moy to deal with?'

'I started off by pointing her towards the media team, but she wasn't interested in talking to them. I stonewalled her when she doorstepped me, but she was rude and unpleasant. Can you believe she came to my house? It's like she has no ideas of what boundaries are, or how to act professionally, never mind self-awareness and manners. She's entitled.'

Stonegrave let him talk before asking another question. 'Did you listen to the podcast she did?'

'Do me a favour.'

'Did you hear from her after she put it out?'

'She's like the shit you can't flush. Once she gets her claws into you, she won't let it go, but it takes two to tango. I've no interest in talking to her, regardless of the stunts she pulls. Let her dig all she likes, she'll get the message eventually.'

He'd heard enough. Thanking Carter, he finished the call. It wasn't a surprise that she rubbed people up the wrong way. Her work was confrontational.

Scanning her website again, it didn't give too much else away. A short biography page told him she'd been brought up in a single-parent family, living in a flat on one of the city's outlying estates. Her social media pages looked to be purely professional, little personal information available. Carter had hit upon the fact she was someone from a different generation, even if his overall assessment was largely harsh. Yaz Moy was someone who would have a different perception of right and wrong, guilt and innocence.

Putting the iPad to one side, he walked over to the window and looked out. His reflection stared back at him. He'd lost weight and aged well-beyond his years. His insides felt like they'd done a summersault and were now twisting around his body like tree roots. It already felt like a situation moving beyond his control. He was living out of a bag, sleeping on his daughter's settee. It wasn't how life was supposed to be, prematurely an old man from an analogue age.

Forcing himself to think harder, he tried to remember how Jake Shaw really looked, not just how he appeared in the handful of photographs that existed online. He tried to remember how his voice sounded, the small tics and phrases that made him who he was, the small human touches unique to him. Working undercover wasn't easy, something you had to learn the hard way on the job. Training could prepare you for it to a degree, but it counted for little when you were out there, selling a lie to criminals. Thinking back, he remembered how the noise at the raves had detached him from his own body and made him feel like he was submerged underwater. You put yourself on the line. It had been easy to flit around in the shadows, no one paying them any attention. People were out for a good time initially with no cynicism and hate. He'd remembered Shaw had taken the work seriously, taken the assignment seriously. There had been no question that Mikey Birch was a justifiable target. No one really cared about kids enjoying themselves, but the drug situation had spiralled out of hand and become a danger. Kids had died from bad batches, or not getting enough water into their system to counteract the effects. Criminals had emerged from the shadows, wanting to monetise the opportunity. Some like Dale Harker traded off the notoriety it gave them, the lowest of the low so far as he was concerned.

There'd been better times. He'd shared a lot with Jake Shaw, on the job and away from it. There'd been long nights in the pub and then nursing hangovers at rugby matches. There'd been the special occasions shared, mutual friends' weddings and christenings, but tougher times too. Jake Shaw was a man he'd known. Closing his eyes, he could see him staring back. A young man frozen in time, one who'd never had the same opportunity, for better or worse, to just live. The memories of that night hadn't faded. People had screamed, a stampede heading for the exits. He'd found himself running in the opposite direction and into the eye of the storm. Screwing his eyes closed tighter, it wasn't going to be enough to block out the image of Jake Shaw bleeding out against the barn wall.

Sitting back down, it was his weight to carry. Violently coughing, his eyes watered. Thumping himself on the chest, he took a moment and wiped his face before drawing up the phlegm into his mouth and spitting it out into a tissue. Picking up his rucksack, he'd arrived on Kelly's doorstep with everything he owned inside it. Rummaging around at the bottom, he pulled out the one item he'd taken care to retain over the decades. Staring at it, Knott was right about one thing. Too much time had passed now. Some things were better remaining buried.

TEN

Yaz stepped off her motorbike and looked around. The area had largely been reclaimed by nature, the abandoned dock she was looking at overgrown and wild. The remaining buildings were so dilapidated, pulling them down and starting again was going to be the only way forward soon enough. The main block would have once overlooked fishing trawlers setting sail from the city for northern waters, plentiful jobs once upon a time. Its crumbling brickwork was now covered in graffiti, windows and doors boarded over. Looking more closely, some had been prised open for access by intruders. If she had to sum it up in one word, it would be apocalyptic. Running alongside, the choppy polluted sludge of the Humber washed up against the dock walls. It had once been the beating heart of the region, but now stood as a reminder that the water gave as much as it took away.

Walking ahead, Yaz heard the broken bricks and glass underfoot, glanced up at the litter piled up on the floor up against the walls of the derelict buildings. It was also a place away from prying eyes. Concentrating, she could hear sounds beyond the creaking of the buildings and the whistle of the wind. She could hear shouting from inside the nearest building, either teenagers flirting with danger, or the homeless desperate for some shelter. It took a moment to get her bearings, but the man was standing where he said he would be. Thirty-five years had passed, but she recognised Stonegrave from the photograph of the undercover team.

He stepped forward and flashed his police identification in her direction. 'I thought we should have a chat.'

'Strange place to meet,' she said, ignoring the ID. He looked gaunt, a decade older than his birth certificate would indicate. The man was starting to shrivel in on himself, being slowly eaten from the inside by whatever illness he was suffering from.

'Let's call it a courtesy so I can straighten a few things out for you. No one will bother us here.'

Stonegrave walked towards the waterfront. She hurried to catch him up, coming to a stop against a low wall at the end of the path. She watched him take a tissue out and cough into it. 'What do you want?'

'A drink, if I'm honest.' He wheezed and thumped himself on the chest before taking out a bottle of water.

Yaz looked around the area as he composed himself. If she needed any convincing the city was dead, this place did the job. Its reason to exist was finished, a footnote in history. It needed smart thinking if there was to be any chance of reinvention and there wasn't enough of it to go around.

'I thought about looking for you at your house,' Stonegrave said. 'Must be tough living there?'

'Why's that?'

'Sharing the facilities with strangers? It's ok when you're a student, but you're old enough to be doing better by now, surely?'

It didn't need an answer. He was fucking with her, seeing how far he could push before getting a response.

'It'll do for now,' she told him. 'You get what you pay for.' It was a place to eat and sleep, little more. Her basic needs met.

'I listened to your podcast. You're good, I'll give you that.'

'I wouldn't have counted you as a fan.'

'I spoke to the detective you harassed during your last series. Fair to say he's not a fan.'

'I'd be worried if he was.'

Stonegrave smiled. 'Fair point.'

'You'll know I'm recording a podcast about Jake Shaw's murder, then?'

'I do.'

'You were colleagues.' A statement, not a question, but Stonegrave didn't rise to it. 'So, what, you've come here to warn me off from doing it?' He didn't respond, instead staring out at the water. 'You're pathetic. We both know you're doing Conrad Knott's dirty work. I'm supposed to be frightened of you, is that it?'

'My own shadow isn't frightened of me these days.'

Yaz reached for her mobile, taking it out of her pocket and placing it down on the wall in front of them. 'I'd like to do this on the record.'

Stonegrave glanced at her before reaching for the mobile. She barely had to chance to protest in the time it took him to remove the rear casing of the handset, going straight for the SIM card. Removing it, he passed the pieces back to her.

'Not a chance.' He nudged the handset away for good measure. 'You have a reputation.'

She folded her arms, trying not to show she was pissed off at being outflanked by him. 'A reputation?'

'I won't apologise for that,' he said.

'Even though I'm coming for people like you?'

Stonegrave pulled a pained face, like it was an outrageous thing for her to say. 'You're not coming for me.'

She watched him take a mouthful of water, stalling for time. 'Says who?' He hadn't denied anything. 'You, Jake Shaw and Conrad Knott were a team working undercover.'

'You think that means there's a story for you?' He shook his head. 'Who's been in your ear?'

'It's none of your business.'

'Kerri Lewis?'

'So what?'

'You need to think carefully if you're getting into bed with someone like that.'

'You think I haven't heard this before?'

'You think it all gets neatly tied up like on your podcasts and Netflix programmes? It's not real life. It's not how a real-world investigation works in the adult work.'

'Don't patronise me.'

'What qualifies you to pass comment on such a thing?'

Yaz held her ground, jutted her chin out and looked him in the eye. 'Time and distance can help you see the truth more clearly.'

'People like Lewis are only too keen to fill your head with rubbish because they've got something to sell. That's the bottom line.'

'You were there, though.' Problem was, she knew there was nothing like the network of security cameras there was now, little in the way of electronic surveillance. If someone didn't talk, it wouldn't be easy to change the narrative. Everything was against her. 'I'm after the truth. Jake Shaw was your friend. You should want it too.' She waited for him to accept the point before continuing, posing another question. 'What do you think happened to him?'

'It's clear what happened.'

'You're sticking with the corruption narrative? It's bullshit and you know it.' It was reaching a little, but she had to draw a line in the sand, if only to see which side he'd stand on. Stonegrave stared hard at her, running the various calculations, weighing her up and forming a judgement. Once a detective, always a detective. She wasn't backing down, either.

'You weren't even born in 1989,' he eventually said, 'so you know nothing. You'd do well to remember that.'

'Enlighten me.'

'There isn't always a mystery, you know? Sometimes things are what they are, and it messes you up. I can vouch for that. You dance near the darkness, and it fucks you up. That's the reality.'

'You sound like you've got something to get off your chest?'

Stonegrave smiled and shook his head. 'You misunderstand me. It's a job that creates a bond between people that you don't break easily. If you work undercover, you have to rely on others to have your back. I'm not being over the top when I say your life depends on them doing their job properly. Can you imagine how terrifying it is to go undercover, to live your life on the edge like that? Going into situations knowing that at any point it can wrong and that someone, somewhere has dropped the ball and you're about to be unmasked? Can you imagine the fear you feel? It makes you paranoid and messes with your head in ways you can't imagine. It's not the kind of thing you shake off, and nor should you. It forms a bond with the men you share it with.'

'You sound like you're speaking from experience?'

'I'm explaining how the job can mess people up. Mikey Birch was a criminal, but he was earning an awful lot of easy money from his events. It was wrong and distasteful, and couldn't be allowed to stand. He was a nomad who'd got himself involved in all kinds of scenes before hitting on the idea of raves. He made a lot of different contacts as he moved around the country and Europe. In fact, he kept some pretty bad company, all things considered. It was our job to put a stop to it.' He paused and swallowed another mouthful of water. 'I've got a question for you. Why this story? Why now?'

Yaz turned away, watched a small ship make its way along the water. If Stonegrave was fishing to find out what she already knew, her hand of cards wasn't strong enough yet to go for bust. The man wasn't an ally of hers. 'The truth is the truth,' she offered. 'Doesn't matter when it comes out.'

Stonegrave made a show of accepting the point, pretending to agree with her. 'It's all about the stories we tell in the end, right?'

'That's one way of looking at things.'

'But stories can change, can't they? Maybe you should think on it?'

'I'm quite happy with the story I've got.'

Yaz pulled up the image on her mobile of Stonegrave drinking with Jake Shaw and Conrad Knott, held it out towards him. 'The lads together?' She watched his eyes narrow, knowing she'd scored a hit.

Stonegrave composed himself and took out a pen and piece of paper, writing his mobile number down on the back of an old receipt and passed it over. 'Don't be a stranger.' He walked away in the direction of his car, leaving her standing at the water's edge.

Yaz quickly followed after him. 'We aren't finished here,' she shouted after him. Stonegrave continued to walk, ignoring her.

He opened the car door and looked back at her. 'It ends here.'

She banged on the window, shouting again as he drove off. 'You don't get to tell me what to do!'

ELEVEN

Yaz humped the large food delivery bag further up her back, trying to find a more comfortable position for it. It was heavy and she was tired, but the world didn't stop because she had a story to follow. She was still brooding on meeting with Stonegrave at the abandoned dock. He'd been sent to warn her off, issuing threats with a smile. There was no doubt in her mind that he'd been sent by Conrad Knott.

Weaving through the city on her motorbike, she'd had time to process and think. It was anger that needed channelling in the right direction. Other than the occasional night bus and taxi, there was little other traffic. It was a place which locked down as soon as the office and shop workers headed home, nothing going on and no vibe. The shop fronts had flashed by; betting shops and charity shops were the only places doing good business, others with boarding over windows, many units standing empty. It was a world away from what she wanted for her own life.

The app on her mobile directed Yaz to an apartment block nestling up against the main road. Placing the delivery bag on the pavement, the murder of Jake Shaw was still on her mind, the only thing she could think about. She buzzed the apartment door, standing back as it opened softly, allowing her inside. Zach had moaned at her when she'd turned up late at the takeaway, ready to work. She took most of her work via an app on her mobile, but he'd always given her hours on the basis she didn't let him down. It paid the bills.

The door in front of her opened and then closed, barely a grunt of thanks from the occupant, the entire process dehumanising. Yaz stood there for a moment, wondering about the people inside who'd placed the order. Maybe they were young professionals working in the finance sector, or something similarly safe and dull. Maybe they worked on start-up projects in the nearby workspaces she was told would drive the city forward. Whatever they did, they still wanted people like her to do their heavy lifting for them and deliver to their doorstep.

Heading back out, a group of youths had congregated around the entrance of the flats, shouting at her as she walked past them. She told them to fuck off and flipped the finger. Working her back to Zach's takeaway, it was more time to think. Thinking about her own research as well as what Kerri Lewis had told her, she needed to speak to more of the people involved. Doing it face to face, she could hear the nuances in their voices, the subtle tells on their face that the person wasn't being entirely truthful, or was holding something back.

Parking her motorbike to the rear of the takeaway, she locked it up and walked back to the front. Numerous bars and restaurants had been packed around ever-more expensive terraced housing, colonising a street once only used by locals for their daily shopping. Heading inside, she dumped the delivery bag on the counter. The grime music he loved played via his Bluetooth speaker, the interior walls freshly covered by local graffiti artists they both knew. Leaning over the counter, she turned the volume down and told Zach to be quiet when he complained. The place was winding down for the night. She watched him move over to the kitchen area, tipping a pile of fries into a paper bag and handing them to her.

'You look like you need to eat.'

Yaz leaned over the counter and ripped open the bag, hungry. 'It's fucked up,' she said between mouthfuls.

'What is?' he said.

'Everything,' she said, pushing the chips to one side and leaning over for a bottle of water.

'You'll need to be more specific, Yaz.'

'Lock up and come upstairs. I'll tell you when you're done.' Grabbing her rucksack from behind the till, she grabbed the food and headed up to Zach's flat. Flopping down on the bed and staring at the ceiling, the only conclusion she'd been able to arrive at as she'd headed back was everything came down to whether she believed Jake Shaw was a corrupt police officer or not. It was all about her gut feeling mixed with what she knew. Hearing Zach walking up the stairs, it was clear to her. Shaw wasn't corrupt, she was sure of that. What she needed to figure out was how to move things forward.

'What are you doing?' Zach asked, lying down next to her.

'Thinking.' His hands went to her. She batted them away.

'You look tired,' Zach said, rolling onto his side to look at her properly.

'I'm always tired.'

'You can't burn the candle at both ends forever.'

'Says who?' Zach didn't look much better on that front. He was as driven as she was in his own way, ready to work the necessary hours to get there. It was the only way.

He sat up and rubbed his face. 'Still hungry? There's more stuff in the fridge downstairs.'

It was tempting. The truth was, she was largely living off chips and toast, food far from a priority. 'I've got a new story for the podcast.'

Zach leaned over her and grabbed the small metal tin off the bedside unit and took out a joint he'd rolled earlier. Lighting it up, he took a long drag and blew the smoke upwards.

'This might be the one.'

'I thought the last one was?'

She nudged him with her elbow, told him to fuck off before taking the joint out of his mouth. Taking a long drag, Yaz let it play around at the back of her throat, wanting to enjoy the slightly hazy feeling and release it would bring. 'It's different this time,' she said, trying to explain it all, telling him about the murder of Jake Shaw, the undercover operation and Mikey Birch's own death. How it didn't sit right. 'It goes higher.' She was thinking about the photograph containing her father and what the consequences would be of sharing it. 'Much higher.'

'Sounds heavy.'

'I need heavy.'

'You need to be careful.' Zach asked for the joint back and took a drag, all the while keeping his eyes on her.

Yaz sat up, pulling the duvet around her. The room had no central heating, just a small electric fan in the corner. 'It's the only way I can get ahead.' Truth was, the city was familiar and comfortable, too easy to know. Small people with small lives, mountains made out of molehills. She needed a bigger canvas, a bigger backdrop.

Zach held the joint back out to her. 'We all need to dream.'

'I've got big ones.'

He laughed and stood up. 'Nowhere will be big enough for you.'

She watched as Zach headed to the bathroom, starting the shower. Standing up and walking over to the window, she looked onto the street outside. She could hear drinkers enjoying the last of the evening, the bars starting to close down for the night. The rain was turning to drizzle and fading away. The drinkers were people the same age as her, but they all seemed so free and so sure of themselves. The rational part of her brain knew she was probably wrong, that they were all as screwed up as she felt, but it didn't help.

Zach walked back into the room, towel around his waist. 'Did you bring me the good stuff?'

'It's in my bag,' she said, pointing to it on the floor. He'd asked for an eighth.

'Nice one.'

She took the money from him, folded up the notes and put them in her pocket. It would help to cover the rent arrears that needed sorting.

Zach towelled himself dry. 'I knew you were trouble from when we met.'

She looked up at him. 'You should have run away.'

'Bit too late for that.' Zach sat down on the bed next to her. 'So what's really going down?'

'What does that mean?'

'You're holding back on me.'

'Am I?'

'I know you, Yaz.'

'You don't know shit yet.'

'Educate me.'

'Conrad Knott is wrapped up in all of this.' Zach's face was blank, the name meaning nothing to him. He wasn't a news junkie like she was. 'Our MP, but he's about to go up in the world.'

'Big man.'

'He's also my father.' She looked away, the words out before she could stop herself.

'I thought you didn't know your father?'

'I don't. Not really.'

'Fucking hell, Yaz. How do you deal with something like that?'

'It's not top of my list.'

'Have you spoken to him?'

'He led the undercover operation I'm talking about on the podcast.'

Zach laughed, unable to stop himself. 'That's perfect.'

'It's fucked up.' The anger in her voice was genuine. Conrad Knott was her biological father, but nothing more than that.

Zach lit up another joint. 'You think doing this podcast will make things better for you? It won't repair your relationship with him.'

'I don't want a relationship with him.'

Zach held the joint out to her. 'This is the chance you've been waiting for, then.'

She took a drag. 'I'm scared,' she said quietly.

'What of?'

It was a struggle to articulate a specific reason. 'Consequences,' she settled on saying.

'I thought your podcast was about the truth? That's the point of it?'

'That's assuming I can get to the truth.' It was about being able to look herself in the eye, knowing she was doing the best she could with the options available. It was the only way she'd be noticed.

'You're playing with fire.'

'I know.'

'Don't rush to make a decision.' He took the joint back. 'Think about it.'

Sitting back on the bed, Yaz pulled up the photograph again on her mobile and looked at the three faces. Her eyes went to Conrad Knott, the casual grin on his face, the same one she'd seen earlier in the day at the BBC. Zach reappeared and called out to her, saying he was going back downstairs.

Heading for the door, he turned back. 'Don't do anything stupid, Yaz.'

TWELVE

Stonegrave glanced across the road towards the marina as he walked. Cranes and diggers continued to probe with surgical precision, prodding at the available space until it yielded. It was a reminder that things were never static, that a city could never fit you like a pair of old slippers. It had always felt like a large village, something he'd liked, but now it felt like a place which would demand more, whether you wanted to give it or not, secrets never fully buried.

Heading down a side street, he found an empty bench looking out onto the river. Many of the warehouses that lined it were long gone. Some industry remained, one site reduced to little more than rubble, one space now a car park. Away from traffic and people, it felt peaceful, a different world. His legs felt like jelly, the cold night air settled on his chest. Coughing, he waited for his breathing to return to something like normal. It was a process. The pain and discomfort needed riding out, letting it pass. Drawing in a breath and wiping his eyes, he stood back up and made his way over to the bar and went straight inside.

The bar was a former warehouse in the Old Town, now converted into a luxury destination to eat and drink. Looking around, it was trying too hard to retain the rustic vibe of its past, but that was the game that needed playing, the acceptable and desirable face of progress in the city. Money talked. Rather than the old boys drinking in Kelly's pub, the bar's clientele all had flash smart phones on display, sharp and expensive clothes and haircuts. A young woman approached him from behind the bar, trying hard to keep the surprise at seeing someone like him in the bar off her face. He didn't fit in.

'I've got an appointment to see Conrad Knott,' he told her, delivering the message he'd been told to give. 'I'm expected.' An update was required, but it was the conversation with Yaz Moy which was weighing on his mind. The place was owned by Knott's son, presumably a safe bolthole for his father to work from. Stonegrave was instructed to stay where he was as the bar worker moved away, picking up a mobile phone and making a call.

Turning away, he let his thoughts drifted back to Yaz Moy. He'd driven away from their meeting needing to put some distance between them. In truth, he'd panicked and bolted. She didn't know any fear and had a certainty to her words that only the young could have. It made her dangerous. The bar worker finished making the call, and grabbed his attention, gesturing to a door hiding away in the corner of the bar.

'The office is up there right at the end,' she said, telling him the code he would need.

Letting the door close behind him, the music faded to be replaced by the sound of his shoes on harsh concrete stairs. Pausing at the office door, he knocked before heading inside.

Knott sprung into action, pushing himself out of the chair, pointing to a fridge. 'What do you fancy?'

'Water's good.'

'Have a proper drink with me.'

'Water's all I want.' Stonegrave pulled up a chair and sat down. 'Looks like this place is going well for Mason?'

'It's what people want these days when they're choosing where to spend their time and money. Bit different to your daughter's place, right?'

'You could say that.'

Knott shrugged and took bottle out of the fridge, tossed it across the room, before reaching back inside for a bottle of beer and flipping it open on the edge of the desk.

'Your lad didn't fancy following in your footsteps?'

Knott laughed. 'Not a chance of that happening. Policing is a mug's game these days.'

'What about politics?'

'Kids aren't interested in that stuff. Blue, red or whatever, it's all the same to them. I doubt he even votes.' Knott drank from his bottle. 'Maybe he'll see it eventually. Who doesn't want the opportunity to shape things and make the rules?'

'Or just serve the public?'

Knott offered his bottle up in mock salute. 'Talk to me about Yaz Moy.'

Stonegrave opened the bottle of water and slugged a mouthful down, an effort not to cough as it hit the back of his throat. He maintained eye contact before giving way and looking around the office. It was small and uncluttered, Knott's mobile placed down in front of him. The skylight window behind the desk would afford a view over the top of the city centre. Knott was still waiting for an answer. He chose his words carefully.

'I'm working on it.'

'I was hoping you'd work on it a bit faster, given the circumstances.'

'I'm doing my best.'

'You should treat it as your top priority. The one thing I'm really trying to do here is make sure there's no fallout for anyone. Is that a fair thing to be doing?'

He was expected to agree.

Knott drummed his fingers on the desk before leaning across, smiling. 'Let's go to the rooftop bar, shall we?'

Stonegrave pushed his chair out. If nothing else, movement after sitting still made him feel better, his insides slowly unwinding again. Heading outside, a member of the security team quietly cleared the VIP area, ushering the last handful of people enjoying it back downstairs to the main bar.

Stonegrave wandered over to the edge and looked out. The yachts in the marina he'd passed were gently bobbing on the water. Further along, the outline of the Humber Bridge lit up the night. In the other direction, the business of the docks continued to turn. The remaining overnight ferry to the continent had loaded up and left, silently cruising out into the dark waters that had always lapped up against the city.

Stonegrave glanced at Knott, watched him drink the skyline in. The building sites down below were creating new opportunities for people like him. They'd been close once, but now they were poles apart. It was hard to imagine they'd find any middle-ground to meet on. He'd been born in the city, had worked it all his life and would eventually die in it. It was something he'd made his peace with. He wanted nothing more than to survive.

Knott took a packet of cigarettes out of his pocket, going as far to put one in his mouth before stopping himself from lighting up. 'Insensitive of me?'

'The damage is done.'

'I tell people I've kicked the habit, but sometimes I just fancy one.' He took a long drag and blew the smoke out over the top of the building. 'Moy doorstepped me at the radio station this morning, tried to get in my face. Can you believe that?'

He could. Although their meeting had been brief, he'd seen enough. 'She's got a photograph of us.'

'Us?'

'With Jake.' He described their younger selves sitting in the pub with Jake Shaw, how he couldn't remember it being taken. 'She's not going to stop.'

'We did what was right,' Knott said eventually.

'Did we?'

'What does that mean? It was the job.'

'We never got to the bottom of the drugs problem at raves, did we? It was always about Birch's partner, right? Dale Harker was the one we were concerned about? He was the one we were investigating and looking to take down, but he walked away without a scratch.'

'You know as well as I do, it's the way it goes sometimes.'

'We didn't save Jake.'

'It was a dangerous job. Don't pretend we all didn't know that. None of us went into it with our eyes closed.'

'We should have had his back.'

'We did what we could. Once the lights went down and the music started, we were on our own.' Knott's face hardened. 'Hardly matters now, does it?'

'Feels like everything's back in play.'

'What happened, happened.' Knott slugged down a mouthful of beer. 'Jake Shaw was a corrupt detective. End of discussion.' Knott turned away before looking away over the city again, flicking the cigarette butt to the floor. 'Yaz Moy's not squeaky clean herself.'

THIRTEEN

Yaz sat at her desk and flicked through the documents she'd photographed in Kerri Lewis's apartment, manipulating and enlarging them as best she could on her mobile. A case of piecing together what there was into something approaching a coherent whole.

Her room was one of six bedrooms in a multi-occupancy house, a large, converted property in an area dominated by transient workers and drifters, the area a relentless shade of battleship grey. The empty room next to hers wouldn't remain unoccupied for long, the house a revolving cast of people looking for somewhere to sleep, shower and eat. There was a single shared kitchen and a pair of bathrooms between all of the housemates. Her own room was small and plain, equipped with little more than a single bed and a tightly squeezed wardrobe into the corner, a desk she'd bought in a nearby charity shop. She'd arranged the rest of her clothes as best she could close to the small radiator in the corner. It was cheap living and added up to time and space to write for the podcast.

The fact Jake Shaw's notepad, which would have recorded what he'd seen and formed part of the evidence to allow charges to be brought, was nowhere to be found grabbed her attention. It felt like a missing piece of the picture. But thirty-five years had passed. All she had to work with was what she would be able to break free. The difficulty of the task hit her. Not wanting to dwell, she turned to looking at Mikey Birch. Birch was considered to be a charismatic man, someone who could charm easily. The inference and morality were clear, though; illegal raves were one thing, but drugs were another level altogether. The reports in Lewis's file, gathered in from interviewing people around the rave scene, wanted the reader to realise Birch was generating a lot of money from his activities. The rave scene was dangerous to be part of and he faced inherent dangers associated with his activities.

Yaz picked her iPad up and turned to FaceTime, hitting up Kerri Lewis. The woman was going to be a night owl like she was. She wasn't wrong, the call connecting immediately.

'You look tired, Yaz.'

'I'll cope.'

'You need to be careful you don't do too much. Take it from someone who knows.'

'I'll cope,' she repeated.

'I'm guessing it's tough to balance the work you want to do with actually making a living? You must be on the go 24 hours a day?'

'You're well-informed.' There was no way she was going to tell Lewis the reality of things, the struggle involved in trying to balance work on the podcast with the need to make enough money to pay the rent. 'I looked you up, too.'

'And what did you see?

'Someone who's had a lot of success in the past.'

Lewis laughed. 'That's a cheap shot.'

It probably was, but she changed the subject instead. 'I've spoken to Conrad Knott again. He said you're a conspiracy theorist.'

Lewis dismissed the accusation with a smile. 'He would do, wouldn't he?'

'He sent Stonegrave to speak to me. He said I shouldn't be asking questions and bringing it all back up again.'

'Make any progress with him?'

'He warned me off, so you could call that progress.'

'If you're upsetting the right people, you know you're on the right track.'

'I spoke with Dale Harker.'

'Harker? He doesn't generally speak about those days.'

'I said I was writing a feature for *The Guardian*.'

Lewis laughed. 'You've got some balls.'

'He was keen to distance himself from Birch.'

'I suppose he would be.'

'He's more interested in his new album and the award that's coming his way.'

'He's the establishment these days.'

'Did you know his son owns a bar with Knott's son? Best mates, it seems.' Lewis nodded. 'You didn't think to tell me?'

'It's that kind of city. You can't hide your secrets here.'

'You should have told me.'

'I thought it best you figured it out.'

Another test and it was beginning to piss her off. 'I need more evidence that Jake Shaw wasn't corrupt.'

'You don't bother with small talk.'

'I have to be certain.' What she really meant was she had to be sure she wasn't being manipulated. It had to be her own conclusion, not the one Lewis wanted her to come to.

'Do you know none of Shaw's colleagues went to his funeral?' Lewis asked. 'It's in the notes you copied.'

She ignored the dig, answering the question instead. 'Why not?'

'Who'd want to be associated with him? His wife had no support back then, nothing. She didn't have any money, or receive any practical help. She had no one to lean on, no one to pick the phone up to. Definitely no justice.' Lewis took a deep breath. 'You can only imagine what he missed out on, the good and the bad. He was spared watching his wife die, but maybe things could have been different?'

'Maybe he can still have justice?'

'This story is the one that can establish your reputation, but you've got to do it right. There aren't any shortcuts to this.'

The words were insulting, but Yaz swallowed back the urge to shout and lose her temper. Buried within what Lewis said was a warning.

Lewis continued to talk. 'There are still lots of opportunities out there for sharp people like you. I meant it when I said newspapers will die. The industry is eating itself and it's about what comes next. The better new media outfits have got a real chance. However they're financed, demand is going to grow for what they do because they tell the truth.'

'You're guessing.'

'Do you know *Inform*?'

'I've heard of them.' It was being economical with the truth. She knew all about *Inform* and the investigative work they did. The reporters were equally impressive, using the platform to write for a variety of publications, online and in the real world and, as well as appear on TV as commentators. Crucially, it was a platform committed to its independence, relying on subscriptions from engaged and curious readers. It meant the writers could stretch their legs, really get under the skin of a subject, and explore it properly. It was anti-clickbait and provided the acid test; if the writing wasn't good enough, the message was sent in the most brutal way. There was lots to like – it was a disruptor to the old-school model – but the change was slow in happening. She didn't have the time to wait for it to gain traction.

'Your podcast is great, but you can do so much more,' Lewis said. 'I can introduce you.'

'I can introduce myself.'

'What they're into is telling stories from fresh angles. Talking about undercover operations is maybe boring, but you can talk about the impact it had in a wider sense, for example. You can talk about the bigger picture and themes. You've just got to be brave enough to see it and find a way in.'

'Why don't you do it?'

'I could place the story if I was to write it, but it's about more than that. What would happen if I did that? Fuck all would happen, Yaz. It would make a bit of a splash, sure, but I wouldn't be able to link it explicitly to Conrad Knott. Any hint of that and he would use his influence to squash it. The story would die on its arse.' She paused. 'Are you with me?' Lewis spoke about having a book to finish, other opportunities to develop for television. 'Believe it or not, I want to send the elevator back down. If I can help you, I will.'

It had to happen quickly. She knew Lewis couldn't see much of her room, or the chipped paintwork around the windows outside, the cracked pavement leading from the gate to the door. Or the overflowing bins on the pavement ready for collection, black bin bags piled up around them, some split open with discarded beer cans rolling down the street. What she needed was the chance to leave it behind, start anew somewhere exciting and vibrant. She had to make something of herself. It was a chance to prove it wasn't contacts that made the world go round, rather what you knew and could do.

Yaz closed her eyes for a moment, making a decision. 'I'm sending you an email.' Scooping her mobile, she sent the photograph of the farmhouse and waited for Lewis to download it. Lewis didn't respond, but Yaz held back from revealing the location. There was a fine line between being trusting and being stupid. 'This is all I've got so far.'

'What's the link to Jake Shaw?'

'I don't know yet.'

'You've been to this place?'

'It's abandoned, but someone has been dossing down there.' It was another moment of no return, another decision to make about how much to say. She explained about her visit. 'I was attacked.'

'Must have shaken you up?'

'I'll live.'

'Have you spoken to the police?'

'Of course not.'

'Men do bad stuff and people like us clean it up.'

'What does that mean?' It was a weird thing for Lewis to say.

'Something to think about.'

One of them needed to blink and say something. Staring at Lewis on her screen, Yaz had gone as far she wanted to. Cutting the call, she leaned over to her rucksack and removed the spy camera she'd collected from the abandoned farmhouse. Setting it playing, she thought again about the place. The camera had been focused on the kitchen area and back door, the layout clear in her mind from previous visits. The suggestion the farmhouse was in the process of being renovated for the holiday market didn't really ring true with what she'd seen. There was no sign of building work underway. There had to be something, though, some ammunition to be used. Kerri Lewis was the woman who was most likely to supply it, one way or another. She was the one who knew the background. There had to be a way of unlocking it, even though she didn't want the woman poking about in her life.

Seeing movement on the recording, she hit the pause button. Replaying it, Yaz watched as a figure moved slowly through the room. Her first thought was that it had to be the man who'd attacked her returning. Slowing the footage down, maybe there was a better facial image to be scraped off the footage. The figure continued to move around the kitchen. She leaned in closer, pausing the footage as the man moved across the window, the moon lighting up his face. She stared, heart beating that little bit faster. Yaz hit rewind watching it a second time and then a third. As the man walked across the path of the camera again, she hit pause. It didn't make sense, but her own eyes didn't lie. Grabbing her denim jacket and heading for the door, she knew exactly what she'd just seen.

FOURTEEN

Pressing the buzzer and taking a step back on the pavement, Yaz folded her arms tightly to her body. She watched the homeless man huddled into the corner of a pub entrance on the other side of the road. She'd emptied her pockets of loose change into his paper cup. Above his head, a weathered 'To Let' sign over the door telling her she could be running the place within weeks. *An opportunity.*

The door released with a soft hiss. Pushing through it, the lights in the communal entrance flickered into life. Into the lift, she stared at her own reflection as it headed up, readying herself. The lift door opened in front of her, the penthouse suite at the end of the short corridor. Conrad Knott opened the door, smiled at her. He was wearing an open neck shirt, suit jacket still on.

He stepped aside, inviting her in. 'Nice to see you, Yaz.'

She entered, quickly taking it in and looking around. The penthouse suite above the BBC building opened up into a sweeping open-plan space, large windows offering a panoramic view of the city centre. To one side, the spires and crooked roofs of the Old Town. To the other, the glass and steel of new shopping centres and offices. Turning away from the window, comfortable furnishings competed with high-end electronics for her attention.

The large television screen attached to the wall showed rolling news, an open laptop on the glass table in front of it.

'Good job I'm a night owl like you, Yaz,' he said, turning the volume down on the music. He pointed to her denim jacket. 'Sure you can't get any more badges on it? How many woke causes do you support?'

'You seem to think you know an awful lot about me?' It was an effort to not rise to his bait. They weren't father and daughter, not really.

'I like to be informed.'

'You've checked me out?'

'No need to take it so personally.'

'Business above all else?'

'I can't make up for lost time, or other factors.'

'Other factors?' Fucking hell. Growing up had been hard. She remembered the way her mother had struggled, working a series of back breaking jobs to make sure they had a roof over their heads, food to eat. Other children had gone to swimming lessons, or ballet classes, or sports clubs. She'd sat on the floor of offices with a piece of paper and a pencil, losing herself in drawing as her mother had cleaned the desks and toilets.

Looking her father in the eye, it was her shit to deal with when the time was right. 'I hope you tipped them,' she said, pointing to the empty takeaway carton and paper wrapping.

'I always do.' He scrunched the waste up and took it to the kitchen area at the back of the space. 'I hear you're in the delivery game, working for your boyfriend?' he shouted to her.

Yaz folded her arms and stared at Knott's back, as he took his time sorting out before walking back through with a bottle of wine and two glasses. 'You set your attack dog on me at the docks and expect to have a civilised drink to discuss it?' He poured her a glass out, but she didn't want it. 'I'm not in the mood.'

Knott placed the bottle and glasses down next. 'Each to their own.'

She took a deep breath. *Men do bad stuff and people like us clean it up.* Kerri Lewis's words had lodged in her head.

'How's work going?' he asked.

She stared at the man, her father, incredulous. The brass neck on him. 'I'm still working on the Jake Shaw podcast, if that's what you mean? It needs closure.'

Knott sipped at his wine before answering. 'Closure for who? It doesn't do anyone any good.'

'Sounds like you've got something to hide?'

'I'm an open book, as you know. Everything about Jake Shaw is on the record.'

She couldn't hold her tongue, cutting in. 'And I'm challenging that.'

Knott smiled, patronising her before sitting down and leaning back into the oversized sofa. He put his hands behind his head. 'You're going to have to lay it out for me, seeing as you know so much.'

Yaz took out a notepad and pen, sitting on a chair arm to the side of him. 'Let's do this properly, then, on the record.'

'I don't think so.'

'I thought being pushy was in the genes?' She watched him shuffle slightly, knowing she'd managed to inflict some minor damage to his personal armour. Putting the notepad back away, it felt good to have done that much. Knott took a bigger mouthful from his wine glass, buying time.

'Things aren't always black and white,' he said. 'You're an adult, you must know that things don't always work out the way you want. It's the way of the world.'

'Like my mother's pregnancy? I was the result of a one-night stand,' she said, knowing it was never going to be purely business. It was beyond that already. 'At best.'

'I'd be very careful what you say.'

'It might hurt your career prospects?'

Knott laughed, his confidence returning. He refilled his glass. 'You've got the wrong idea about politics and politicians, you know? It's not about that stuff these days. You think the public are really interested in what I do, or what anyone else does? That boat has well and truly sailed. No, all people are concerned about is whether they're being heard. They don't even care what's being said, just so long as it appeals to their gut instinct and prejudices. No one has any expectations of politicians these days.'

'Maybe it'd be different if they knew about me?'

'You wouldn't do that.'

'Wouldn't I?'

'It's not in your nature. You don't want to be the story, you want to write it and explain it. You want the glory.' He tipped his glass in her direction, a fake cheer. 'Imagine if you did go public? Assuming anyone actually cared, and they really wouldn't, you'd be clickbait. The media would rip you apart whilst making me sound like the victim. I'd make sure of that.'

His words made her feel aggrieved, not least because she knew he was right. He was a powerful man who could bend the media to his whims. She didn't have the same platform.

'You should be careful, that's all. We've all got our secrets.'

'I haven't.'

'Sure about that? Why don't you tell me how you top up your earnings?'

'That's none of your business.' She bit back the urge to say something more, knowing it was a veiled threat.

'We've all made errors of judgment, Yaz. They don't have to define us.' Knott let a pause linger between them for a moment. 'I don't believe you're naive about how things work, not for a moment. It doesn't need to be this way, though, does it? I certainly don't want it to be this way.'

'You're offering me fatherly advice?'

'I'm probably not qualified to give you that.'

'Fucking right you're not.'

'Are you going to ask if I regret things? I try not to live my life that way, but like everyone else, I've done things I'm not proud of. I've made mistakes, I know that much. Maybe I can do better in the future.' Knott's mobile sounded, his attention straight to the screen.

She watched him stand up and head to the bedroom at the far end of the living space, closing the door behind him. It gave her another opportunity to look around. Straightaway she moved across to his laptop. The screen had gone to sleep, but waking it up, it needed a password to access any data on it. He'd left nothing else out. The more she looked around and took it in, the more the place felt like an empty shell. It had probably been decorated by his staff or the initial developer, a place to stay when he wasn't in London. A small number of photographs lay on the arm of another chair, ready for framing. Flicking through them, she stared at one of Knott with his son in his new bar. Her brother. Folding it in half, it went into her pocket.

The door Knott had disappeared behind opened. He stared at her as he reappeared, stuffing his mobile back into his pocket. They both knew she'd been poking around the room. She waited it out, daring him to say something. He glanced at his laptop, the screensaver still lit brightly, betraying the fact she'd touched it. If he was going to say something, he let it go, picking up his glass again and sitting down on the sofa.

'I'll level with you, Yaz. It could be embarrassing if my name is linked to something like Shaw's story, that's true, but shit doesn't stick in politics, or anywhere, these days. People don't care. Bottom line is that there's no story here for you.'

'Everything's political?'

'No, everything's a culture war these days. You think people care about Mikey Birch and Jake Shaw? Not a chance. The public were against the raves back then and they still are. We saw that during lockdown when they sprung up again. The media painted it as feckless kids sticking two fingers up to the law. It's behaviour like that which pisses people off.'

'I'd hate be as cynical as you.'

'It's how it works.' His mobile sounded again, but he rejected the call, tossing the handset down next to him. 'Don't you want to be on the winning side?'

'You think you're winning?'

'I know I am.'

'What is your agenda?' She couldn't resist cutting in. 'Really?'

'You want the truth?'

'Always.'

'It's what the PM says it is. It's as simple as that.'

She snorted, disgusted by his brazen lack of principles. 'Shameful.'

'It's reality and you're peddling fantasy stuff. It's not going to get you where you want to be. There are better options for you.'

'Is that so?'

'I'm a friend to many people,' Knott eventually said. 'It's what makes the world go round. Do you really think Kerri Lewis is your friend? Do you really think she can help you?'

'Maybe I don't need her help? Mikey Birch isn't dead,' she said, wanting to wipe the shit eating grin off his face.

He laughed. 'You definitely have been listening to too many conspiracy theories.'

'He's alive and kicking.'

'I don't believe you, Yaz.'

'I've got proof.'

'What proof have you got?'

'A photograph.' She took her mobile out without thinking, found the image from the camera in the farmhouse and held it out to show him. Knott went to grab it, but she pulled it back. Letting him see it was enough. Mikey Birch had aged, but it was definitely him. There was no doubt in her mind. The fear she could see on her father's face told her she'd hit the bullseye. It confirmed she had a story.

PODCAST EXTRACT – EPISODE TWO

NOT YET UPLOADED

In this second podcast in the new 'CrimeTime' series, we'll explore the world that undercover detective, Jake Shaw, had started move within ...

The Second Summer of Love started in 1988 and Mikey Birch and Dale Harker were smart enough to take what they'd seen going on firsthand with raves in London, making all the contacts they needed, and put them on locally ... although the legality of hosting them was murky at best, you could argue Birch and his team weren't initially doing any harm ... they didn't have licences, that's true, and drugs were certainly involved, that's also true, but if we're being adult about it, it's hardly anything new ... it was a reaction to the times, and like now, the government of the day offered little for youngsters. The prevailing culture was one of individualism meaning the raves were political in nature ... there's plenty of anecdotal stories available online describing the rave scene, how they took on the establishment, communal gatherings that helped create an amazing experience. It was certainly the case to start with ...

Where Birch and Harker succeeded was in making sure they controlled the nature of the punters attending the raves ... he would hand out flyers, or invites as they had to be, to people as he moved around the rave scene, people who were trusted, costs kept to a minimum. People would then congregate at designated meeting points ahead of been given the actual location ... if you didn't have the invite, you didn't get access ...

Like all DIY cultural scenes, the raves quickly changed as they outgrew their origins and initial ideals ... what became obvious was that they needed bigger premises ... it had to be places sourced off farmers, large but private buildings, big enough to meet demand ... it's quite clear that Birch and Harker weren't fools and were certainly switched on enough to realise that if you got yourself a space legitimately leased off the owner, you were halfway there ... they had it largely sorted and their Bliss nights become hugely popular, too big for their own good, you might say ...

The use of drugs might have been normalised in the minds of their punters, but the wider picture was changing. The media changed that for the police, decrying what they saw as a moral panic, a danger to the youth of the day ... raves were springing up all over the UK and the perception was that they were dangerous ... the government of the day didn't understand the youth culture and only saw it as a threat. Referring to the promoters as 'drug barons' in relation to the sums of money involved, police action was enthusiastically supported by the government ... the country was starting to change, too, darker clouds beginning to gather away from the rave scene ... The Gulf War, Poll Tax protests and wide-spread social disorder ... it was all waiting around the corner ...

As the mood changed, things were about to spiral out of control ... when anything becomes big business, it automatically attracts attention ... some of that attention was maybe welcome, but some of it certainly wasn't ... it became routinely harder to hire equipment, as it would be regularly impounded by the police ... road blocks became more frequent, radio signals jammed and even helicopters scrambled in an attempt to stop young people attending ... the government even went as far to change the law, giving the police the tools to shut down the raves, and more importantly, they had the public support they required to act, including the undercover operation mounted by Detective Constable Jake Shaw and his colleagues ...

Serious money was in play, and despite best intentions, criminal gangs started to pay more attention to the raves. This was partly because of the supply of drugs was increasingly lucrative, but also because there was a perception that the cash the raves generated was in some way fair game, not totally legal ... there was also a fair assumption that the police wouldn't be too inclined to help the promoters ... stories spread about the use of guns, forceful raids on safe houses containing the money, even kidnapping of family members wasn't unheard of ... the message was very much that the promoters were no longer in charge ... at best, they were now in partnership with serious people, the threat of violence always hanging over something that had once been so peaceful and beautiful ...

What's clear is that Mikey Birch ultimately moved in dangerous circles, finishing a long way from the ideals that had once fired him up ... it's against this backdrop that Jake Shaw was working ... undercover work by its nature is difficult and dangerous, always at the whims of changing circumstances ...

it was likely events were moving fast for both men with Mikey Birch having to decide which side of the line he was operating on ... running illegal raves was one thing, murdering an undercover police officer something else entirely ...

FIFTEEN

Yaz looked around the village again, taking her time and letting her gaze settle on the farmhouse at the top of the hill. Sleep hadn't come easily after watching the footage of Mikey Birch in the farmhouse and the subsequent argument with her father. Sitting in her room, she'd replayed the film several times, checking again and again the image against ones available online of Birch. Even allowing for the passage of time, she was in no doubt it was him. Buzzing and wide awake, she'd recorded more thoughts for the podcast; passages that would link up the interviews and perspectives she wanted to capture. Her notepad was full of scribbled notes outlining the structure it would take. The temptation was to push the audio out immediately, package it up with the photograph. She'd put the brakes on herself, think strategically. Once the image was out there, she was no longer in control of the story. Birch was still alive, but she needed more. She needed a conclusion. Mulling it over in her room, failing didn't bare thinking about.

A man in an oversized hoodie and pyjama bottoms closed the door to the village shop behind him, a pint of milk in his hand. She'd already been inside and bought chocolate on the pretext of hearing the local gossip. The woman in the shop had stonewalled her, not biting. Yawning, she swallowed the remains of the energy drink in her hand, throwing it away in the bin at the side of the road.

Walking towards the village hall and the photography exhibition she'd visited once already, her mobile vibrated in her pocket. Staring at the screen, Kerri Lewis was calling. She'd called more than once, leaving voicemails and sending text messages. Yaz stuffed the handset back in her pocket, ignoring them for now. Sharing everything she knew with the woman was a big decision to make. It came down to trust and the only person she really trusted was herself.

The door to the exhibition was open for the day, Yaz shouting out as she walked inside. No reply. She stepped further inside, looking again at the images on the walls. The power of them still taking her breath away, the voices of rebellion speaking to her. Staring at them, she knew she wanted her words to have the same effect on people.

'I knew you'd come back,' Bella said.

Yaz turned to face her. 'Really?'

'It's not somewhere you pass through without a good reason.'

Yaz smiled. 'Guilty as charged.' She delved into her rucksack, taking out the bar of chocolate she'd bought. 'It's not much, but it's a small thank-you for trying to help yesterday.' And hopefully for help you're about to give, she thought. 'And you're eating for two.'

'Very kind.' Bella unwrapped it and snapped it in half. 'Only right to share.'

Yaz waved the offer away, explaining it was dairy. 'It's a proper test of my willpower, though.' She pointed to the photographs on display. 'Must have been an unconventional upbringing for you, moving around with your mum?'

Bella considered the question. 'You don't really appreciate that it's different as a child, I suppose. It was just normal to me. I look back on it, though, and I really enjoyed it. I wasn't always cooped up in a classroom, I was out in the world learning.' Her hand went to her stomach. 'I'll probably put this one into a regular school, though.'

Yaz pointed at the photographs of the New Age Travellers. 'I'm guessing you're about the right age to have shared those times with your mum?'

Bella nodded. 'I was a baby, so I haven't got any memories. Looks pretty wild, though.' She threw the empty chocolate wrapper in the bin. 'You're back to ask about the farmhouse?'

'I can't stay away.' Instead of directly asking, she waited as Bella took her time with the chocolate, wanting her to speak, see if she'd offer anything first.

Bella took the bait. 'No one knows anything about him.'

Yaz pulled up the image of Mikey Birch for Bella to look at. Giving her the man's name and explaining who he was had been an option, but it felt like information she should keep close for now.

'That's him.' No hesitation. Bella looked up. 'How did you get it?'

'I left a camera there.'

'You're good.'

'I have my moments.'

'I asked around after your visit yesterday.' Bella pointed at Birch's face. 'He was acting weird in the shop the other night. Turns out he bought a bottle of brandy and some cigarettes.' She shrugged, like it was unusual behaviour. 'They said he was agitated and distracted when they tried to speak to him.'

It was interesting to hear that Birch had been unsettled. Something had triggered events and then his disappearance. She turned, hearing the door open. Nell Heard walked into the hall, a carrier bag of shopping in her hand. She stopped when she saw Yaz.

'She's got a photograph of the man from the farmhouse,' Bella said.

'Is that so?' Nell Heard placed her shopping down and asked to see it. Taking the mobile from Bella, she studied it for a moment. 'Have you got a name?'

'I'm hoping you'd both like to speak to me for my podcast.'

'I don't think there's much to say if you haven't got a name, do you?'

'Think of it as background.'

'I'm not here to do your work for you.' She turned to her daughter. 'And you've got jobs to be getting on with.'

'I want to know more about the man,' Yaz said, taking back her mobile. 'Have you seen him around?'

'Can't say I have.'

'Bit weird, given you live in the same village?'

'I mind my own business. Always have done.'

'Bella's seen him in the pub and he was using the shop the other night. He doesn't sound like a hermit to me.'

'I can't help you.'

'You don't seem curious about him?'

'I'm really not. I've had a lifetime of people in authority telling me what to do. It makes me wary of listening to anyone.'

'Someone I know said to me that men do bad stuff and people like us clear it up.' She waited for a response, not getting one.

'I won't keep you any longer,' Heard said. 'I've got an online presentation to prepare for tonight.'

Yaz picked up a leaflet from a nearby table and folded it up and put it on her coat pocket. 'Where would we be without Zoom?'

'It's a chance for people who can't visit in person to see the work.'

Yaz nodded her agreement and picked up another leaflet before taking out a pen and scribbling down her name and number on the back of it. 'In case you want to talk.' She placed it down on the table. There was something there, but it would need drawing out. 'I'll leave you to prepare for your event.'

Nell Heard waited until her daughter was out of sight and unable to hear them. 'Get the fuck out of our faces and keep it that way.'

SIXTEEN

Taking an unoccupied bench outside of the market hall, Stonegrave watched people walk in and out, happy to wait. Whenever the automatic doors opened, he caught the mixed smell from inside; fresh fish and meat, the earthy smell of fresh produce. It mingled with the global aromas coming from the food court, the shadow of the imposing Minster flooding the plaza.

There were things he didn't want to think about, though. Things were never black and white, always shades of grey, but he was certain Conrad Knott was holding things back from him. That was a given. It threw him back to their relationship all those years ago and the power imbalance, knowing nothing had really changed. It was something to be swallowed down if he wanted to keep his job. He'd dealt with hundreds of people during his career, probably thousands, from the top of society all the way down to the human sewers in the darkest corners of the city. He'd looked evil in the eye, tried to make sense of people he'd happily erase from the planet. He was owed something for those years, regardless of what Yaz Moy might think about him.

There'd been plenty of time over the years to think back to Jake Shaw's murder, to try to put events into some kind of orders. The story had slowly died and faded from memory and the front pages. That should have been the end of things. It shouldn't be resurfacing thirty-five years later. Once Mikey Birch was in the wind, it had been all over for them, lucky to still have their jobs after the internal investigation. The public didn't know about an undercover operation, something that would never be confirmed or denied, but that didn't mean it didn't happen. It didn't mean what happened was right. Jake Shaw was a name from a previous life, one that Stonegrave had mentally boxed up and stored away, no chance of doing any damage in the present day. It was where he wanted it to remain.

He'd eaten breakfast downstairs in the pub as quickly as he could, hoping Kelly would stay in bed and not hear him. She was a light sleeper and could read him like a book, knowing exactly how unsettled Knott's visit had left him. He'd tried to make light of things, easy lies falling out of his mouth before heading out for the day. What he did know was that there were different ways a story could be told and shaped by people like Yaz Moy, none of them ending well for him. He knew full well what he'd done. Or not done. The story might initially go out via per podcast, but it would spread like fire. It would take hold and spiral out of control until it burned down everything. It didn't need to be said that it wouldn't care who it took with it.

He swallowed back the coffee he'd bought in the market, wincing as it went down. One thing was certain, though. If his police pension went, he was fucked. It was that simple and Knott had made it his problem. Another bout of coughing welled up in his lungs. Pulling out a handkerchief, he spat out the remaining phlegm in his mouth. Staring at the blood, he balled it up and put it back in his pocket. He wiped his mouth, knowing he was sailing far too close to the wind. If things went wrong, it would be game over.

'Interesting place to meet,' Kerri Lewis said, sitting down next to him.

Stonegrave scrunched up the empty cardboard cup and threw it in the nearby bin, pushing the thoughts to one side. Lewis continued to stare at him, quietly judging. He wiped his mouth and coughed, looking away. 'As good as anywhere, I suppose.'

'Don't you still use the police station for meetings?' she asked.

It didn't need to be said they were off the record. Lewis was too long in the tooth to need it spelling out. 'You've come a long way from the newspaper when we first met,' he said to her. 'I thought we could have a chat privately, like two adults.'

'Like old friends?'

'If you like.' Stonegrave coughed again, eyes watering. 'You're working on a new project?'

'I'm always working on projects. It's the nature of my business.'

He looked up at the sky. It was never going to be an easy conversation. But it wasn't one he could avoid, either. He levelled his gaze on her. 'We need to speak about your new friend, Yaz Moy.' It was inevitable he'd have to speak to Moy herself again, but the groundwork needed laying first.

'What about her?' Lewis asked.

'You're working together?'

'You've been speaking to Conrad Knott?'

Lewis stood up and looked down on him. He mirrored the move, not quite as tall she was, but not prepared to allow her to literally talk down to him. It was an old school tactic. 'He has concerns.'

'Concerns.' Lewis rolled the word around. 'That word covers a multitude of sins.' She stepped to the side before quickly turning back to face him. 'You best outline his concerns, then, as I can't imagine what they are.'

'Don't overplay your hand here.'

'I didn't realise I even held a hand.'

'Jake Shaw was a friend and colleague of mine.' He made sure Lewis accepted the point before continuing, sure he wasn't imagining her sniffing in the air as she did so. Like she was seeking out a lie. 'The story is out there in the open,' he added. 'You know it inside out, just like I do.'

'Jake Shaw was corrupt? How does that make you feel, seeing as he was your friend?'

Stonegrave paused and smiled, wanting her to know she was pushing her luck. 'We're not here to talk about my feelings. Let's cut the shit, shall we?'

'I'd like that very much.'

'It is what it is, but that doesn't make it any easier.'

'It's about your feelings?' Lewis's eyes narrowed. 'It would be convenient for Knott if the real story remained buried for now, given his political ambitions?'

Stonegrave held her stare. 'He's an important man in the area.' He told her about the Cold Case unit work, how it was bringing closure to families in the area, answering questions and delivering justice, often decades later. That it was work with value. 'Who do you think makes sure it's funded? Say what you like about him, but we'd be poorer without his influence.'

Lewis scrutinised his face, a smile settling on her own. 'Influence is certainly an interesting choice of word. He's not above the law.'

'Of course not.'

'And nor are you.'

'If I didn't know better, that sounds like a threat.' He turned away and coughed, his body feeling like it was folding in on itself. He straightened back up, letting the pain pass, trying to ignore the biting cold seeping inside him. The meeting should have been set for indoors, but he hadn't wanted anyone listening in. 'No one is above the law,' he said to her. 'Why would they be?'

'Is this the point when you mention the cases you're working on, how they'd make for good stories, maybe books or documentaries? How I should speak to Yaz Moy, suggest she does something on them instead? A win-win?' Lewis looked at him like he was something she'd scraped off her shoe. 'Or did Knott send you to offer me something that will make me look the other way?' Lewis crossed her arms. 'I'm not for sale and neither is Yaz Moy.'

'It's not a case of being for sale or not.'

'Everyone has a price.' Lewis continued talking. 'Crazy times back then, right? It was a good job your senior officers had the ear of my editor at the newspaper. I was told very firmly to leave things alone.'

'Above my pay station back then.'

'It happened and it fucked me off.'

'So this is about you and your feelings?' Stonegrave laughed and rubbed his face. 'Fucking hell. All these years later and here we are.'

Lewis stepped closer. 'It's about the truth. You and Conrad Knott still don't get it. You think you know me, and fair enough, you maybe do. But you don't know Yaz Moy and what she's about. You can't control her like you can control a newspaper. We're not working together, but I'm going to hugely enjoy seeing what she can do.'

'Finished?'

'Not by a long chalk. Have you any idea how powerful podcasts can be? They give people a voice, whether it's direct actors or those on the periphery, maybe those who weren't heard previously. Nothing's off limits. The game's changed whether you like it or not.'

'Do you believe what you're saying?'

Lewis took a deep breath. A smile forming on her face. 'Intimidation doesn't work these days. You can pass that message back to Conrad Knott.'

SEVENTEEN

Yaz weaved through the cars heading towards the sea front on her motorbike. The bins outside of amusement arcades were starting to fill with the day's discarded fish and chip wrappers, seagulls swooping in to take what they could. Rolling into the grounds of the caravan park, an elderly couple gardening looked up and stared as she passed, children playing on the grass to the side paid her no attention.

Helen Pullman's caravan was to the back of the site, hidden away on a plot in the far corner. She'd worked through the information Kerri Lewis had sent, trying to figure out where she should start. Going back to the people who were around and involved made sense. Lewis had kept a tab on all of them over the years. Pullman had once been Detective Inspector Pullman, South Yorkshire Police. She'd been the one who'd led the investigation into Jake Shaw's murder.

Pulling up, Yaz took her helmet off. 'I need to speak to you about Jake Shaw,' she said. Pullman stared back at her, a hard look on her face. A look that said she was used to facing down strangers, a part of the job that didn't leave you. Pullman was in her early seventies, which tallied with what she'd read in the files. Yaz walked over to her knowing she needed to face things head on, be more direct if need be. Two garden chairs had been set down next to the caravan, Pullman sitting in one, the man next to her presumably her husband. A bottle of wine was between them on the outdoor table, two upturned paperback books on it.

'There's a name I haven't heard for a number of years.' Pullman toyed with her wine glass. 'Who are you?'

'I'm a podcaster,' she said, introducing herself.

'Is that right?' Pullman smiled. 'If you know who I am, you'll know I don't talk to journalists. Never have done.'

'Maybe it's time you changed that.'

'I wouldn't be so sure about that. How did you track me down to here?'

'I spoke with Kerri Lewis.' Pullman had retired a decade earlier, and looking around at the leisurely caravan park, she had no reason to be getting involved again. It wasn't a given she'd care so far down the line. But the woman was curious. It was written all over her face. The scans of newspaper reports marking the former-detective's retirement confirmed the woman was planning on moving to a seaside resort. Pullman had no presence on social media, but with a bit of patience, she'd found family members sharing information and photographs online. Working out where the caravan was, it hadn't been hard to get the details she needed.

'Jake Shaw wasn't a corrupt detective,' Yaz said. 'I think you know that, too.' Pullman didn't respond. Yaz held her ground. She needed Pullman to acknowledge the same doubts she'd had when conducting her investigation. Pullman stared at her, neither of them speaking.

Pullman weighed it up before turning to her husband. 'You were going to get us fish and chips?'

He read the script, giving a small nod to his wife and heading off, leaving them alone.

Pullman pointed to the now empty chair, inviting Yaz to sit down. She poured herself a glass of wine. 'I would offer you one, but not if you're on your motorbike.'

'I'm fine.'

'And you've gone to the trouble of finding me to say Jake Shaw wasn't corrupt? That's it? Have you got something new to back this up?'

'I'm getting there.' It was all she wanted to say. The photograph of Mikey Birch wasn't for sharing. Yaz turned back to look at the former detective. 'I'm not talking about the official record.'

'What does the non-official record prove?'

'It proves that if you scratch at the surface, things come to light.'

'That's true.'

'You were parachuted in to investigate Shaw's murder. Must have been tough?'

'I was a newly promoted DI back then.' Pullman shrugged. 'It was the short straw, the job nobody wanted to do. Who would want to investigate the murder of a corrupt detective? Maybe I was unlucky to be free at the time, maybe it was what they wanted, but I wasn't naive. There were never going to be any good answers.'

'The narrative was already set?'

Pullman stared at her, a thin smile on her face. 'Your words, not mine. I did the job to the best of my ability.'

Yaz waited for more, but it wasn't forthcoming. She prompted the woman to say more. 'Shaw had some close colleagues?' She let the words hang there wanting Pullman to pick up on their significance. 'The rest of the undercover team?'

'That's a bold statement.'

'Let's not bullshit each other.' Yaz pulled up the photograph she had of the three men on her phone; Shaw sitting in the pub with Knott and Stonegrave. Detectives off-duty and relaxing. 'These were the men. If I was betting, I'd say Conrad Knott was the leader, the rest following orders.'

'You're well-informed.'

'He's a senior politician these days.' If Pullman was surprised, she didn't show it, keeping her poker face in place.

'I remember them,' Pullman eventually said. 'You think he's the story?'

Yaz waited for Pullman to look at her before answering. 'Jake Shaw's the story.' They both fell into silence. A football rolled past them, two young boys chasing after it.

'Those men treated me like I was stupid,' Pullman said. 'Like I was dirt.' She took a deep breath. 'Policing has always been a man's world, none more so than when you walk into a scenario like that. They didn't make it look like a big deal, but they closed ranks on me. They knew what they were doing.'

'They wanted you to fall in line?'

'Again, that's your conclusion. Not mine.'

Yaz accepted it with a nod, knowing she'd made her point. 'Mikey Birch was murdered himself in the aftermath.' Yaz waited for a tell on the woman's face, something to suggest she knew more than was on official record. There wasn't so much as a flinch from Pullman. 'What did you make of that?'

'Birch moved in certain circles.'

'That makes it ok?'

'No.'

'You must have been curious about his partner at the raves, Dale Harker?'

'It wasn't within my remit.'

It was a lie, she was sure of that, but it was also an answer to designed to close off the line of questioning. 'What did Jake Shaw's colleagues say to you?'

'They didn't say anything. They weren't interested. They supported the suggestion Shaw was a bad apple, a rogue case of policing gone bad.'

'Do you believe in coincidences?'

Pullman considered the question. 'I try not to if it suits my own narrative.'

Touché, thought Yaz, taking her mobile out. The woman was still sharp, still capable of seeing through bullshit. 'Do you recognise this place?' She showed Pullman the photograph of the farmhouse she'd been sent to, thinking again someone had gone to the trouble of seeking her out. Someone wanted the story to resurface.

Pullman studied it, asked where it was before shaking her head. 'I've not seen the place before.'

Yaz lowered her phone, one last try to shake something loose. 'You're retired now, no part-time work or consultancy? No cold case work?'

'I've been totally out for almost a decade.'

'You can speak truth to power, then. What can they do to you?'

'What can they do to me? Have you not heard a word I've said?'

'It sounds like you're scared to me.'

Pullman eased out of her chair, ready to greet her husband who was at the far end of the path, slowly walking back towards them. 'It sounds like you know nothing about what happened to Jake Shaw.'

Yaz held the woman's stare, angry at being denied. 'I need you to go on the record here. You can help me make a difference. Otherwise, you're a footnote in someone else's wrongdoing, just another person who turned her back and didn't do the right thing.' She cut Pullman off from speaking, not caring that the woman was angry with her. It needed saying. 'Regardless of what you think of him, Jake Shaw hasn't had justice. That's the bottom line. You either stand for what's right or you stand for what's wrong.' Pullman wasn't meeting her eye. 'I can change the narrative.' Yaz scribbled down her mobile number and email address on a scrap of paper she found in her pocket. Placing it down underneath the paperback on the table, she'd made her case. 'Don't take too long thinking about it.'

EIGHTEEN

Walking across the city centre, rain pooled in the broken pavement underfoot, the few late-afternoon shoppers braving the weather seeking any cover they could find. Yaz glanced at the hopeful artistic impressions plastered on the side of former-department store, selling a vision of urban living that she doubted would ever come to fruition. Coming to a stop outside of Fresh Juice, the building had once been a discount supermarket, now repurposed. The charity's website advertised the place as giving young people an opportunity to explore their potential and find their path in life.

Pushing at the door and heading inside, she picked up a leaflet and looked around. The aims were all encompassing and ranged from advocating about legal rights through to assistance for young people in relation to accommodation, training and jobs. The organisation was founded and operated by Carolyn Seymour, Mikey Birch's girlfriend at the time of his murder. It offered a recording studio for musicians and space for those who wished to explore the visual arts, as well as workstations and computers. It was a one-stop place for those in danger of falling through the cracks of society.

Seymour's social media pages were unlocked, the woman not particularly security conscious online. Scrolling through the hundreds of photographs that she'd shared, Yaz paid particular attention to the scans of Polaroid photographs taken at raves in the region. They were generic shots of crowds, rather than of anyone specific, but it gave her the confidence to drop the woman a private message online, asking to speak further.

Pointed towards the office in the far corner, Yaz knocked and walked in. Carolyn Seymour was in her early-fifties, vivid red hair piled up on top of her head, a leopard-spotted coat hanging off her shoulders. Her desk was a mess of paperwork. Digging deeper online, the woman was a force of nature. Her media campaigns and refusal to accept no for an answer had the kept the lights on when fighting against biting financial cuts. It was impressive.

'I appreciate you taking the time to see me,' Yaz said, taking the seat she was pointed towards. 'It's good of you to talk.'

Seymour gestured to a stack of paperwork on her desk. 'You're saving me from myself.'

Yaz took out the spare mobile phone she used for recording and placed it on the desk. 'Are you ok with me recording our conversation?'

A small hesitation from Seymour before a shake of the head. 'No.'

Yaz let it go and didn't argue. The woman had been warm enough when exchanging messages on Facebook Messenger. Talking to her was enough for now. Putting her mobile away, she got straight to the point. 'You were Mikey's girlfriend?'

'Long time ago now.'

'You meet through the raves?'

Seymour nodded. 'Different times, but good memories.' She glanced at her paperwork. 'Life was definitely more fun back then, I can't deny that. I was seventeen years old and on the inside of things. Maybe the fact it was all a bit edgy added some spice, but it was the first time I understood what it meant to be part of a community. The country was fucked up back then and not much has changed. I can confirm that much.'

'I went to a few raves myself recently.'

'During lockdown?' There was a twinkle in Seymour's eye. 'You can't legislate against people having a good time, can you? Kids who've been fleeced for university fees they're not getting any benefit from? Kids cooped up in a classroom all week and then told they have to stay home all weekend? I'm not having that. If running this place has taught me anything, it's the importance of good mental health. It's complicated, but I'm seeing a lot of people who feel angry and let down, just like we were all those years ago. I'm not saying it's right, but there aren't many opportunities out there.'

'You don't need to tell me that.'

'Sometimes you have to kick back.'

'That's what you were doing with the raves?'

Seymour thought about the question. 'It wasn't political to start with, though it obviously went that way soon enough. We were in it for a good time and that's the truth. He was a pretty shit boyfriend in many ways, but he knew how to have a good time. We travelled all over for raves at the start. I remember going down to London to the ones being held in warehouses on the docks, then up to Manchester which were the best, but other places you wouldn't necessarily expect, like Blackburn. Happy days.'

'So it was Mikey's idea to start them around here?'

Yaz let the woman talk, wishing she was recording the

conversation. Snippets of the back story would give the podcast the context and colour it needed.

'It wasn't easy at first. You'd think you could find a warehouse that wasn't being used, but it was slim pickings around here. Fair play to Mikey, he hit on the idea of talking to some farmers and it worked perfectly. They had the large outbuildings and barns we needed. All you had to do was pay them enough to go on holiday for a few days and make sure you cleaned up afterwards. It was an easy earner for them, everyone was happy.'

'But it turned darker?' She took a breath and rolled the dice. The woman would either answer her next question or shut down. 'Drugs got in the way with Mikey? He was involved with bad people?'

Seymour sat back again in her chair, scanning the room as she thought through an answer. 'It was part of the scene back then.'

'Sure.'

'All good things eventually get hijacked and become something else entirely. Ultimately it all went wrong. Everyone took ecstasy, and it seems a bit ridiculous to say it now as a middle-aged woman, but it was an integral part of what was happening back then. It was a good thing for the vast majority. All those clichés about how it made you feel are absolutely true. I wouldn't be doing the job I am now without that start. It made me value people more.' She shrugged theatrically. 'It changed people's lives, certainly mine.'

A silence settled, Yaz knowing she needed to get the conversation back onto the territory she needed to explore. 'I don't disagree with what you've said, but there must have been a dark side, too, given the money floating around?'

'That's fair comment.'

'How about Dale Harker? He was best friends with Mikey?'

Seymour stared at her, clearly weighing up how far she was willing to go. 'It wasn't what Mikey was interested in. Some things are only built to last a short while, maybe light a fuse in other people. That's their job. They become gateways to other things. They naturally change when money takes over. Once raves went indoors and legal, it was over. Those who were interested in money won big time.'

'You didn't get on with Dale?' Seymour didn't respond, but the vibe was clear. She'd said all she wanted to on that topic. 'Mikey's death must have hit you hard?'

'It did.'

'Whose toes did they stand on?'

'The police seem pretty certain they know what happened. I'd leave it at that.' Seymour toyed with her mobile, distracted before speaking again. 'That kind of scene was nothing to do with me. I wasn't into it at all.'

'Other drug dealers?' Yaz let the suggestion hang there for a moment, but got nothing back. Instead, she took out her mobile and pulled up the photograph of the farmhouse, held it out to Seymour to look at. 'Do you know this place?'

'No.' A shake of the head. 'Should I?'

'Not if you don't.' She tried a different approach. 'How did you feel when you heard about Mikey's death? That he'd murdered a police officer?'

'How do you think?' Seymour held her hands up, apologised for being so blunt. 'It's a long time ago now.'

There was nothing more, just like with the retired detective. To them, Mikey Birch was long dead and would stay that way, however painful the memories it stirred were. 'Jake Shaw was an undercover detective.' She put it out there, wanting to see a reaction. Seymour didn't so much as blink. 'That's not a surprise to you?'

'Nothing surprises me these days, but Mikey didn't murder anyone.'

'It's not what the official account says.'

Seymour smiled. 'People lie, don't they?'

NINETEEN

Closing the front door behind her and using the wall to guide her in the dark, Yaz walked up the stairs. The terraced house had been split into two small flats, one of many on the long street populated by slowly crumbling properties bought by landlords looking for an easy profit. The door at the top opened, Sarah Shaw waiting for her. Talking to the Sheffield detective who'd led the investigation into Jake Shaw's murder had planted a seed, but no more. It had been the same story with Mikey Birch's girlfriend. Thirty-five years down the line and there was a lack of willingness to talk. It felt like she was chasing things, but she needed to make some progress.

Heading inside, the smell of fried food in the air, Yaz watched the woman disappear into the kitchen. Alone, she took the opportunity to look around, immediately going for the collection of framed photographs on a table in the corner of the room. Picking them up one by one, they showed a side to Jake Shaw she hadn't seen before. It was Shaw the family man, Shaw the friend and Shaw the happy police officer. Taken together they chronicled a life. The only image she'd seen otherwise was the one used by the media in the aftermath of his death, the one that had stuck. The photographs also told Sarah Shaw's life; the happiness of her parents holding her as a baby, growing up in school uniform, the smile on her face looking increasingly forced as her father leaves her life. The pain was clearly etched on her mother's face, more recent photographs showing the toll illness was taking before her death. Yaz turned as Shaw walked back into the room, putting the photograph back down.

Shaw sipped from her glass of water, glancing at the images herself. 'I'd offer you a drink, but I don't have alcohol in here.'

Yaz turned away, said she wasn't thirsty and took the rest of the room in. The furniture was threadbare and mismatched, but with some throws and cushions, it had been made homely enough. The television in the corner was on, sound muted.

Shaw picked up a framed photograph and considered it. 'This is all I've got left.'

'No brothers or sisters?'

'No.' She placed it back down. 'I always thought my mother might remarry, but I think they both died that day, really.'

It was a sobering thought and one Yaz hated herself for thinking it was a hook for the podcast. She walked over to the window and peered out and down onto the street below. A car door slammed somewhere out of sight, a cat dawdled across the road. Drawing in a deep breath, she turned back. 'You're wondering I can carry this story, if I can see it through?'

'I've not interested in timewasters.'

'I'm not a timewaster.' What she didn't want to say was how they were connected by their fathers. It had to be about business. 'Did your mother ever talk about the work your father was doing?' What she wanted to hear about was the stuff that wouldn't be on the record, the insight that was only available to people close to things. The question was considered for a moment.

'My mother said they never spoke about his job. That was the deal they made with each other. It stayed out of the house.' She shrugged. 'Worked for them, I guess.'

'She must have known he was working undercover, though?'

'She said not.'

It was a stalemate. Maybe it was the truth. Maybe Jake Shaw played his cards close to his chest. Maybe ignorance was bliss when it came to his wife's position. Yaz pulled up the image of Jake Shaw in the pub with Conrad Knott and Stonegrave, held it out. 'How about his work mates? I think they were a team working undercover together.'

'My mother spoke to them, but they weren't interested.' Shaw's daughter pointed at the screen. 'Can I have a copy of this?'

Yaz ignored the question, knowing Conrad Knott was her leverage. He was the one who would care if it was in the public domain. She was regretting sharing the photograph, acting before thinking. Stuffing the mobile back in her pocket, she wanted to steer the conversation away from the image. Shaw's daughter headed into the kitchen and refilled her glass with water. Yaz stayed where she was and waited. The repetitive thud of dance music started up from downstairs.

Shaw shook her head and placed her glass down on the windowsill. 'It starts up every night at this time.'

'You should tell them to wind their necks in.'

'Have you spoken to the men in the photograph you showed me?'

It hadn't been forgotten. Yaz weighed up how much to say, calculating how she should hold back. 'One of them is still serving a detective. Works cold cases now.'

'My mother said he was a weak man. He was a good friend of my father's, but once it all happened, he cut all contact and didn't want to know.' She picked up her drink and swallowed it back. 'What kind of friend does that?'

'A scared one.' It was as charitable as she could be.

'You know the other one is a politician now?'

There it was. Yaz nodded. 'I do.'

'He won't want you poking around in his business.'

It was an understatement, but she wasn't going to disclose their relationship. They were connected in a way neither of them would have anticipated. It was fucked up. 'I never knew my father growing up, either.' It was as close to the truth as she was willing to go. 'I know it's tough.'

'He died?'

Yaz didn't miss a beat. 'He was always dead to me.' She allowed herself a moment to take a breath. 'I know how important your mother becomes.' She picked up a framed photograph and looked again at the damage illness did. 'They died pretty much at the same time, same thing,' Yaz said, putting it back down again. 'It's just me now.'

It meant she'd been kicked out of the flat they'd shared, the landlord unwilling to extend the lease to her. It had been bullshit, and there was only so long you could sofa surf for until your luck ran out. The podcast had been a distraction, a way of satisfying the urge to tell stories. What she hadn't expected was the way it had gotten under her skin so quickly. It had been hard to make sense of, but looking around Sarah Shaw's flat, it simplified things. Amplifying marginalised and silenced voices was what she needed to do. It helped Yaz make sense of the world around her, a way of making a mark on it when the cards were stacked so firmly against her. People like Conrad Knott couldn't be allowed to make their own rules.

Pushing the thought away, she made her pitch. 'We're back to the question of whether you think I can see things through. I'm committed here are, but are you?'

'What does that mean?'

There was an edge to the response, but Yaz was past trying to woo. It was time to move things forward. 'Do you trust me?'

'I don't know you.'

Yaz picked up a leaflet from the coffee table. ReStart was another local charity she was aware of, much like the one Carolyn Seymour had started up. Glancing at the details, this one engaged with people struggling with addiction, aiming to help get them back into accommodation and employment. On the back, a name and mobile number had been scribbled down. Things started to make sense. Yaz placed it back down where she'd found it.

'I'm going all in here and I'm doing it for the right reasons,' she said, straightening back up. 'I don't believe your father was a corrupt detective, but I need your help to prove it. I can't do it all by myself.' She pointed to the framed photographs she'd looked at when first walking into the room. 'I need those for my website and social media because they'll start to change the narrative. Rather than the image of him everyone knows, it shows the truth. It shows him as a husband and a father.' Yaz picked one up and stared at it for a moment. 'I'm trying to tell his story for you so you've got closure, but you've got to decide if you believe if I'm doing it for the right reasons.' Yaz stopped there before she said too much and couldn't stop. The case had been made and laid out. She took her second mobile out and started the voice recording app going before placing it down between them. 'You're either in or out.'

TWENTY

Pushing her notepad to one side and reluctantly hauling herself up off the bed, Yaz headed to the front door. Her housemate had already gone back into his own room, leaving her to deal with whoever was asking for her.

She had various names written down with arrows between them, trying to make connections and sense from the information. People's memories would fade, but past crimes were always due a reckoning. She'd chopped and parcelled up the story as clearly as possible, playing on the unresolved issues in the story, figuring out the structure the podcast would take. But if she promised a game-changer in relation to the story, she had to share the photograph of Birch from the farmhouse. What she couldn't shake was the fact someone wanted her to know about his reappearance. Sarah Shaw had set her story down, the direct connection it needed with the reader. It would change the story from a dry retelling of history to an emotional connection. It would open the right doors, though it felt more important than that now. It came with a price tag, as she'd lied to Shaw's daughter by omission, not connecting the dots between both their fathers. It didn't feel great, but she could swallow it down for now. It was a story that promised to resonate now and have consequences for senior public figures. It was also about personal truths and justice.

Kerri Lewis waited on the doorstep, arms folded. 'I thought we should have a catch-up.'

'What do you want?'

'Can I come in?'

'Why?' Lewis had tracked her down. It wouldn't be the hardest thing in the world to do, but it would still take a bit of effort. They both turned at the sound of a door opening somewhere in the house, loud music exploding out, a snippet of an argument before the door slammed closed. She was letting the woman into her territory.

Yaz led them through the house and the kitchen, a pile of discarded pans and plates still festering in the sink. Opening the back door, they stood in the yard. A crumbling brick wall marked out the space, weeds poking through the cracks in the concrete floor. 'It's a dump, but welcome to my world.' They could both hear the repetitive thump of music from one of the rooms.

It was life in a multi-occupancy house.

'I need more and you're holding back on me,' she said to Lewis. She was thinking about the conversations she'd had and the need to make progress. 'You've been chipping away at this story for years. Don't take me for a fool.'

'No one's taking you for a fool.'

'Sure about that?'

'It's becoming personal for you?'

'Why would you say that?'

'I know Conrad Knott is your father.'

Yaz chewed the words over. There it was. Lewis kept files on the story and seemed to know plenty. 'I don't want to talk about it.'

'We're on the same side here.'

'It doesn't feel that way.' Her buttons were being pushed; fuck Lewis and her sense of what was right and wrong. It was easy to be sanctimonious when you had the cushion of money and privilege. 'Far from it.'

'Knott's scared of the truth,' Lewis said. 'Most people are.'

Yaz chewed on that, not liking what she was hearing. 'Are you saying I'm scared of following the story?'

Lewis smiled and paced the yard. 'You seem rather defensive.'

'You don't know anything about me.'

'Don't you want to talk about it?'

Yaz levelled her gaze, not having it. 'It's none of your business.'

'I'd say it is.'

'It's not important.'

'Let's not lie to each other.'

Yaz didn't reply. Conrad Knott might be her biological father, but that was far as it went. 'I've never had a father in my life.'

'Same here.'

'I don't need one.'

'Your mother brought you up alone?'

'Dragged me up.'

Lewis smiled. 'They say it takes a village to raise a child. My mother worked in the fish processing factories, back in the day. Pattie slappers, they called them.'

Yaz took the bait, wanting to hear the story. 'You'll have to explain that to me?'

'Read up on them. There were some amazing women working in those places, but it was proper work. Long hours and tough conditions. I'd go to neighbour's houses, the library, or be allowed to stay at home as I got older. It's where I started to write, something to lose myself in.'

'And you're bitter about that?'

'Bitter?' Lewis shook her head. 'That's not the word I'd choose. We had no money, but I was happy. It was only as I became an adult that I really understood the sacrifices my mother made so I didn't notice or go without. If anything, it helped shape me.'

'And you think it shaped me?'

'There's only you who can answer that question, but you've got an opportunity to even the score up.'

'You think you know an awful lot about me.'

'We're not that different when all's said and done. I hate corruption and abuse of power just like I know you do. I hate injustice. We can both sniff out when a story doesn't add up.'

'Is that so?'

Lewis was laying it out for her and wasn't being subtle about it. There was a decision to make. Yaz took her mobile out and glanced at it, checking the social media notifications. It felt like the weight of the world was crushing her – Knott on one side, telling her to drop things. Lewis on the other, demanding she followed it through. She needed to make the right decision for herself first and foremost.

'I don't think Mikey Birch died thirty-five years ago.' She presented it as a fact to Lewis, wanting to see the woman's reaction. Lewis didn't respond immediately, the suggestion hanging between them.

'I think you'd need some serious proof of that.'

'What if I had it?' Yaz teed up the photograph from the spy camera on her mobile and showed it, explaining how she'd obtained it.

'Impressive work,' Lewis said. 'Have you told your father this?'

'I have.'

'That's a brave move. He'll come for you.'

'I don't care.'

'I never thought Mikey Birch was dead,' Lewis said. 'Not for one single moment. His disappeance never added up, but no one wanted to question it. They certainly weren't interested in carrying a story about him.'

'You could have let me in on the secret.'

'Would you have believed me?'

'Maybe.'

'Bullshit, Yaz. No one has wanted to listen to me. If I'd come straight out with it, you'd have laughed at me.'

'No I wouldn't.'

'You would, and I wouldn't have blamed you. Doesn't matter what we're talking about, it's always comforting to accept the easy option in life. It's human nature.'

Yaz paced the yard. She knew Knott and Stonegrave were making decisions and talking. It meant they had something to hide and it added up to collusion. It would also lead to mistakes and cracks would appear, and she'd be the one waiting to slip in between the gaps and probe. What she had in front of her was a jigsaw puzzle that had been throw into a box, all of the pieces shaken up, daring her to put them back together again in the right place.

'You're thinking of putting this image out?'

Yaz tuned back into the conversation and nodded. 'I am.'

'Don't do it. Fuck all will happen, Yaz. The photograph of Mikey Birch will make a bit of a splash, sure, but you won't be able to link it explicitly to Conrad Knott. Any hint of that and he'll use his influence to squash it. It'll die on its arse, and you'll be stuck where you are.'

'I've got to do something.'

Lewis took out a card and handed it over. She glanced at it. It was an invite to the VIP event being held at the bar owned by the sons of Knott and Harker, a soft opening launch. Dale Harker was providing a set on the decks.

'Very cosy.'

'I need a plus-one, Yaz.'

TWENTY-ONE

Stonegrave headed straight towards the private door in Mason Knott's bar, catching it as a member of staff walked back out into the main space. He wasn't announcing his arrival to Conrad Knott. No one had paid him any attention, invisible to people in such a place. He'd seen the way Kerri Lewis had looked at him, something like pity at his condition. Not that she'd held back with her words. Hearing voices, he stopped as he was about to knock and peered inside the office. It was only a glimpse from the back, but there was something familiar about the man Conrad Knott was talking to.

Stepping back into the shadows, Stonegrave watched as an agitated Knott paced the room, the other man sitting calmly in front of the desk. Knott walked over to the door and attempted to close it. It didn't catch, slowly easing itself back open. He moved closer, finding the right angle to see inside from, but far enough back to remain in the dimly lit corridor. Knott plucked two bottles of beer from the small fridge next to the desk, opened them and passed one over. Leaning in, Stonegrave managed to put a name to the other man, remembering Dale Harker as Mikey Birch's partner in the raves. The watch he could see on the man's wrist wouldn't have been cheap, nor were the clothes he was wearing. Harker had moved onwards and upwards, but the foundations of his career had been built on illegal activity. Stonegrave edged forward again to hear better, able to get a sightline into the office.

'You should have called.' It was Knott talking. He placed the beers down on the desk. 'This isn't a social club.'

'Some things are done better face to face,' Harker said. Harker shuffled back in his chair and put his feet on the desk. 'And better now than at tonight's event.'

Stonegrave held back the cough that was building in his chest, bending over in an attempt to stifle it. Concentrating on Knott and Harker, the undercurrent of the conversation was clear. Knott was uncomfortable at being dictated to. The politician was the one used to calling the shots.

'I'll tell you what's ironic,' Harker said, continuing to talk. 'People like us wanted to use abandoned and unwanted warehouses back in the day and were run out of town. We had no choice but to go out to the fields for our raves. Youngsters use a place like this to open a bar and it becomes big business.' He laughed. 'What a world. Suppose this is what happens when a place runs out of options and has fuck all left?'

'That's regeneration for you.'

'It's bullshit if you ask me, but funny how some things turn out, isn't it? One minute we're on opposite sides, the next we're both successful men with empires, proudly watching our lads make their way in life. Promotion beckons for you, right? You're heading towards dining at the top table at last. But you always were ambitious, weren't you? You were always going to get what you wanted.'

'What other way is there to be in life?'

Harker laughed and offered a warning. 'It can sometimes eat you up, though. You have to make your peace with the fact it's all about the journey. Who knows where we'll both be in a decade's time?'

'I didn't have you down as a philosopher.'

'Hidden depths, my friend. I'll tell you something else too. It's the kind of position that needs you to be squeaky clean. No offence, but politicians are scum. We both know that.' Harker paused. 'But even these days there are still some scandals that are just too big to survive.'

A silence in the room settled. Stonegrave took another step towards the door, wanting to hear more. Knott was taking back control of the situation, outlining Harker's position to him.

'I hear you could do with your new album being a hit?'

'Where did you hear that?'

'Just on the grapevine. You've got a lot of money riding on it and you're not the hot property you once were, awards or not.'

Stonegrave didn't need to be in the room to know Harker was pissed off with the way the conversation was going.

'A few poor business decisions that are taking their toll on your wallet,' Knott said, continuing to talk. 'It happens, but add in the music industry slowly dying, and it's tough. I get it. It's like everything, the world moves on to the next bright young thing.'

'Don't you worry about me.'

Beer bottles clinked, Knott proposing a toast. A truce was being brokered.

'You people thought you were so clever back then,' Harker said, 'thinking you were blending in. But you stood out like a sore thumb. It was obvious. Shame it didn't turn out differently, of course. Who would have had Mikey down as a murderer?'

'It's the way it goes sometimes,' Knott said. 'Things happen when people are pushed. It's in the past where it needs to be, though.'

Stonegrave listened as the office fell quiet. Something was happening. Things had taken a different turn. He edged forward again, trying to get a better view.

'Recognise her?' he heard Harker ask Knott. Knott was looking at something on a mobile phone. 'She told my PR that she's a journalist at *The Guardian* and wanted to talk to me about my new album.'

'Must happen a lot.'

'It does, but she was sloppy. She didn't do her homework and check it out. Turns out she's a true crime podcaster.'

Stonegrave winced in recognition. Yaz Moy was putting herself about. Knott wouldn't be happy.

'She's having a sniff around, so what?' Knott said. 'Mark her card and send her packing.'

Stonegrave heard a mobile sound, Knott saying he needed to return the call. Chairs scraped on the floor, the two men done. He moved towards the corner of the corridor, staying out of sight, as the men walked to the doorway.

'We both came out ahead,' Knott said, 'even though things got out of hand. We weren't to know what was going to happen, right? Mikey Birch and Jake Shaw both made their own decisions. All we did was react to them.'

Harker had the last word, making sure to face Knott. 'This podcaster needs shutting down.'

Stonegrave waited as they walked down the stairs and back towards the bar before heading into the office. Looking around, it was Knott's son's space. The only paperwork he could see was a file of invoices. His mind went back to something he'd heard – *our lads*. Pulling up the bar's website, he saw it immediately. Mason Knott and Riley Harker were business partners. Years of being a detective taught him to think slowly and clearly. It didn't have to mean anything, but it felt significant. It was a small city, but an undercover detective moving in the same circles as the man he was surveilling? Men now in conversation with each other?

The door behind him swung open, Knott walking back into the office. Knott immediately stopped in front of him.

'What are you doing in here?'

'We crossed as you were downstairs.' He didn't mention Dale Harker, letting Knott stew on things.

Knott closed the door and took a bottle of beer out of the fridge in the corner of the room. 'I'm celebrating.' He ignored his mobile phone sounding in his pocket. 'You're talking to the new Minister of State. The deal has been rubberstamped. It's just down to waiting for the official announcement.'

Stonegrave continued to stare at the man, not really listening as Knott spoke about his political plans. 'I want to talk about Yaz Moy,' he said, cutting in.

'I take it you spoke to Kerri Lewis?'

'She says she's not working with Yaz Moy.' He'd replayed their conversation in his head again, the way she'd looked him in the eye and all but said, *fuck you*.

Knott took a drag on the bottle of beer, a small shake of the head. 'Did you make it clear to her that she shouldn't indulge Moy?'

'She didn't want to hear it.' His eyes went to the window, too dark to see out of. If he could, he'd see a city that had never looked so grey to him, a place slowly squeezing his insides to the point he couldn't breathe. Everything was complex and interconnected.

'Do you remember Dale Harker?' He watched Knott carefully to see what the reaction would be. Knott played it with a straight bat, saying nothing. 'He was Mikey Birch's partner, but went legitimate afterwards. He's now a music producer. I looked him up. Seems he's still making new stuff from time to time. Got a new album out, apparently.'

'What about him?'

'Maybe I should speak to him?'

'Why?'

'Maybe Yaz Moy has spoken to him?'

'I want you focusing on the podcaster.' Knott jabbed a finger out. 'Do as you're told.'

TWENTY-TWO

It was easy, as Kerri Lewis said it would be. Yaz showed the invite she had in her hand and was granted access to the bar, no questions asked. The security on the door were more interested in chatting to the young women trying to make their way in without an invite. Moving through the crowd, Yaz scanned the faces for ones she recognised. Some were movers and shakers in the city, big fishes in a small pond. Others she had no idea who they were. Dale Harker was on the decks, an elevated stand on the stage in the corner of the bar, making sure no one was going to miss him. He was concentrating on the job in hand, mixing vinyl the old-school way by hand, two minders discreetly standing either side of him. The room buzzed with conversation and laughter, Harker sound tracking it with an electronic backbeat. The younger people in attendance were no doubt Mason Knott's friends and those he wanted to impressive, the reflected glory of political power and a famous DJ in the building.

Staying on the move, Yaz finally spotted Conrad Knott. He was in dressed in casual clothes that were too new to look as relaxed as he wanted them to. It seemed you could take a man out of a suit, but you couldn't take the suit out of the man. He was talking to a small group of people she recognised as the city's other Members of Parliament; money and champagne as they toasted all their mutual success. Their eyes locked together for a moment, Knott unable to keep the surprise at seeing her off his face before he quickly glanced in the direction of Harker.

She wanted to speak to both men, wondering if it was a strange quirk of fate that had brought them together. The fact they were both present suggested something else to her. It suggested a level of familiarity and comfort if they were happy to be in the same room together. Scanning around, their sons were similarly holding court with an audience. One was her half-brother, one she only knew through social media. They'd never spoken, no need to. What could they say to each other? Even the thought of doing so made her feel sick.

Yaz felt an arm on her shoulder and turned to look at Kerri Lewis. 'You didn't say the guest list was an A to Z of wankers?'

Lewis smiled. 'What did you expect?' She nodded in the direction of the stage. 'I'm sure his thugs will keep a lid on things, assuming they're not just for show.'

Yaz watched Conrad Knott make his way through the crowds, heading towards Dale Harker, watched them talk to each other. She let Lewis guide her towards a quiet booth at the back of the room. Lewis grabbed two glasses of champagne from a passing waitress and held one out. 'It's the good stuff.'

Yaz waved it away and sat down. She shrugged her denim jacket off and threw it to one side, leaning in to drown out the loud hub of chatter and thump of dance music. 'You always knew that Conrad Knott is my father.' It had needled away at her. 'We don't have a relationship. He's a piece of shit.' If she stopped to think about it for too long, the anger bubbling inside would spill out.

She glanced across the room towards him, Knott with a cupped hand around Harker's ear, shouting something to him. He pointed in her direction.

'Something else happened that night, and I can understand why people want it to stay buried, but that's not happening on my watch.'

Yaz sat back against the leather booth. 'There's more to this.' She was thinking aloud.

'How do you mean?'

It was hard to articulate, but Yaz was thinking about the contradiction around money. She'd been told Mikey Birch cared nothing for money and that he was all about the money. No middle-ground. There was no way of putting her finger on it, but it all felt wrong.

Lewis pushed her drink to one side and took a piece of paper out of her pocket and passed it over.

Yaz glanced down at the name scribbled down, Maneesh Kapoor, and his number. Kapoor had reputation for being a media disrupter. He was the public face of the *Inform* collective.

'I told him about you, Yaz. People like you are rare, so don't throw it away.' Lewis paused. 'They're not just about politics. They're looking to beef up the investigative journalism. Call him and have a chat. Take the opportunity. Explore the story, see if there's something mutually beneficial for you both here.'

Yaz scanned the room again, not listening closely. Conrad Knott was staring straight at her. He moved towards a door in the corner, turning back to her as he opened it. The message was clear. She left Lewis where she was and walked over, heading up the stairs. The office at the end of the corridor had a light on. Inside it, a large desk dominated the space.

'We didn't finish our conversation last night,' he said, closing the office door behind them, the music from the bar area fading away.

'I'm pretty sure we did.' Yaz looked around, figuring the place was her brother's. She kept the thought to herself.

'I've always watched you from afar, you know?' Knott said. He grabbed a beer from the fridge behind him. 'You're exactly like your mother, you know? She was always confrontational and aggressive, far too stubborn to accept any help. She always though she knew best.'

'You don't get to talk about her like that.'

Knott held his hands up, accepting the point. 'You're an adult, you can understand that things sometimes just happen. I tried to do something to help you, but I had to respect the fact your mother didn't want any help.'

'It made life easier for you and your conscience, though.' There was no disguising the anger in her voice. 'Spare me your concern. Now she's dead, I consider myself an orphan.'

'We can't change the past, can we, but we can look to the future?'

'A social media meme is the best you've got to offer?' There was the slightest hesitation and flinch as he worked hard to mask his irritation at her calling him out. 'We're well past that stage.'

'Doesn't mean I don't want to do right by you.' He offered a smile. 'We don't need to be enemies here. We can be friends.'

'Is that so?'

'I could help. I've got contacts who'd be interested in hearing from you.'

'Not on your terms.'

He sighed. 'I really don't understand you, Yaz. Why would you even want to be a journalist? Everyone knows they're scum of the earth, following their own agenda and attacking people just trying to get by. But even allowing for that, I'm trying to accommodate you.'

Yaz laughed. 'A politician attacking journalism? You've got some balls. You'd do well to get your own house in order, get yourself some integrity.'

Knott settled back in his chair, a smile on his face. 'Messing about with a podcast gives you integrity?'

'It does.'

'It certainly doesn't give you an audience.'

'You'd be surprised.' Watching him shrug like it was no big deal brought things back into sharp focus. They both knew he was on the back foot and couldn't control things. Yaz returned his smile. 'You sound scared?'

'Scared?' He shook his head at the suggestion. 'I'm about to become a Minister. My inbox is already overflowing with things I need to worry about. What I won't worry about is a minor issue from so long ago.'

'You're expending a lot of energy on something that's not important to you.'

'This is my moment. I don't want it ruining by a distraction.'

Yaz rolled that around before speaking again. 'That's an interesting choice of word? The murder of a former detective and colleague of yours, a friend, is a distraction to you?'

'Don't take words out of my mouth.'

'That's exactly what you said.'

He loosened his collar, playing for time and staring back at her. 'You think it's important? You're wrong. If it came out, it would be embarrassing for me, but I'd ride the storm out and it'd be forgotten within a news cycle. There's no real story here.'

'You'd take your chance on that?'

'People are talking to me.' Yaz took her mobile out and held it up to him. 'I've tracked down the detective who investigated Jake Shaw's murder and heard how you scared her off. I've spoken to Mikey's girlfriend back in the day and heard her story.'

'So what?'

'I've also spoken to Jake Shaw's daughter.' Yaz stood up and pocketed her mobile again. 'She hasn't had justice yet.'

Knott dismissed her words, not caring for what she'd said. 'Do you still think Kerri Lewis is your friend? I bet she didn't tell you she'd spoken to me? She called me and set up a meeting. Being curious, I agreed to it, and we had a frank exchange of views. It seems she wanted me to know all about you. I'd say she was trying to pump me for more information, like she thought it was a live story for her. Last warning for you. She's going to fuck you over, Yaz.'

TWENTY-THREE

Down the stairs and into the heat and noise of the main bar area, Yaz hadn't stopped to see if Knott was following her. Pushing her way through the crowd, she glanced over at Dale Harker. He had his head down as he teed up the next record. Her head felt like it was going to explode. Her father's words were going around; the job offer she didn't want to entertain. The fact she couldn't trust Kerri Lewis.

'How was your father?'

'He sends his regards.' Yaz leaned in, getting straight into Lewis's face. 'You didn't tell me you've been having comfy chats with him.'

Lewis smiled. 'I like to stir things up.'

'You didn't think to tell me?'

'I go back with him. I thought I'd rattle his cage.'

'You said this wasn't your story?'

'It's your story, but if I can shake something loose, why not?'

Yaz sat back, tried to think clearly. 'Why are you doing this? What's your bottom line?' They'd been over it, but she wanted Lewis to say it. It needed to be out in the open, everything on the table.

Lewis plucked another glass of champagne from a passing waiter and drank it before speaking. 'Forget everything else, Yaz. I want the truth to emerge and you're the only person who's going to deliver it.' She stood up. 'Give Maneesh a call at *Inform*, step things up. Put your podcast out through them and grab the moment. Seize the fucking day.'

'You're very keen to tell me what I should do.'

Lewis picked up her cigarettes and mobile from her bag. 'Can I borrow your jacket?' It wasn't really a question as she grabbed at it. 'Have a think about it.' She took out an unlit cigarette and twizzled it like a baton. 'When you're calmer.'

Yaz watched Lewis make her way through the crowd and towards the exit. Scanning the room again, Knott was back out from the office, working another group of people, all smiles as he posed for selfies. Turning away, disgusted, she looked at her mobile phone, wanting a distraction. Scrolling through her social media feeds, she wasn't taking it in, idling instead on the countless memes and jokes. Hitting Google, she pulled up *Inform's* website and glanced through the recent stories, knowing it was impressive stuff.

They'd exposed a Member of Parliament's family links to a private company winning government business without the correct tendering process. It was worthy, but didn't float her boat. A recent expose on police violence against environmental protestors was much more eye-catching. It lived up to the website's promise to speak truth to power. When they got it right, the work was insightful and pissed off all the right people. The nagging doubt at the back of her mind was that it didn't reach enough people. It was like shouting into the void.

Putting her mobile back down, there were other frustrations to deal with. She couldn't shake off the thought that Nell Heard hadn't wanted to talk to her, or about the farmhouse. There was something she couldn't quite put her finger on. It continued to nag at her, the increasing certainty she wasn't quite managing to connect the dots. She was also thinking about what she definitely knew, how Dale Harker's connected to her father, how the relationship between the illegal rave organiser and undercover detective spanned the generations. It was another layer of the story to peel back and explore. Taking in the room, her brother had never missed out on a single thing. He had a guaranteed future. She was owed something. Grabbing Lewis's bag from under the table, she wanted to continue their conversation, argue it through and make sense of things.

Pushing her way through the crowds and towards the exit, ignoring the people who swore at her as she did so, she threw herself against the wall and breathed in the night. The bouncers she'd seen on the way in pointed at her and laughed. Turning away, she wasn't in the mood. The street was quiet, the low hum of a bar on the opposite side of the road. It looked to be empty inside. She watched a couple stagger past it, heading for the idling taxis. The driver of the one at the front of the queue folded up a newspaper and started up his engine.

There was no sign of Kerri Lewis. Her best bet was that she was somewhere on the cobbled street running down the side of the bar, smoking her cigarette in peace. Pushing herself off the wall, the bouncers were gathered around a mobile phone, laughing at whatever they were viewing.

Yaz had to double back to spot the small cut-in running behind the bar, a narrow alleyway leading to a pair of offices. The brass plaques detailed them; a recruitment company and an IT support firm. Kerri Lewis was face down on the pavement between the doorways, a pool of blood trickling away from her like the tide going out.

Yaz's head started to spin. She placed her hand against the wall to remain balanced, forcing herself to slow her breathing down. Instinct kicked in and took over. She bent down and felt for a pulse, finding one. Rubbing her face, it was something. Standing back, she took her mobile out and called the emergency services.

Her call connected, Yaz listening as she was told to slow down by the responder. She asked for an ambulance, explaining the scene in front of her.

'The police will also attend,' the voice at the end of the line said. 'Can I take your name, please?'

Yaz hesitated, knowing the call would be recorded. She'd used her own mobile, the one that would be traceable. It wasn't what she wanted. Killing the call, she stayed rooted to the spot, a decision to make. She'd made a mistake.

Her first thought was to head straight back into the bar, fuck the bouncers on the door. She'd march straight back into her father's office and confront him. It would be a stupid move to make, she knew that, but she'd always acted first and thought later. It was her nature, but it needed to change. Staying where she was, she tried to play the scenario out. Jumping straight in wasn't always the best option.

Hearing sirens, speaking to the police was the right thing to do. Whatever was happening was spilling outwards with serious consequences. Looking down at Kerri Lewis, Yaz thought again about the link between actions and consequences, seeing what she should have immediately recognised. The truth of the situation hit her. She bent over and dry heaved, this time slumping down against the wall, tears in her eyes. The sirens grew louder, focusing her mind, knowing the police would be arriving ahead of the ambulance. She wiped her eyes with the back of her hand and stood back up, looking down at Kerri Lewis. Taking a deep breath, she knew what she had to do. Blue lights started to flash at the top of the road, reflecting off the walls of the buildings. Hearing a car door open and slam shut, she made her decision. Head down, she quickly hurried away in the opposite direction.

TWENTY-FOUR

Yaz stopped and looked around. Taking a breath and settling herself, she took the keys to Kerri Lewis's apartment from the woman's bag. The feeling of paranoia was irrational. No one was watching, no one cared. Slipping inside, she walked up to Lewis's apartment and stared at the door. Going inside would be crossing another line.

Yaz quickly closed the door behind her and leaned against the wall for a moment, looking again at Lewis's apartment. She was still processing what had happened in the bar and outside of it, what Lewis was trying to tell her before she'd gone outside to smoke. What she didn't know was what happened in the time between Lewis stepping outside of the bar and calling the emergency services. What she didn't want to think about was how Conrad Knott and Dale Harker had watched them talking. The muscle they had on the site. Walking over to the kitchen sink, she poured herself a glass of water, wanting to get it straight in her head. Looking out over the marina from the window, the one thing she didn't want to do was stay in her own room.

Yaz picked up her mobile, and using Google, called the numbers for the region's hospitals until she'd found the one Kerri Lewis had been taken to. The response was that Lewis was stable, but hadn't regained consciousness. The voice at the other end of the line was reluctant to give her any further details. Instinctively, Yaz knew she shouldn't say too much, either. Heading back into the living space, she unzipped her tracksuit top and threw it down onto a chair.

Sitting down, Lewis' laptop was on the coffee table. Instinctively she tapped at the keyboard, watching as it sprung into life, no password required. Lewis wouldn't be expecting anyone other than herself to be using it in the apartment. Searching through the folders, most related to a novel Lewis was working on. Scrolling through the rest of the folders, Yaz focused on the one marked with Jake Shaw's name. A lot of the documents inside were scans of Lewis's own contemporary newspaper reports. One file was an audio recording. It was tagged as *Conrad Knott. mp3* and dated two days previously. It was the same date she'd approached Lewis wanting to talk about Jake Shaw's murder. It was the conversation Knott had told her about, twisting the knife. Lewis had written it off as rattling the man's cage. Hitting the play button, the recording started with background noise she couldn't make immediate sense of. Kerri Lewis's voice and the sound of crockery confirmed the conversation had taken place in a restaurant.

'It's not every day you get to dine with a soon-to-be Minister of State,' Lewis said, voice slightly distorted.

The recording cut out briefly, a muffled blast of white noise, before the restaurant came back to life. If she was guessing, Lewis had set the voice recorder going on her mobile before placing it down between them on the table, maybe pretending to check a text message. It was a ballsy gamble.

'I would have thought your interest was in crime, not politics,' she heard Knott say.

'They're often the same thing in my experience.'

Knott laughed. 'I assume you've been working on that line?'

Yaz could read between the lines, knew Knott would have hated that comment.

'My father was my role model, both as a detective and then a politician. Why not keep it in the family?' A pause. 'Are you going to take your coat off?'

Yaz tuned into the background noise as the conversation dipped. She tried to imagine where the meeting had taken place. Chances were, it would have been somewhere away from prying eyes.

'I was surprised to hear from you,' Knott said, restarting the conversation. 'I'm intrigued to hear what you think we've got to talk about.'

'I made that clear when I left the message. I want to talk about Jake Shaw.'

'You're like a dog with a bone. It's been, what, thirty-five years?'

'People don't forget.'

'I read your latest book, you know? *Murder Around The North*. Fair play, it wasn't as sensationalist I thought it was going to be, even if it didn't sell.'

Lewis cut in. 'It tells important stories from a female perspective. People like you have been allowed to set the agenda for too long.'

'And that's important, but it lacked the police perspective. You're only telling part of the story.'

'That's because no one will speak out.'

'Good writers find a way.'

Yaz sat back and drew her knees into her body, the tension across the table all too easy to picture.

She heard Knott laugh, knowing he was trying to needle to Lewis. 'Neither confirm, nor deny,' he said.

'You know the way it works. It means the police can continue to do their important work.'

'It also means they can continue to hide their wrongdoings.'

'Not at all.'

A third voice drifted in briefly, a waiter making small talk with them for a moment.

'Ladies first,' Knott said, presumably pointing to something the waiter had brought over to the table before continuing. 'There's nothing more to say about Jake Shaw's murder, I'm afraid. You know that because you've written about it. I'm only talking to you because he was a friend and colleague of mine.'

'I remember what it was like covering the story back in the day, how difficult it was made for me. It was all about the outrage over young people daring to have a good time, wasn't it? The drugs and the money involved made it easy to suggest Jake Shaw was corrupted by it all.'

'I assume you're familiar with the idea of Occam's razor? Things just are what they are most of the time. There doesn't have to be a grand conspiracy.'

'No one believes that for a minute.'

'It's a matter of established fact.' Knott paused, the sound of a mobile. Yaz heard him say the call wasn't important before continuing. 'I'm not sure why we're having this conversation, unless you've got something new to say?'

'What do you know about podcasts?' Lewis asked him. Yaz shuffled forward, listening closely.

'I know enough to say they're not for me,' Knott said.

'You're old-school and prefer the traditional media, right? I'll tell you about that world, shall I? When I covered Jake Shaw's murder I was stopped from doing my job. Some of those barriers were quite aggressive, some more subtle. Did you know the paper's editor at the time played cricket and golf with some of the police's senior people? They were all drinking mates. You might think that's the way of the world, but the world's changing rapidly. Jobs for the boys and trading favours are on the way out. The future is here now, and podcasts are one part of it. Podcasters aren't waiting for permission, they're going out and telling the stories they think are important. All bets are off.'

'Finished?'

'Not by a long way. I want the truth. It's as simple as that. I was a young reporter when I tried to write the story. I was bullied and harassed, but I didn't know how to fight back against it. I do now, though.'

'This is about you?'

'It's about a lot of things, isn't it?'

Yaz listened to the sound of a chair being pushed backwards, scraping along the floor. The sound distorting as the mobile was picked up.

'We both know the truth about what happened that night at the rave hasn't been allowed to surface,' Lewis said.

'You sound like a conspiracy theorist.'

'You didn't ask who I'm helping with the podcast.'

'It's irrelevant to me.'

'You might know her?'

'I shouldn't think so.'

'Yaz Moy.'

There was a moment of silence between them before Knott spoke. Yaz leaned in, wanting to hear his reaction.

'I don't know her.'

She knew what he would say, his words a lie, but they still carried enough poison to inflict a wound.

'She's good,' Lewis said. 'She'll get to the truth of what happened that night.'

Yaz leaned across to the laptop having heard enough and hit stop. Clicking on the file, she scrolled back through the conversation. There was something she'd heard, but it was only now hitting home. Finding it, she listened again.

'This is about you?' Knott said.

'It's about a lot of things, isn't it?'

Hitting stop, Yaz sequenced it in her head, reading between the lines. The only conclusion to draw was that Lewis had valid reasons for staying involved. It was frustrating, too many unanswered questions. Pacing the room, one thing she was still thinking about was why Kerri Lewis had given her help with the story, why she didn't want it herself. The position Lewis had outlined made sense. It was a story suited to a podcast, not a newspaper. It also didn't make sense, though. It wasn't an altruistic decision, that much felt right. Sitting back down, Yaz's mobile sounded. Picking it up and glancing at the screen, the number wasn't one in her contact list. She answered without speaking, a force of habit.

'Am I speaking to Yaz Moy?' The voice speaking to her was female and young, plenty of background noise. The caller was outside somewhere.

'Who are you?'

'Detective Constable Oberman.'

'We haven't met.'

'Not yet.'

She hesitated. 'What do you want?'

'Do you know Kerri Lewis?'
'Why?'
'Shall I assume you do?'
'You can assume all you like.'
'We need to talk, Yaz. Now.'

TWENTY-FIVE

Picking out the headlights coming down the track, the vehicle swept into the car park next to her. Yaz turned away, staring out into pitch black nothingness, cold. Stepping off her motorbike, she removed her helmet and waited. The car came to a stop, the engine killed, headlights following. A woman in her late twenties got out and walked across to her.

'You're the detective who called?' Yaz said.

'Detective Constable Oberman,' she said, briefly flashing identification before pocketing it again. Oberman took a step forward, looking around. 'We could have done this somewhere warmer?'

Yaz didn't reply. There was no way she was having the police in her room, or in Lewis's apartment. Hessle Foreshore by the Humber Bridge had been the first place to come to mind when the detective had pushed. By day, the beauty spot was populated by dog walkers and families eating ice-creams on the shingle beach. By night, the car park area was used for darker deeds, sexual activity prevalent. Maybe she'd hoped on some level that it would put the detective off.

'Kerri Lewis was attacked tonight, and it's touch and go,' Oberman said, explaining that Lewis had been transported to hospital. Her head had hit the pavement as she'd fallen. What would happen next was anyone's guess. 'I'm not going to bullshit you here. It was lucky someone found her and called an ambulance.'

Yaz stared at the detective, silent, weighing up what she should say. She swallowed it down, thinking about the choice of words by Oberman. *Lucky.* Fucking hell.

'I was hoping you'd have a moment to talk about it,' Oberman said.

'I can't help you.'

'Let's not get off on the wrong foot here. You were out drinking with her at an invite-only party, one for the city's beautiful people. I'm not judging, but I was surprised. You have a certain reputation, shall we say?'

'What would that be?'

'You're certainly not very popular with the old-timers I know at the station. I've looked at your website and can see the link to the podcast that pissed them off. They're not fans of yours.'

'I'd be more concerned if they were.'

Oberman smiled. 'Fair point.' They both watched a vehicle sweep into the car park. It stayed where it was, engine running and headlights on. Oberman spoke first. 'It was called in by a young woman off her mobile.'

'Could have been anyone.'

'Are you going to tell me what happened?'

'I was in the bar.'

'What are you working on with Lewis?'

'We don't work together.'

Oberman sighed and got to the point. 'You two are in communication with each and then this happens? I don't buy coincidences.'

'That's your lookout.'

'That doesn't answer my question.'

'It's the best answer you're going to get.' They were at an impasse. 'Made an arrest yet?'

'Not yet, but there's not much to go on, which is unfortunate. And just so we're completely clear on this, we're totally off the record here. If any of this turns up anywhere, I'll know where it came from, and I'll make your life a misery. Understood?'

Yaz smiled, but didn't bite. Instead, she asked if any witnesses had come forward.

Oberman said not. 'There might be something on the cameras in the wider area, but it's needle in a haystack stuff. Who knows? You can never tell until you start knocking on doors and rattling some cages, but don't take the piss. I might be inclined to help you if you give me something back. Maybe I'm too nosy for my own good, but there's more going on here than I know at the moment, and I don't like sweeping up other people's shit.' Oberman's mobile sounded and she walked away out of earshot to take the call.

Yaz took out her own mobile and went online, first searching for any new information about what happened to Kerri Lewis. There was nothing official, too early for the mainstream media to be covering it. It would need the police's media team to spoon-feed them the basic details first. Turning to social media, it was a case of narrowing the search parameters down. There was also little to be gleaned, still too early in the process. Once people knew Kerri Lewis was the victim, it would gain some traction and become more newsworthy.

Glancing at Oberman's back, Yaz ran a quick online search for information on the woman. The results referenced court cases in the local media. Scanning through, the main reference was to an investigation that had gone wrong, Oberman commended for her part in bringing down an organised crime gang. Reading more critically, it had come at a personal cost to her, an injury sustained during the operation.

Having read enough, Yaz pocketed her mobile and turned to look out over the water again, thinking about Kerri Lewis and what had happened to her. People had watched them, but who had seen Lewis step outside? Recognising the truth, even if she didn't want to face up to it.

Oberman finished her call and walked back over to her. 'You should come in and speak to me,' she said, 'get your information down as a statement.'

'Maybe I'll do that.'

'Don't make me coming looking for you, Yaz. That's not how it works.'

'Men do bad stuff and people like us clean it up.' It was what Kerri Lewis had said to her, the words out before she could stop herself.

'You'll have to explain that to me?'

'It doesn't matter.' She watched Oberman head back to her car, headlights illuminating the water in front of her, the scene reverting to darkness as Oberman reversed out of the parking space.

Heading away, Yaz pulled on the motorbike's throttle, increasing her speed as she turned onto rural roads. She was going too fast for the stretch she was on, but didn't care. Weaving past a car, she ignored the blast of its horn and the aggressive flashing of headlights, leaving it behind her. None of it mattered. She went faster, approaching the bend, momentum seeing her straddle both lanes. The car on the other side of the road swerved, clipping the pavement. *Shit*. She eased off, pulling to the side of the road. Removing her helmet, she breathed in the cold night air, adrenaline pumping around her body. The car she'd overtaken slowed as it passed, the passenger lowering his window to shout out that she was a fucking idiot. It was a reflex action to throw some abuse back in his direction, but the car had already driven away. The driver also wasn't wrong.

Maybe it wasn't wise, but looping back into the city, Yaz found herself heading for the one-bedroom flat she'd been brought up in by her mother. It was the place she'd told Sarah Shaw about, a featureless satellite estate on the tip of the city. It was grey and drab, anonymous, doing its best to make use of what crumbs from the table of government spending fell its way. Just staring at it from a distance brought back memories; some welcome, some not so welcome. The same streetlight she remembered flickering had broken again. The block of flats was arranged in a rectangle with concrete staircases in each corner, a car park in the middle. Closing her eyes and zoning out, Yaz could hear her own footsteps echoing off them from when she was a child. If she had time to walk along the balcony, the lingering aroma of that evening's cooking would be in the air, kitchens packed in densely next to each other through thin walls, people living shoulder to shoulder.

Deep down, she knew why she was angry. Kerri Lewis had spoken to Conrad Knott and made her a pawn in their ongoing game stretching through the decades. No one got to use her like that. Kerri Lewis had picked up and worn her denim jacket as she left the bar and headed out into the night, but she was the one who'd waved her mobile in Knott's face and said she had the story on it, that people were talking to her. Lewis had been the victim of the attack, but she shouldn't have been. There was no reason for it to have happened to her. It was a case of mistaken identity. Yaz knew she was the one who should be lying in hospital, fighting for her life.

PODCAST EXTRACT – EPISODE THREE

NOT YET UPLOADED

In this third podcast in the new 'CrimeTime' series, we'll explore in more depth the night of Jake Shaw's murder ...

The three-man undercover team was headed up by the then Detective Inspector Conrad Knott ... Knott was already a high-achiever, young for such a role, but on the path to fast career advancement ... of course, the name may well be familiar to you ... shortly after Shaw's murder and the winding down of the undercover work, Knott left the police force, and after a spell in the private sector away from the region, he returned to the region and moved into politics, elected to Parliament in 1997 when his own father retired from a safe seat ... since then, he's built a second career and stands on the cusp of becoming a Minister of State ... this podcast has tracked down the other man who was part of the undercover team alongside Jake Shaw and Conrad Knott, but he didn't want to talk to this podcast about his murdered colleague ...

It wasn't a team of equals, that much is clear ... being younger and not as experienced, Jake Shaw certainly wasn't on the same footing. He was also very much in thrall to Knott and his colleague, looking up to them with genuine respect and admiration ... but there was a side to Jake Shaw that was troubled, too. From talking to friends and family, it's clear at the time of the undercover operation he felt concerned that he was in trouble and facing danger ... it's also clear he didn't feel able to share his concerns with the rest of the team ...

The night of Shaw's murder was chaos ... the alarm was raised by a reveller, a young woman taking a short break from the rave. Heading behind the barn and away from the crowd, Shaw was found slumped against the wall, dying ... the raves were successful partly because people couldn't easily or quickly spread word of where they were happening, but that cut both ways ... there was no fast way of calling for an ambulance ... instead, when word started to spread, people naturally panicked and streamed away from the site, a stampede towards the exit and the field that cars were parked up in ...

Attention quickly shifted to finding Mikey Birch ... we know he shared a flat with his girlfriend, a corner property on the bottom floor of a two-storey block to the north of the city ... finding no one there, police undertook a search of the local area ... facing resistance from residents unwilling to assist them, one neighbour spoke out ... Birch had been seen returning to his flat, visibly distressed, before leaving shortly afterwards with a bag ... good riddance, his neighbour had said ...

Kicking the door of the flat in, the police weren't prepared to wait ... inside, the place was a chaotic mess that mirrored Mikey Birch's lifestyle ... detectives found nothing that indicated where Birch had fled to, but they did find the knife that killed Jake Shaw ...

Dale Harker quickly surrendered for questions to the police, but Birch was a different matter ... he was in the wind ... put yourself in his shoes for a moment and try to understand the panic that must have been coursing through him ... why would he run? ... what was he scared of, or more pertinently, who was he scared of? ...

TWENTY-SIX

The bench next to the pier towers instinctively felt an unusual place to set a meeting for. It was public yet private, no choice but to wait it out as instructed. Withernsea was nominally a seaside resort, but the handful of amusement arcades looked forlorn and locked down, a small number of hardy families wringing some fun out of being on the beach together, all wearing coats and hats as the wind whistled around them.

Yaz checked her mobile, waiting. The nurse on the ward hadn't allowed her access, as she'd expected. Kerri Lewis was conscious, but sleeping heavily and frequently. Instead, spinning a story, she'd handed over an old mobile with a new SIM card, hers the only number stored in it. The nurse had been reluctant at first, but eventually took it from her with a promise to pass it on.

Ordering her thoughts, Yaz had seen both Conrad Knott and Dale Harker in the bar. She'd seen them with their heads together, her presence more than noted. Worse, she'd waved her mobile phone around, telling Knott she had fresh interviews recorded on it. She'd made herself a target before it had all gone wrong. Oberman had quickly worked it out, the denim jacket Lewis had grabbed to keep her warm enough to confuse her attacker in the darkness. Unable to settle in the woman's apartment, Yaz had worked her way through Lewis's laptop. Lewis had made piles of notes on various stories, downloaded links from websites, seemingly developing ideas to pitch. It had looked like she had a number of balls in the air. Yaz had wondered if any were going to stick. Lewis had been fastidious in wiping her online trail, no website history to look. She'd raked though Lewis's bookshelves, flicked through a copy of the woman's latest book, imagined leading the same life. What she couldn't shake was the thought she should be the one lying in a hospital bed.

Someone sat down next to her on the bench, taking her by surprise. Yaz glanced to the side at the woman. 'Bit cloak and dagger?' she said.

'You can't be too careful.'

'I guess so.' Helen Pullman had sent a text message, saying they needed to talk urgently. 'Credit to you, this place is certainly low-key.' They had a full view of the main promenade, everyone approaching from both ends. It would have been an hour's drive down the narrow coast road from her caravan, easy enough to make sure you arrived alone and hadn't been followed. It meant the woman who'd been parachuted in to investigate Mikey Birch's murder had taken every precaution. Once a detective, always a detective. Either she had something to say, or was paranoid. Yaz looked glanced across the road at where she'd parked Kerri Lewis's car. Finding the keys and debating with herself whether it was ethical to use it, the thought of having to travel around on her small motorbike swung it.

'We moved out to the coast for the peace and quiet, you know?' Pullman said to her. 'We wanted to be near the sea and have somewhere for the grandkids to come and visit so they could play on the beach.'

'Makes sense.'

'It's also somewhere away from where people know who I am, if you follow?'

'I follow.' Pullman had fallen silent for a moment, wanting her words to be understood. She might look like any other retired grandmother, but she had a past that could come back to hurt her. Pullman lived in the shadows in a way she hadn't really considered. She was vulnerable, probably more so in retirement with none of the protection she'd once enjoyed. Some people would never forgive or forget.

'I can't help you.'

'Don't say it.'

'I don't have to justify myself to you.'

Yaz scrolled through the photographs on her mobile, finding the one of the farmhouse she'd been sent. 'I was sent this anonymously.' She asked if the location was familiar, if it flagged anything up in her mind. It was a desperate attempt to keep Pullman invested and interested.

Pullman glanced at the image and shrugged. 'I don't know it.'

'Do you believe Mikey Birch murdered Jake Shaw?' Pullman's eyes were darting around, her foot tapping against the floor. There was no disguising the fact she was seriously on edge, despite everything.

'I never got to put the question to him.'

'What do your instincts say?'

Pullman didn't answer immediately, sitting back against the bench. 'It doesn't matter what I think.'

It was maybe reckless, but finding the image of Mikey Birch, Yaz held it out and waited for Pullman to react. Pullman's face told her all she needed to know, eventually nodding her agreement. 'You don't seem that surprised?'

'Very little surprises me.'

'You always knew.'

'Says who?'

'You wouldn't be here otherwise.' Yaz laid it out, the bullshit that had been sown in the aftermath of Birch's supposed death.

'I'm sure you don't need me to tell you about Knott and the places he's heading.'

'I wouldn't be doing it if I wasn't certain. Mikey Birch wasn't murdered in the aftermath of Jake Shaw's death. He went to ground.'

'People don't just go to ground.'

'It happened.' Yaz left it at that, knowing that although the photograph she had of Birch said one thing, explaining the intervening thirty-five years was much more difficult. She'd made her point. Pullman could shrug it off, but she'd scored a hit.

'Maybe you should think about joining the police?' Pullman suggested. 'Make something of yourself?'

'I don't think so.'

'You'd rather stick to delivering takeaways?'

Yaz smiled and folded her arms. 'You've checked me out?'

'Of course I have.'

'I don't think Jake Shaw was corrupt, either.'

'You can prove that?'

'I'm getting there.'

Pullman stood up and turned to look out at the sea which had been to their backs. 'This is a mess.'

Yaz mirrored her move, eyes fixed on the wind turbines in the distance, the tugboat making slow progress. 'You're not wrong.'

'The way I was treated left a bad taste in my mouth.'

'It's why you've got to treat the root cause. Otherwise you're just going to continue picking at the sore. It's not what you went into policing for.'

Pullman straightened back up, staring down at the pavement. 'You want the story?'

'I do.'

'Everything has a price tag. It's the way it works. You have to decide if it's a price worth paying.'

Yaz looked out to the sea again, trying to read the woman's thought process. 'I think you can help me answer my questions and you know I'm serious.' She turned away from the water, hands in her pockets. 'I won't let you down.' Pullman didn't respond. 'But I can't do it all by myself.'

'I've told you what I can.'

Yaz wasn't having it. 'You've got to tell me what you know.'

'There's nothing more.'

'Bullshit.'

'Don't play games with me, Yaz.'

'I'm not playing games.'

'I've been warned off.'

Yaz looked up to the sky and swore. Of course Pullman had been contacted. 'Who by?' She needed to hear the name.

'It doesn't matter.'

'It matters to me.'

Pullman sighed. 'People associated with Conrad Knott, even if they won't say as much.'

'They threatened you?'

'Not in so many words. They didn't need to.'

'Your pension?'

'Don't even think about judging me.'

'They can't do that.'

Pullman laughed. 'Don't be so naive, Yaz. People like Knott can do what they like, and don't tell yourself otherwise. You need to leave me alone. It ends here.'

'Do you remember Kerri Lewis?'

Pullman looked puzzled for a moment, thought about the question. 'The journalist?'

'She covered the story back in the day. You must have spoken to her?'

'Can't say I did. I tried to minimise my dealings with people like that.'

'She's in hospital.' Yaz explained what had happened, but stopped short of mentioning she was the intended target.

Pullman held a hand up, told her to stop talking. 'People are attacked all the time, unfortunately. A scumbag sees a nice mobile phone, or spots someone carrying cash, that's all it often takes.'

'It didn't happen like that.'

'You're guessing.'

'So Knott gets to win?' Yaz quickly tried to formulate a plan to win the woman around, needing to find the right words. 'I thought you wanted the truth.'

Pullman headed away. 'Don't make this awkward or difficult.'

TWENTY-SEVEN

Still angry from the way Pullman had folded, Yaz walked across the marina in the direction of the waterfront, heading for the benches next to the sculpture of the migrant family. It symbolised the millions of people who'd passed through Hull on the transmigrant route to North America. Staring at it, she understood. Everyone was passing through.

Carolyn Seymour took a seat next to her on the bench and sipped at her takeout coffee. Yaz couldn't push Helen Pullman out of her mind, the way she couldn't persuade the former detective to work with her. It was self-preservation, cowardly. But Seymour would know something if she could find the right words to win her over. Seymour also had a right to know her then-boyfriend was still alive. It was a card to play, one that would have to change things. Someone had helped Mikey Birch go to ground and Seymour was high on her list of candidates.

'Not a bad view, is it?' Seymour said, breaking the silence.

Drawing in the smell coming off the water, there wasn't much she could imagine missing about the place. Not really. Not when she really thought about it, but being close to water was the one thing she instinctively liked about the city.

'Did you want a coffee?' Seymour gestured to where the nearest cafe was.

'I'm fine.' Pushing her chin down into her coat, Yaz waited. Seymour had set the meeting, the woman checking around them with little finesse, her eyes scanning the small pockets of people in the area. 'Problem?' Seymour didn't respond. 'You should say whatever it is that's on your mind.'

Seymour sipped at her coffee before speaking. 'I wanted to help you with the podcast, but I can't.'

Yaz noted the past tense and rubbed at her face, squinted against the low-lying sun.

'I can't help you.'

'You're choosing not to help me. That's a big difference, right there.'

Seymour sipped at her coffee again, considered her words. 'I suppose that's fair enough.'

'You told me very clearly that you still wanted justice for Mikey.'

'You want to leave this city, Yaz?'

The change in direction surprised her. 'I hate it.' She glanced again at the sculpture, knowing she wanted to pass through and leave the place in the rear-view mirror.

'I had dreams, too. Big plans for myself. It didn't work out for me, and here I am, thirty-five years later. Still trying to make the best of things.'

'Conrad Knott's got to you.' She didn't even dignify dressing it up as a question. It was what had happened to Pullman too. Her father was burning the ground underneath her feet.

There was a short nod of the head. 'I'm static and my clients are static. None of us are leaving this place anytime soon and many don't want to.' Seymour sipped at her coffee, buying time. 'You either bend to living in a small place or you leave it behind. We all make our own choices.'

It was a pointed comment Yaz rolled around in her head, thinking of Jake Shaw's daughter and how she'd engaged with a similar organisation in an attempt to get back on her feet. 'Some things are bigger than that, though.' Seymour didn't respond. 'You think I'm naive? Is that it?' She stared at the woman, but Seymour didn't divert her gaze from out at the water. 'Maybe it's just I've got the courage of my convictions?'

Seymour shook her head. 'You think it's that easy? It's easy to have principles when you're young and have nothing invested, that's a fact. You have nothing to lose.'

'You had convictions and principles once, I know you did, but you're selling them out. How do you sleep knowing that?'

'Now I know you're being naive.'

Yaz fell silent, frustrated. Things were unravelling fast around her. 'I'm being threatened because of this story and I'm not going to stop.'

Seymour stood up and threw her empty coffee cup in a nearby bin. 'I can't help you.'

Yaz stared forward, watching a slow boat make its journey, like it was also trudging through treacle. She stood up and faced Seymour, told her what had happened to Kerri Lewis. 'It should be me lying in the hospital bed.'

'That sounds like another conspiracy theory.' Seymour quickly apologised. 'I hope there's better news soon.'

'That justice will be done?'

'How do you feel about that?'

'Probably the same as you did last night when you were leaned on?'

'Sometimes you have to be pragmatic and walk away.'

'Like you're doing?'

'Something like that.' Seymour sighed, said she'd spell it out. 'My place is a charity, and it relies on funding. That's the reality of it, that's the bottom line for me. I help a lot of people who desperately need it. If I close, there's nothing for them. Can you imagine how little help is available for those who fall through the cracks in a place like this? It's my life's work and I'm not walking away from it.'

Yaz listened knowing it was emotional blackmail and she hated it.

'I'm sorry, but you can't use what I said to you.'

Seymour had angled herself away slightly, looking down at the floor. At least she was embarrassed by what she was saying. Yaz chose her words carefully. 'You know there's something to hide here, right? You implied I didn't have the full picture.' She paused for breath. 'So help me.'

'I can't.'

'Off the record.'

'I'm sorry, Yaz. I can't.'

'Do you think Mikey's really dead?'

Seymour stared at her. 'What kind of question is that?'

'One that requires an answer.' She watched Seymour walk away without any further comment, back in the direction of the city centre and her office and charity work. There was nothing more she could do. Yaz kicked out at a stone underfoot, frustrated and started to walk away. It was far from over. She had to make things happen for herself if she wanted the story and the truth, divide and conquer. If she let it, the story would slip back into the shadows.

She followed Seymour, catching her up. 'Mikey wasn't murdered afterwards.' The words were out before she could stop herself, as impulsive as ever.

Seymour stopped and turned to face her. 'Not true.'

'You think?' Seymour wasn't meeting her eye. 'I can prove it.'

'Don't be stupid.'

'How did it work?' Yaz asked, not letting it go.

'You're mad.'

'He'd need help from people he trusted, right?' She'd scored a hit. Seymour increased her pace, trying to get away. 'Who could he trust more than his girlfriend? Surely she'd be the one person who'd help? Maybe he'd made promises about what would happen down the line?' It felt like a strong theory, but that's all it was. Seymour wasn't giving her anything back. 'How did it work? Tell me what happened? Mikey would have needed money and contacts, a safe place to stay.' Still nothing. 'Talk to me. Put it on the podcast.'

Seymour shook her head. 'Let sleeping dogs lie, Yaz.'

'Don't let men like Conrad Knott take advantage of you!' she shouted at Seymour's back as she walked away from her again.

TWENTY-EIGHT

Staying hidden out of sight, there was a clear view of the train station from where Yaz was standing. The walls were all bulky concrete, nicotine and weather embedded into them, the entrance gate to an end of the line city that couldn't change even if it wanted to. The way Carolyn Seymour and Helen Pullman had been silenced proved the point.

The woman sitting on a blanket in the entrance, head bowed, hadn't moved. She'd only had loose change in her pocket to offer her. Yaz's eyes locked onto DC Oberman approaching. She killed the call and switched her mobile to silent. Oberman was moving slowly, a slight limp on her right leg. She was also scanning the scene in front of her. Yaz stepped forward and waited to be spotted. She'd made the call to Oberman, setting the meeting before cutting the detective off from talking, saying when and where she'd meet her. It hadn't been a negotiation. There had been a smile on her face as she'd done it. It was about control. She'd told Kerri Lewis she had no interest in working with the police, but was learning fast that you had to make tough choices.

Oberman came to a stop in front of her, hands in her pockets. 'This isn't how it works. If you've got something to say about what happened last night, you need to come down to the station and do it on the record.'

Yaz shook her head, making it clear that wasn't going to happen. 'This is how it works for now.'

'Is that so?'

'I read up about you.'

'What did you read?'

'Officially, not a lot. Between the lines, I can see it all.' The detective was trying to stamp her authority on things, but she wasn't having it. They were going to help each other out. Yaz had tried to find out more about Oberman away from work, looking for something online, something that would help explain what made the detective tick. There'd been nothing to find. It was inconceivable Oberman was a blank page. There was probably a social media profile somewhere, but it wasn't uncommon for people doing such a job to hide behind truncated or disguised names. It effectively locked people like her out.

Oberman folded her arms. 'Enlighten me, why don't you?'

'No one goes from being a detective in Major Crimes to working the night shift like you're doing. You fucked up.'

'I didn't fuck up.'

Yaz smiled. 'It wasn't your fault, then?'

Oberman lowered her voice and moved in closer. 'My career is none of your business.'

'It is if I can help you get it back.'

'Who says I want to go back?'

'I do.'

'You think you know me?'

'Am I wrong?'

Oberman stared hard at her before relenting a touch. 'You're a dangerous woman to know.'

Yaz smiled. 'Have you listened to my podcast?'

'I have.'

'What did you think? Be honest.'

'The last one was an interesting listen.'

'That's it? Interesting?'

'What do you expect me to say?'

'It's just us two talking. You don't have to be the detective here.'

Oberman turned away, watching a train pull out, before speaking. 'I joined the police to right wrongs.'

'It makes us the same.'

'Does it?'

'My podcast is about righting wrongs, that's the bottom line. Our aims are the same, it's just that our methods that are different. We're on the same side, but you've got your doubts about me? That's fine. I'm not hiding, am I? I'm putting my name to these podcasts and I'm looking powerful men in the eye.' She eased off the rhetoric, knowing the words were hitting home. It was a roll of the dice. She needed to give something to receive something back. It was ok to shout from the sidelines, but Kerri Lewis's advice was on the money. Sometimes you had to work with others.

'I'm lucky to have a job,' Oberman said.

Yaz glanced at the detective's leg and eased off. 'How did you do it?'

'Let's just say it was in the line of duty.'

There was a tinge of bitterness in Oberman's voice. 'It's held you back, right? People have taken the piss out of you?' The question didn't need an answer. It was written all over her face. 'You deserve better.'

'And you're not convincing me.' Oberman turned and walked away.

Yaz had no choice but to follow. Walking alongside her, she continued her pitch, but was cut off from talking.

Oberman stopped and folded her arms. 'What were you and Kerri Lewis doing at the launch for the bar last night?'

'Do you know who owns it?'

'I do.'

'You know who their fathers are?'

'I do.'

Yaz knew Oberman was on the hook, 50/50 if she would help or not. Yaz straightened herself back up and looked the detective in the eye, laying out things about Jake Shaw's murder and Mikey Birch's involvement, checking Oberman knew the story. 'Birch is still alive,' she said, finishing up her explanation.

Oberman shook her head, disbelieving. 'Sounds like fantasy stuff.'

'It isn't.'

'Let me guess, though. You can't prove it yet?'

Yaz took out her mobile and pulled up the image of Birch from the spy camera. She laid out how Stonegrave was linked to Knott via the undercover work at the illegal raves. It sounded mad, but she hoped the conviction in her voice did the heavy lifting for her.

'What have you done with the photo?' Oberman asked.

'Nothing yet.' It was her exclusive, her decision on when to release it. The timing needed to be right. She put her mobile away.

'You haven't shared it with anyone?'

'No.' She told the detective how the story had started. 'Someone sent me to the farmhouse knowing Mikey Birch was living there.'

Oberman dismissed it, not interested. 'So what's your bottom line here? Mikey Birch didn't murder Jake Shaw, but went to ground instead? You're going to need a lot more than that. I don't want to hear a conspiracy theory. I want to hear facts.'

'And I'm getting them.'

'What do you expect me to do for you, Yaz? I'm a police detective and you're a journalist when all's said and done. We're not on the same side and we don't have a relationship. Information flows to me, not the other way round.'

'No one will talk to me.' It came out more as a whine than she'd wanted it to. Her options were being narrowed and she was powerless.

Oberman softened slightly. 'With respect, that's not my problem. All you can do is go through the official channels and the Media Team.'

'That's bullshit.'

'That's reality. You haven't got anything, Yaz.'

'This is about police corruption.'

Oberman leaned in, lowered her voice. 'You're talking about something that happened decades ago.'

'And that changes things for you? Justice doesn't count after so many years?'

'Don't take the piss here and don't twist my words.'

'This is important.' Yaz wasn't having it, continuing to argue. 'Conrad Knott is about to move even further out of reach, isn't he? He needs stopping before it's too late.'

'You're making assumptions. You've offered me nothing to say the attack on Kerri Lewis was anything other than random. Shit happens, doesn't it?'

'You don't believe that anymore than I do.' It didn't matter. She was talking to Oberman's back as the detective walked away.

TWENTY-NINE

Heading through the maze of light industrial units, Yaz came to a stop and knocked loudly on the heavy pub door. She'd called the hospital again and received the same message. Kerri Lewis was conscious, but going nowhere fast from the trauma ward. Nor was she was going to be allowed to speak to her.

Helen Pullman and Carolyn Seymour had both been warned off from speaking with Yaz, or offering any help. That much was clear to her. The investigation had been deliberately fucked with, as had the detective. Pullman knew something about the night Mikey Birch had been murdered, but the former detective had been nervous, indicated by the fact she'd set the meeting in an anonymous seaside town well away from home. She'd been fucked over and had more to say, but it hadn't been forthcoming. Seymour was too close to things to not have knowledge to share. It wasn't a massive jump to realise they'd been silenced, that Oberman thought she was some kind of crank. The conclusion she'd drawn was that Conrad Knott was closing off as many avenues open to her as possible. He didn't want people involved with the rave all those years ago talking. He was more than prepared to use his position and power to shut them down. It was wrong. Something needed to change, and something needed to happen. She needed to wrestle back control of the situation.

The area hummed to the beat of industrial work, the rhythm of steelwork and the occasional sound of shouting. A small lorry inched past, a piercing alarm sounding as it backed into a nearby yard. She was going to find Mikey Birch and speak with him for the podcast. He was the key that would unlock everything, but she needed some to shake things up and disrupt them first. A crow swooped down from the top of the roof and landed in the gutter, pecking at the debris it contained. The paintwork around the door and windows had faded, chipped away. She could see the decay, the money it would cost to put things right. It was another back street pub that would wither and die sooner rather than later.

The locks on the pub door released. A woman with large curls piled on top of her head stared back, a larger-than-life presence about her that was probably worn as armour when working. Yaz put her in her mid-thirties. She offered a smile. 'Is it Kelly?' She'd checked out Stonegrave's daughter on social media. Her Facebook page was unlocked, meaning she knew all there was to know. The fact she liked true crime podcasts had immediately caught her eye. Stonegrave and Knott thought they knew all about her. It was time to return the favour. She had a plan.

'Who's asking?'

Yaz introduced herself. 'I record a podcast called *CrimeTime*,' she said, going into her rehearsed routine. 'I'm here about a murder in this area back in the 1970s. You might have heard of it?' She'd quickly read about it online, knowing there was nothing there, but it was her way in. A man had been jumped and beaten by a gang in a work yard, his body found the following morning. Arrests had quickly been made, the victim had been conducting an affair with a former-colleague's wife. It was an uncomplicated case of revenge being taken in the most brutal form. 'Can I come inside and talk to you about it, please?'

Kelly stood aside. 'I know who you are.'

Yaz closed the door behind her, not sure if the woman's words were positive and welcoming. It felt unnatural to be inside the place when it was closed to the public. The faint smell of alcohol was in the air, ingrained into its walls. The fridges behind the bar were half-empty, the tables in need of a wipe down. Giving it six months felt generous she decided. Pulling out a stool at the bar, Yaz didn't sit down and instead watched as Kelly started to restock the crisps, opening multi-pack buys into the empty cardboard boxes in the corner of the bar.

'Cheaper to buy them from the supermarket these days,' Kelly said, catching her staring.

Yaz smiled, saying she understood. 'Can I use your toilet before we get started?'

'Up the stairs and turn right. Go ahead, there's no one home.'

Thanking her, she headed straight up. Instead of turning right, Yaz turned left and walked into the living space. It was untidy, clothes piled on top of the settee. A pile of magazines on a coffee table. Looking at the photographs on the wall, they all showed what she assumed was family. None of them included Stonegrave. There was little sign he lived in the place. Looking at the badly folded duvet pushed into the corner, he appeared to be more a squatter, the pub a place to lay his head. A weathered rucksack had been pushed into the opposite corner. Peering inside, it held his clothes, mainly underwear. Satisfied there was nothing else to see, Yaz took her mobile out and quickly filmed a scan of the rooms and added a few photographs, before heading into the bathroom to flush the toilet. Back downstairs, she sat down on the stool and placed her mobile on the bar, pretending to record their conversation. 'It'd be good to get some background from you, given you're a big part of the area.'

'As much I liked your last podcast, I'm not sure I can help you much. A few of the regulars still talk about the murder, but it was well before my time. I'm a big fan of true crime podcasts, but I can't imagine there's much mystery around it, if I'm honest.'

'You'd be surprised what reviewing the past can throw up.'

'I suppose that's true enough. You're always hearing about miscarriages of justice, aren't you?'

'Your dad is a retired detective, right? He looks at cold cases?' Kelly's face darkened at the question, and for a moment, she thought she'd blown it, but the woman relented with a shrug.

'He won't talk about old cases.'

'Maybe he knows someone connected to it?'

'Not to my knowledge.'

'Be good to speak to him, though.'

Yaz grabbed at a leaflet on the bar and scribbled down her name and number, wanting Stonegrave to know she'd been here, poking around in his home. The pub door behind them opened, loudly ricocheting off the wall. They both turned as Stonegrave walked in. Yaz smiled at him, knowing she'd caught a break at last. There was no need to wait for him to get the message that she knew how to find him, how to insert herself into his life. Kelly made the introductions, explaining why Yaz was there before going back to her work, but Stonegrave didn't take his eyes off her. His face changed, setting into a much harsher stare, something much more difficult to read. He was resetting himself, ready to deal with her. She maintained eye contact and waited for him to say something. Inviting it.

Stonegrave broke the spell first and turned to his daughter. 'I'm not sure I can help your guest all that much, but I can certainly show her where it all happened.' He headed for the door and opened it. 'Shall we?'

THIRTY

Stonegrave closed the pub door behind them, his expression changing to one of anger. 'What do you think you're playing at?'

'Not so keen on someone stepping into your life and sniffing around?' Yaz said. 'Two can play at that game.'

Stonegrave shook his head, but didn't move or follow. 'You're playing games?'

She jabbed a finger out at him, also angry. 'I'm not playing games.'

They stared at each other. Lorries continued to move goods in and out of buildings, small groups of people emerged from workshops and factories laughing and joking, huddling together and smoking cigarettes. No one paid them any attention.

Yaz headed away down the street, a calculated gamble that he'd follow. Stonegrave lunged forward and grabbed her arm, pulled her into an empty yard. She shook him off, told him to keep his hands to himself. 'You're going to do yourself a mischief if you're not careful.' He was breathing heavily. 'You haven't asked how Kerri Lewis is doing yet?'

'I heard she was attacked.'

'You're not following the investigation?'

'Why would I be?'

The ghost sign on the brick wall said the place had once been occupied by an electrical wholesaler. A more recent sign said a printing company had set up camp there, but the broken glass and wooden pallets pushed into the corner, the weathered *For Sale* sign clinging on to the front of the building, told her that things had changed again.

Stonegrave coughed and composed himself. 'You don't bring this to my home and attempt to blindside me. Are we clear on that?'

'You've already said that, and I wasn't interested the first time.'

'What did you say to Kelly?'

'We bonded over podcasts. She's a fan of mine.' Yaz leaned back and made herself more comfortable against the brick wall. It was an opportunity to shape the conversation and back Stonegrave into a corner, let him know how it was going to play out. She wanted his help, but he had to commit to doing it for the right reasons.

'You don't speak to Kelly again,' Stonegrave said. 'Are we clear on that?'

'You don't get to decide who I speak to. Your daughter's an adult who can talk to me if she wants to. You're the one dossing down in her place, like some sort of tramp.' Yaz kicked a stone out from under her foot. The smart thing to do was swallow down what Stonegrave was saying, let him think he was winning, and then make her move. But her mouth always acted before her brain. It was a blessing and a curse.

'You're out of your depth here, Yaz.'

'Help me out, then? Knott isn't your friend or ally.'

'Help you out?'

She laid it out, wanting Stonegrave to see the truth for himself, but knowing she was only going to get one shot at it. 'Jake Shaw wasn't corrupt,' she said. 'Let's take that as the bottom line, shall we?' He looked away, not wanting to meet her eye. 'It's just you and me in this shitty yard,' she said, arms out wide. 'I'm not recording it, no one's listening, no one's watching. You can just admit it so we both know.'

'You're talking nonsense and wasting my time. Give it up and walk away.'

'Not going to happen.' He was still there, still listening and engaging.

'You should get out of this city and get ahead. This place is dying. That's my advice to you.'

'I'm not walking away from this story.'

'Why not? Leave it at that and find another one.'

'People still care.'

'Who?'

'People like Mikey Birch's girlfriend back then, Carolyn Seymour. No one has listened to what she's got to say. You don't walk away from something like that without some damage. She deserves better. Jake deserves better, doesn't he?'

'Seymour was no angel back then.'

'Maybe she's ready to talk about it.' Yaz knew she was reaching, a stretch to imply Seymour was on her side, but Stonegrave was rattled. 'Once she starts talking, I bet she won't stop.'

'We've all got our own version of the truth. She's no different, but she's also wrong.'

'You don't even know what she's said to me.'

'I can guess. Mikey Birch was an angel and ran those raves for the greater good and so on? It's bullshit, Yaz. She's playing you because it makes her feel better about what happened all those years ago.'

'Why would she be playing me?'

Stonegrave shrugged. 'Maybe her charity needs some publicity?'

'And you think this is the way she'd choose to do it? Fucking hell, you're cynical.'

'It's a small world in these parts. You do what you need to do.'

Yaz took out her mobile and pulled up the photograph showing him with Knott and Shaw. 'You were part of the gang.'

Stonegrave glanced at it. 'Gangs? There were no gangs.' He dismissed her words. 'Do you think it was the Wild West, or something? We were the police.'

'I think you should reconsider talking to me for the podcast,' she said. 'Get ahead of the story, rather than let it consume you.'

'Why would it consume me?'

Yaz smiled. Stonegrave's eyes flickered for a moment, the first time he'd shown any doubt. He was unable to hold her stare. 'Conrad Knott wasn't your friend, not really.'

'You think you know an awful lot, don't you?'

It felt good to take her time, watch his reaction, knowing she was making some progress. She'd rattled his cage and was slowly boxing him in, giving him a decision to make about his next move. 'Jake Shaw's long dead, so that only leaves you,' she said, closing the gap between them. 'If you're not careful, you'll end up the carrying the can for other people's sins. You've got one shot with this and that's it. I'm the one who's on your side.' She wanted him to say something, but he remained silent. 'Do you think Mikey Birch murdered Jake Shaw? I don't.' It was the question she'd spent too much time thinking about, increasingly sure she was right. Jake Shaw had been described as a good detective, solid and dependable. Yet he was portrayed as having gone rogue, the proverbial bad apple. It didn't sit right. None of it did.

Stonegrave made for the gate at the end of the yard, ignoring what she'd said. He turned back and jabbed a finger out in her direction. 'You keep away from me and my family, or there'll be trouble.'

Yaz followed, shouting at his back. 'We're not done here. What do you really know about Conrad Knott? Tell me. How much do you know about your friend?'

Stonegrave stopped and turned back to face her, checked they were alone in the street. 'I know he's going places and is going to be even more powerful than he already is.'

She couldn't help but laugh. 'That's what you're scared of? The fact he's powerful? What about decency and the truth?' Yaz shook her head, disappointed in him. 'I'll tell you what you're scared of, shall I? You're scared you're going to be collateral damage when the shit hits the fan. You're scared that what little you've got is about to disappear.'

'Don't be naive about how the world works. Reality is, everyone has their price.'

'Do you know about his children?'

The question stopped Stonegrave from walking, confused by the direction the conversation was taking. 'Mason? I know him. He's a good kid. So what?'

'Interesting that he owns a bar with Dale Harker's son?'

'They're friends.'

She'd scored a hit. Stonegrave's words didn't carry any force. They both knew it was bullshit. 'Bit too cosy,' she said. 'If I was you, I'd be asking questions about their relationship.' He stared at her, not speaking. 'Did you clock what Kerri Lewis was wearing when she was found last night?' The question didn't prompt a response. 'It was my denim jacket she put on when she went outside for a cig. All the badges and patches make it distinctive. Are you following me?' Still nothing. 'You must have a theory?'

'Why would I need one?'

'I was the target.'

'She's probably made plenty of enemies.'

'Not this time.'

'You're guessing.'

'How about Knott's other child?'

'You're not making any sense.' Stonegrave turned back towards the pub and started to walk away. 'You're wasting my time.'

'I'm his daughter.' Stonegrave hesitated for a moment, but continued to walk on. She shouted at his back again. If he wasn't prepared to look at her, he could still hear what she had to say. The point needed reiterating. Knott wasn't his friend. 'If he hasn't told you that, what else hasn't he told you?'

THIRTY-ONE

Taking a breath, Yaz hesitated for a moment before heading through the door and into Mason Knott's bar. Trying to force Stonegrave's hand was one thing, but what she really needed was an insurance policy if she was going to push forward and rattle more cages.

It had been a quick turnaround from the previous evening. Instead of the city's great and good partying, the place was now serving late breakfasts, some people enjoying a coffee, through to a group conducting a business meeting in the corner. Instinctively, she didn't like the place now she could see it properly. The way its past was being used – the bare brick wall and tasteless use of original features – felt obvious and basic. It was lazy regeneration, baffling to think people paid a premium to visit.

The conversation with Stonegrave was a deliberate attempt to stir him up, provoke a reaction. In his shoes, she wouldn't be happy if the man he was shielding hadn't been honest. He now knew Conrad Knott was her father, a dirty secret shared between them. She'd chosen to weaponise it, a feeling she needed to work through later on. The immediate priority was seeing what Stonegrave would do with the information. It was something she couldn't control, but she wanted it to create division between the two men. Stonegrave would have to decide where his own line was drawn. The gamble was in widening the number of people who knew the truth. It created the risk that things could spiral out of her control. It was a gamble she was willing to take.

Mason Knott was sitting in the far corner, slightly hidden away by the curve of the seating booth. He was hunched over paperwork with a calculator in his hand, sunglasses pushed to the top of his head and a casual shirt undone at the top. His dark hair was pushed back from across his eyes and clearly benefitted from an expensive cut. There was little between them in terms of age, something that made their shared father's indiscretion feel even worse to her.

She marched straight over, ignoring the woman who'd appeared at the bar, ready to serve her. 'Sorry to bother you.' Yaz extended her hand towards him and introduced herself, watching carefully for any kind of reaction. It felt weird and wrong. Beyond his momentary confusion, there wasn't one. It confirmed Conrad Knott hadn't mentioned her to him. He didn't recognise her.

'Nice to meet you,' he said, ignoring the hand being held out towards him.

She went into her pre-prepared speech, telling him that she'd been commissioned by the local newspaper to write a piece about the city's new movers and shakers. 'You were top of my list.' She carried on talking, knowing it was pure bullshit, but flattery was a powerful tool. 'Didn't you get the message I'd be dropping in today?'

He cocked his head to one side, intrigued. 'Who did you speak to?'

'I didn't get a name, I'm afraid.'

He hesitated for a moment before gesturing that she should join him in the booth. 'Not to worry.' The paperwork went to the side. 'Can I get you a drink?'

'Just a water, please.' She watched him make his way over to the bar, mobile in hand, knowing he'd be doing his best to quickly check her out. She turned away not wanting to get caught staring at him. The gamble was hoping that he didn't contact the newspaper directly, but she figured he'd have to be seriously suspicious to do that when he was being made the centre of attention. Equally, there wouldn't be much to find without a deep dive. The podcast had separate social media channels. All he'd see in relation to her were shell accounts, nothing that contained personal information. If anything came up, she'd style it out. There was no chance he'd clocked the fact she was snooping on his accounts with fakes of her own. All it had needed was a facial image from a website that generated fakes, making sure she chose a young woman who looked likely to frequent his bar. She was inside both his Instagram and Facebook profiles with them, quietly watching.

Her mind wandered, considering whether she could see anything of herself in him from their shared DNA. It didn't seem likely they'd share much beyond that. He'd had everything handed to him on a plate by their father, she'd received nothing. Risking another glance over her shoulder, she wasn't sure if she even wanted to know him.

Mason Knott walked back over with two glasses of water, both piled up with ice and slices of lime. 'Cheers,' he said, taking a sip from his.

She thought about mentioning Kerri Lewis and what had happened outside of the bar the previous night, but stopped herself. It might give him reason to look at her again, place her alongside Lewis. Instead, she mirrored his manoeuvre before placing her spare mobile between them and made a show of saying she'd record their chat. 'For future review and quotes.'

'Fair enough.'

'Nice place you've got here?'

He sat back in the booth, spread his arm across the back of the upholstery. 'I'm very proud of it, and the wider area. People have always said the city's a dump and been quick to knock it, but I've never seen it that way. I could always see its potential.'

Yaz smiled and zoned out as he continued to talk, not really recognising the place he was describing. Her experience of it was very different. She waited for him to finish before leaning in to ask another question. 'Must have been hard work getting a place like this off the ground?'

He nodded. 'Incredibly hard, but I strongly believe you do what it takes when it's your dream. Nobody gives you anything on a plate.'

'How about your business partner? His father is quite famous?' She was thinking about Dale Harker and his entourage.

'I guess he is. We go back a long way, our fathers are good friends. It was particularly good of Dale to come along last night and DJ for us.'

'Was your own father a help, too?' Our father, she thought. It was as polite as she could phrase the question, swallowing down his utter lack of understanding when it came to privilege.

'My father's a great man, he really is, and I'm very proud of what he's achieved in his own career. He's very supportive of me and someone I can always turn to for advice and help. He expects a lot of me and I'm repaying that as best I can.' He smiled, like he was being generous with his words.

'I'm sure.' There was every chance Knott had financed the place and used connections most people could only dream of. 'How about siblings?' she asked. 'Does he support them equally?'

He picked up his drink, drinking through the straw and shaking his head. 'I don't have any.'

Yaz did the same, her mouth dry and in danger of threatening to run ahead of her brain. She placed the glass down, knowing she needed to dial it down. 'How about future plans, then? Tell me about them.' A smile reappeared on his face from being on much more comfortable territory. She zoned out again as he spoke about his desire for more bars, a chain based on the place she was sitting in. There was no doubt he'd get it, too. He was a big name in a small town and that gave him opportunities and protection. It was how life would work for him.

He continued to talk, confidently holding court. 'It's important to work with the newspaper and other media outlets, so the positive stories are out there to promote the good things we have to offer. We're all in this together, in my opinion.'

Yaz only half-listened as he carried on talking, knowing he was creating sound bites for his own purposes and his own aims. It wasn't journalism. She'd rather work endless takeaway delivery shifts than write up what was being recorded on her phone.

'Are you new to the paper?' he asked, dragging her back into the conversation.

'Freelance,' she said with a smile. 'Just getting my feet under the table, if I'm being honest.'

He raised his glass. 'To a beautiful friendship.'

She was saved from acknowledging his toast by his mobile sounding. He took the call, saying he'd call back before placing it back down on the table between them. 'I've got to go, I'm afraid.'

Yaz scooped up her own mobile, stopping the recording. 'I've got plenty, don't worry.' She stood and made her way around the booth to stand next to him, subtly blocking him from being able to leave. 'Do you mind if we take a quick selfie? I like to have a record of everyone I've interviewed. Just a daft superstition I've got.' He shrugged and quickly offered a smile as she raised her mobile into the air. 'Thanks,' she said, stepping aside to let him out.

'My pleasure.'

Watching him go, Yaz quickly gathered her things together and headed out of the bar herself. Rounding the corner, she leaned against the wall and allowed a moment to compose herself. Attaching the selfie with her brother to a text message, she found Conrad Knott's number and hit send. The message she typed to go along with the image was clear; do not fuck with me.

THIRTY-TWO

Stonegrave turned his mobile over and placed it down on the bar, ignoring the call coming in from Knott. Yaz Moy and their conversation was on his mind, the bombshell she'd dropped on him. Maybe he should have been more alert to what was happening around him, but any news about Conrad Knott was something he'd conditioned himself to zone out and ignore. Yaz Moy was right about it, though. It had implications. There was plenty to chew over, but he couldn't ignore the way she'd stepped into his home, or the nearest thing he had to one, and taken aim. She had known exactly what she was doing when spinning a bullshit story to Kelly about researching for a podcast. More than that, she'd looked him in the eye and levelled with him. *What else isn't he telling you?*

The pub was too quiet, as ever, Kelly standing at the other end of the bar, toying with her own phone. The lunchtime crowd had dwindled to next to nothing, people hunkering down and keeping whatever money they had in their pockets for now. Kelly was a fighter, but there was still a limit to how long she could keep the place trading. She'd asked about his conversation with Yaz Moy, satisfied with his lie about being willing to help her out. Thankfully, no further questions had been forthcoming.

Catching him staring, Kelly moved along the bar in his direction. 'You don't look well, Dad.'

'I'm fine.' He stretched his arms out, like that would be all it would take to convince her. She'd seen through him from the first day he'd pitched up at the pub looking for somewhere to sleep.

'You need to take it easy.'

'I need to help you keep this place going.'

'You've done enough.'

Shame burned through him, knowing it was nowhere near the truth. The divorce had been costly for them all on every level. 'I haven't done enough for you.'

'You've taught me right from wrong.'

He considered that for a moment unsure what to do with it. 'I wouldn't go that far.'

'Don't talk shit, Dad.'

'I'm not proud of lots of things.'

'You know full well what I mean.'

'I thought I was the parent here?' He offered a smile that wasn't returned. 'People might not say nice things about me when I'm gone.' He'd done things in the last couple of days, necessary things, if he wanted to justify them to himself. Things that wouldn't look good in the harsh light of day.

'Hold that thought.' Kelly pushed herself off the bar and prepared to serve the customer who'd walked in.

He'd spent the night downstairs in the bar until Kelly had come down, thinking he was a burglar. She'd removed the glass from his hand with a sigh, a warning about behaving himself. The first whisky had been enough. He'd thought about telling her more about Conrad Knott and Jake Shaw before clamming up.

Putting the money into the till, Kelly turned back to him. 'You need to stop talking like you're going to die on me tomorrow because you're not. You'll get fixed up and then you can enjoy a proper retirement.' She cut him off, told him to stop talking in such a way. 'You should be proud of what you've done over the years. You've taken plenty of bad people off the streets. Not many can do the job like you can.'

He wasn't going to sail off into the sunshine of retirement. His consultant had made that perfectly clear when they'd spoken. He still hadn't told Kelly about the conversation. There wasn't going to be a happy ending, a year to eighteen months maybe. Two years if he was lucky, or unlucky depending on how drawn out it would be. Fingering the letter in his pocket, he didn't want to think about the implications. All he had to look forward to was the inside of a hospital. His mobile sounded again. Flipping it over, he stared at Knott's name on the screen.

'You best take it,' Kelly said. 'Someone wants to talk to you.'

The text message sent between calls told him all he needed to know. Kelly headed through to the back, saying she was going to finish restocking the crisps. He grabbed his coat and slipped out of the door. Walking, he passed the multi-cultural shops that lined one of the city's main arterial roads into its centre. Head down, it was only when he arrived at his destination that it felt obvious and natural.

Standing at the gate, he unscrewed the lid on the bottle of water he'd stopped to buy, swallowing the first mouthful a struggle. Some things had to be done, though. He stretched his back, cold wind scratching at his face. His eyes watered followed by a violent burst of coughing, thumping himself on the chest as the liquid went down. Taking a moment, he wiped his face before drawing up the phlegm into his mouth and spitting out into a tissue. Heading into the cemetery, the volume of headstones packed into every corner of space was disorientating and confusing.

Carefully picking his way through, it didn't take long to find the grave he wanted to see. Kneeling down, it was an effort to look at it, even though he knew the words on it by heart. Truth was, the news from the consultant still hadn't struck him. It was a death sentence, but it felt like an elaborate practical joke. Staring at the headstone, he'd experienced what death felt like when holding Jake Shaw's hand as he slipped away. He wanted a better death for Kelly's sake.

'I haven't seen you here before?'

Stonegrave turned and stood up. He hadn't seen the elderly woman tending a nearby grave. 'It's my first visit.' It was the truth. He'd only seen Shaw's grave via photographs previously, staying away feeling like the right thing to do. Guessing she was somewhere in her late seventies, he watched her struggle to stand, using one hand and arm to lever herself upwards. By the time he thought to help, she was done. The headstone in front of her carried a man's name, one who'd been dead for over twenty years. Chances were it was her husband's grave, a tribute to him as a husband, father and grandfather. It had probably been an ordinary life lived as well as you could. Or he hoped as much.

'I sometimes see his daughter here.'

Stonegrave nodded. 'That's good.' It was another person he'd lost touch with. Sarah had been a girl when he'd regularly visited their home. She'd be a woman approaching middle-age now, hopefully settled and at peace.

'I often wonder about him, you know?' She was pointing at Shaw's grave. 'I've read all about him in the paper.' Her voice trailed off.

'You shouldn't believe all you read in them.'

The woman was puzzled. 'Why ever not? Why would they lie about things he'd done?' She pulled her coat tighter around her. 'I'm not particularly pleased to have my husband lying so close-by, but what can you do about it?'

'My friend was a good man.' Stonegrave had turned his back on the woman, staring again at Shaw's grave and headstone. Weeds were growing around it, needed some attention. Maybe he'd be the one to do it. 'He was a good man,' he repeated to himself, knowing he was right.

THIRTY-THREE

Heading through the city centre, Stonegrave wondered if he'd bother to see it again or not, lift his head up and look at the imposing buildings that told the region's story. Maybe familiarity bred contempt. Only a handful of shoppers passed by, moving between indoor shopping centres in various needs of repair.

The place he wanted was off the main drag, even cheaper space to rent. A window was boarded over, graffiti covering it. Whitewash paint had been splashed over the racist abuse hurled on it. Heading inside Refugee Assist, the main floor space was a shop selling second-hand clothing. Further back, the offices were used to offer help and legal assistance to those needing their services. To the side, a pair of young boys played with toys, giggling as they did so.

There was no one working the shop till, on hand to help. Stonegrave turned as a woman approached from the side, asking if he needed some help. 'I'm looking for Bob.' The woman knew what he was immediately. Police. Bob Sander had been a Detective Inspector, the man they'd answered to back in the day.

'He's in the stockroom at the moment.'

'I'll go and say hello.' There was a trace of uncertainty in her voice, but he didn't stick around to let her think on it any further. He certainly didn't want his arrival announcing.

Walking through the shop and stepping over the boys playing, he pulled back the curtain to the stockroom and stepped inside. It was the place the charity kept donations ready for sorting and filtering out to the shop floor. Sander looked up and did a double-take. 'It's been a while, Bob.'

Sander placed the pile of clothes in his hands carefully down on the floor and stood up, taking his time. His face was set neutral, years of training to give nothing away. 'It's been over thirty years now.'

It didn't need to be said that their ties had been cut on the night it all went wrong. Sander certainly wasn't offering a handshake. 'You're looking well.' Sander would be the wrong side of seventy, but he looked a decade younger; tanned, slim and healthy. 'Still as fit as a fiddle.'

'I'd like to say the same.'

'I'm dying.'

Sander considered the words, tried to find the correct response. 'I'm sorry to hear that, really.'

'Life's a lottery, isn't it?' The man's words of condolence meant little. Instead, Stonegrave looked around the room again, trying to put it together. 'I didn't have you down as a bleeding-heart liberal?'

'Neither did I until I met Joyce, my second wife. She opened my eyes to a lot of things, not least the way these poor bastards are suffering. It's hard and we get no funding and rely on donations, but we do what we can.' His stopped himself. 'You think we saw some shit back in the day, but this is something else, I can tell you.'

'Funny how we change.'

Sander's face darkened. 'I assume this isn't a social call. Maybe you're here to volunteer your time?'

Stonegrave shook his head, said he'd leave a fiver in the collection tin. 'We need to talk about Jake Shaw.'

'I thought as much.' Sander paused. 'I wasn't involved, as you well know.'

It was a fair comment and the truth. 'But you knew us all and was part of the chain of command. Conrad Knott answered to you.'

'Not that time.'

'But generally.'

'He won't even remember my name now.'

It wasn't the point. Stonegrave leaned against the wall in an attempt to make himself more comfortable. 'Jake died in my arms.' He didn't need to describe how the night unfolded. The point had been made.

'I remember.'

'It was like a part of me died with him. I was terrified I couldn't help him, terrified about what would happen afterwards. Terrified our cover had been blown and we were in danger.' The list goes on. Even now it was as clear as the night it happened. There'd been no way of communicating and getting an ambulance out, no one to ask for help. All he could do was sit there and wait. 'You don't forget.'

'Justice was done in the end.'

'You think so?'

Sander picked up the pile of clothes and started to sort them again. 'It was a long time ago, but Mikey Birch, the rave organiser and drug dealer did it, right?'

'Doesn't it annoy you that Conrad Knott walked away from his own shit show without a mark?'

'Everyone walked away. No one wants to talk about a corrupt police officer anymore than necessary.'

Stonegrave took a breath and coughed, pain thumping against his rib cage. 'He walked away because of who he was. Jake took the fall for him.'

'It's the way of the world.' Sander looked up from his work. 'You should remember the positives from the situation.'

'The positives?' He managed a weak laugh. 'You'll have to explain them to me.'

'The main one was that you were spared your job after the shit hit the fan. You've still got a job, I understand?'

'It's not right.'

'It's the way of the world, my friend. It belongs to people like Conrad Knott and we're just the supporting cast. Our job is to just get through it in one piece and not make a mess of things.'

'Tell me what happened the next day?' It was something he'd been thinking about since Knott had knocked on the pub door. He could remember what had happened on the day, but no one ever stopped to look again at the aftermath. It was like asking what happened the day after The Armistice. Things didn't return to normal, as if by magic. 'I was out of the loop.'

'For good reason.' Sander considered the request. 'What good will talking about it do now?'

'I need to know because it ripped me in half. I was told not to contact his wife, a friend of mine. I was told I had to stay away.'

'It was for your own good.'

'Maybe I was prepared to believe that back then, but not now.'

'You remember the DI coming in from Sheffield?'

'We all spoke to her.'

'I was pleased it wasn't my problem.'

'It was everyone's problem. He was our friend.'

Sander looked him in the eye. 'A corrupt detective wasn't my friend.'

Stonegrave pushed himself off the wall, telling the man he didn't get to rewrite history.

'Knott ran the operation, right?'

Stonegrave nodded.

'There you go, then. Your questions are for him. I didn't get involved back then and I don't want to get involved now. The order to keep things tight and say nothing came from over my head, so that's what I did. It's the way it worked.'

'You didn't kick back at all?'

'Why would I?'

Stonegrave paused, thinking. Sander's attitude appalled him. 'You knew Jake.'

'Like you said when you walked in here, people can surprise you.' He stood up and placed the clothes on a portable rack, the items ready to be wheeled out for sale. 'Evidence was found.'

Stonegrave folded his arms and cocked his head to the side. 'I looked up to you, you know? I thought you was a decent detective.'

'I was.' Sander pulled back the curtain, ready to leave the room. 'You'll be retiring soon? My advice to you is to find something to enjoy, a new hobby. Maybe consider volunteering somewhere. Keep your head down and take your pension. Remember that you earned it.'

'That's what you'd do?'

'That's what I'm doing.'

Stonegrave stayed where he was for a moment before following Sander out onto the shop floor. 'I can't do that,' he said to the man's back.

THIRTY-FOUR

Yaz paused in front of Kerri Lewis's door, noticing the damage to it. It was slightly open, a chink of light at the bottom. Quietly stepping back, she listened, unsure if she could hear anything inside or if it was her mind playing tricks. No one lived with Lewis, no one had any reason to be inside. She was on edge, too much shit happening around her. Looking again at the damage, it wasn't paranoia.

Fight or flight, she toyed with her options. Flight was safest, but she had to go inside to satisfy her curiosity, if nothing else. It was another obstacle that needed navigating. There was no choice in the matter, nowhere else she could head for. Looking around the communal space, a desk of some sort had been broken down and left outside of the door to another apartment. Picking up what had once been a table leg and feeling its weight, she edged inside Lewis's apartment, fumbling around for the switch. Finding it, she braced before flooding the room with light.

Nothing happened. Heading further inside, books had been ripped off shelves and tossed to the floor. Lewis's vinyl records had been given the same treatment. Looking around, the place was a mess. Stepping over the books on the floor, Yaz moved slowly into the kitchen. The cupboards had been emptied onto the floor, containers with pasta and coffee upturned, mess everywhere she looked. It didn't make sense. The low-hanging fruit; electronic items, cash, keys, even alcohol, hadn't been taken.

Starting to tidy as best she could, it was clear the place had been turned over by someone looking for something specific. Her eyes were drawn to the framed retro book cover print of *In Cold Blood* on the wall. She had a tatty paperback of Truman Capote's true crime masterpiece in her room, one she returned to time and time again.

Finding a file of personal and financial documents, it didn't require an accountant's eye to realise Lewis was in a financial hole. The bank statements she was holding didn't paint a pretty picture of the situation. Lewis was at the end of her overdraft, charges being levied for direct debits that had gone unpaid. Yaz placed them down and rubbed her face. It was something to think about another time.

Thinking logically about the state of the apartment, the pieces started to fall into place. Walking over to the kitchen sink and pouring herself a glass of water, Yaz wanted to get it straight in her head. She was the one telling the story, the one who should be a target. Her world was digital and fluid, everything backed up safely to an online cloud, but the way things had been raked over suggested something else. The murder of Jake Shaw belonged to a different world, one of copy print and scribbled down notes, hastily taken photographs which were the exception rather than the norm of people having them on their mobile phones. The visit had been for a specific purpose, she was sure of it. Someone was scared by what Kerri Lewis might still be holding in her apartment. Looking around, the problem was, she had no idea what it might be.

Shuffling into a more comfortable position, Yaz opened her own laptop and crossed her legs on the settee, stared at her notepad and the scribble of notes in it before hitting record on her mobile, wanting to capture her own thoughts. Looking at the puzzle in front of her, she might cut and splice elements of it later for the podcast, knowing she was making sense of it as she worked. She couldn't stop her mind from wandering.

Hitting pause on her mobile, she headed into the kitchen and poured another glass of water, not managing to push her own issues to one side. Returning to the front room and using her fake profile, she searched for her brother's Instagram page. You couldn't miss what you'd never had, but you could change your future. Staring at his face, any action she might take would have consequences. She quickly dismissed the thought, knowing it would be one more complication she didn't need at the moment. But the seed about her own family and background had been planted and wasn't going to go away. Scrolling down the screen, he'd posted an update earlier in the day saying he'd been interviewed by the local media. He seemed pleased with himself at being highlighted as a player in the city's future. She felt a pang of guilt at having played him. Hitting the record button again, Yaz looked at the image she had of Mikey Birch from the spy camera in the farmhouse and tried to put herself in his shoes, figure out what had happened all those years ago. Maybe he was guilty of murder? Maybe he had killed Jake Shaw and then disappeared. It was perfectly possible.

Conrad Knott wouldn't want the story resurfacing, certainly not at this moment in time. It would be embarrassing for her father. It needed more proof and there were parts of the puzzle she still didn't have. Looking again at the image of Mikey Birch, the story around him felt like a submarine resurfacing for the first time in decades.

Toying with her phone, she called the number for the mobile she'd passed along to Kerri Lewis, surprised when it connected. She needed to talk to someone.

'Hope you're looking after my place, Yaz.'

Yaz straightened up and rubbed her face, struggling for an answer.

Lewis laughed. 'It's what I'd do in your shoes. You've got my keys, right? Bet you're using my car too?'

She answered with her own question. 'You spoke to Conrad Knott about me?'

Lewis paused. 'You had a look at my laptop?' She sighed, spoke to someone else, a nurse, before returning to the call. 'I wanted to rattle his cage.'

'Someone's been inside your place and turned it over.'

'There's nothing to find.'

'Sure about that?' Yaz scanned the room, unsure if Lewis was still holding out on her. They were still playing games with each other, fucking about.

'If there was, you'd have found it by now,' Lewis said.

Yaz smiled, accepting the barbed comment. 'I should be where you are.' It wasn't her fault, but it weighed heavily.

'I'm glad you're not, Yaz. You're the one who needs to be pushing and finishing the story.'

She closed her eyes for a moment thinking about Helen Pullman and Carolyn Seymour. 'No one will talk.'

'What are you going to do?'

'I don't know yet.' She was waiting for Stonegrave to make a move. He was the key now she'd given her father something to think about. She wasn't taking his shit lying down. She thought again about the photograph she'd sent her father, how it dangerous and escalated things.

'Have you thought about *Inform?* They're the right home for you and the story. Make contact. They'll respect and value what you're doing.'

It wasn't a conversation she wanted to have right now. Finishing the call, Yaz stood up and paced the room. Her mobile sounded again, another incoming call, the number withheld. Listening to the silence at the other end of the line, she waited. 'Who's there?' she said eventually. More waiting, more background noise.

'Conrad Knott here, Yaz.'

'What do you want?'

She'd been checking his tweets regularly. He was getting ready to head to the sports stadium for a large charity function. Following the hashtag, it was a black-tie event, mandatory evening dress. Having checked the details, the event was invite-only and guests were expected to have deep pockets for the fundraising auction. They would be the quiet power behind the region.

'We should talk,' he said.

'I've got nothing to say to you.'

'I'm waiting outside,' he said, before killing the call.

THIRTY-FIVE

The black 4x4 idled in the shadows, parked up discreetly against the main entrance to the block of apartments. The engine gently hummed, headlights illuminating the path in front of it. She stared at it, but didn't make a move. The driver got out and opened the rear door for her before getting back in himself. She paused before walking over and got into the vehicle.

The car pulled away, heading out onto the dual carriageway that ringed the city centre. Commuters were heading home, clogging up the roads and filling buses. Crawling through the traffic, the vehicle turning towards the train station, cruising slowly through the roadworks and lights.

With a divider in place between the front and rear seats to give them privacy, Yaz made the first move, turning and talking to Knott. 'Did your people find whatever it was you were looking for in the apartment?'

'I've no idea what you're talking about.'

'Sure about that?'

'Do I look like the kind of person who breaks into places?'

There was no point dignifying the question with an answer. It wouldn't be something he'd do directly, but there was every chance a man like Dale Harker would have the contacts to make it happen. Her father would be complicit. She turned away, looking again out of the car window. 'Unless you want to talk to me on the record, you're wasting your time.'

'I tried to find you in that place you live. It's a proper shithole, isn't it? One of your housemates let me in.' He shook his head sadly. 'You don't get much for your money these days, do you? All that damp and patched up furniture. It's a bit grim.'

Biting, she turned back, ignoring the smile on his face. 'Maybe you should be using your position to look at regulating the rental sector properly?' There was no point asking how he knew where to find her. It didn't matter. 'It's not forever.'

Knott laughed and sat back and stretched out. 'Maybe I'll whisper it into the right ear.'

'My life is none of your business.'

'Not strictly true, but that's why we're here.'

Yaz shook her head, quietly fuming. 'Kerri Lewis is in hospital.'

'I heard.'

Of course he had. 'Shall I pass on your best wishes?'

'What happened?'

'Why don't you ask the police?'

'You seem to be in the picture.'

He didn't respond to the prompt. 'Did you get it wrong?'

'Get what wrong?'

'Kerri Lewis was wearing my jacket when she was attacked.' She waited for him to catch up with her train of thought. 'I was the target, wasn't I? You and Dale Harker don't like me poking around in your business, but tough shit. I've got no plans to stop.'

Knott laughed again. 'You love the drama, don't you? The world revolves around you, right?' He cut her off from speaking. 'It was most likely opportunist. Someone saw Lewis on her phone and thought they'd have it. Maybe they thought they'd have what cash she had on her, take her bank card. Whatever.'

'You made it happen.'

Knott stared out of the window, his voice low. 'I'd be very careful about repeating that in public.'

'It might set off a chain reaction? If I go down, you're coming with me. It's as simple as that.' They locked eyes, her father knowing exactly what she was talking about.

He leaned in closer, hissing into her face. 'If you pull another stunt like that with Mason, I won't be so lenient with you.'

She wasn't in the mood to back down. 'Worried about what I'll tell him?' She'd scored a hit. He was her brother, but it was too much to think through clearly, conflicting emotions that would need dealing with when the time was right. 'Who'd have thought he'd own a bar with Dale Harker's son?'

'It means nothing.'

'What if Stonegrave talks to me about the night Jake Shaw was murdered?'

'You think he'll do that? Behave yourself, Yaz. He's got far too much to lose by talking to you. I'll make sure his pension goes and that his daughter's pub fails. He's not going to get involved. It's not how the world works.' He took a business card out of his pocket and passed it over. 'I'm your only friend.'

She glanced at the details, the name and number of a national newspaper's editor.

'They're looking for someone like you to join them.' He sat back and relaxed again. 'Not many opportunities like this around.'

Yaz toyed with the card. 'You just said journalists are scum.'

'Some are worse than others.' He shrugged. 'I don't care, but it's what you want. Best thing that can happen for everyone is that you take what's on the table and let this go.'

She glanced out of the window as the vehicle indicated and turned onto the road that edged around the northern tip of the city centre. Things would change in an instant if she accepted the offer from Conrad Knott. The kicker was the podcast would have to disappear, her work with it. It would be selling herself out to him, just like Carolyn Seymour and Helen Pullman had done. 'Not interested,' she said, looking him in the eye.

'Sure about that, Yaz? Not many newspapers run serious investigative units these days. You're being offered a rare opportunity.' He gestured out of the window. 'It gets you away from here and down to London where the action is. It's the dream, right?'

'On my terms.'

'This is on your terms.'

'It's selling out.'

Knott laughed. 'That's your problem, right there. You see things in black and white terms. You need to get away from that before it ruins you. This isn't just about a moment, it's about all the work you've done so far. It's the reward for that. You've earned your big break and here it is.'

'How do you sleep at night?'

'Comfortably.'

'You disgust me.'

'I'm putting it on a plate for you here, and that's how you respond? What's the alternative, Yaz? You scrape around in a city that has nothing for you until you ultimately give up when it's not sustainable?'

'That's my business.'

'You need to think very carefully about my offer here.'

'I'm good, thanks.'

'You won't be if you carry on.'

'Is that a threat?'

Knott shook his head. 'It's the reality of your situation, that's all. If you pursue your story, whatever you think it is, you become part of the story. There's no way you can avoid it happening.'

'I'll take my chances.'

'Are you sure you want people poking around your life? I'm not sure you do. And it won't just be you. They'll start talking about your mother and she's not around to stick up for herself.'

'Let me out.' She yanked at the door handle, the vehicle at a stop. She'd heard enough. Knott leaned across, grabbing her by the wrist. 'Get your hands off me.' He twisted, really hurting her, but she eyeballed him. She wasn't going to show any weakness.

'Make the right decision here, Yaz.'

THIRTY-SIX

Hammering on the buzzer and stepping back, Sarah Shaw had called and left a garbled message on her voicemail, making little sense. The overall sentiment was clear, though. Looking up, a light was on in the flat. Hitting the buzzer again, Yaz thumped on the door and shouted at the window.

Despite the job offer he'd brokered, her own father was actively working against her, moving pieces around like a game of chess. It meant her feelings were complicated, something she didn't want to unpick immediately. She felt a mixture of emotions – hate for him, but also disappointment and sadness at the thought she'd never know him. Except she did know him. She knew exactly what he was about. He was prepared to use her dead mother against her. He was prepared to ruin her life if she continued with the podcast.

Pushing at the door, it wasn't locked. Heading straight up the stairs, the door to Shaw's flat was also unlocked. Walking in, Yaz looked at Sarah Shaw and the pile of tissues on the table in front of her, the woman's red eyes. Her gaze went then went to the bottle of vodka also on the table. Picking it up and shaking, it had been opened.

Shaw wouldn't meet her eye. 'He got to you.' Framing it as a question was unnecessary. She placed the bottle back down. They both knew they were talking about Conrad Knott.

'I make my own decisions.'

'What did he offer you?' Yaz sat down on a chair. 'Was it money?' It was an effort to keep the anger out of her voice. The moment she'd clocked the voicemail and listened to it she'd known something was wrong. 'Where does money get you?'

'He said he'd have my father's murder investigated again, start again from scratch and look at the evidence with fresh eyes. He said he'd be in charge himself.'

'He's lying to you,' Yaz said, rubbing her face. 'He's a liar. It's what he is.'

'How do you know?'

'I just do.'

Sarah Shaw reached for a tissue and blew her nose. 'I don't want anything to do with your podcast.'

'It's too late for that.'

'You can't use what you recorded. You don't have my permission anymore.'

'He told you to say that, did he?' There was no answer. Yaz swore to herself under her breath. The podcast needed Jake Shaw's daughter voice for it to have power. Her head was spinning to work out if what she was hearing was a game-changer or not. The podcast certainly needed the woman's approval if nothing else. It had to be authentic and serve a purpose.

Looking at Sarah Shaw, Knott had done a number on her. He'd reduced her to a wreck and left her with a bottle of vodka. It was reprehensible. It also showed how scared he was of the woman speaking out.

Sarah Shaw looked up at her. 'Who the fuck are you, Yaz?'

'I'm Conrad Knott's daughter.' The words were out, no emotion behind them. It was nothing more than laying the facts out.

'Don't lie to me.'

'I'm not lying and it's not going to stop me telling this story.' She was picking at her nails, not as confident as she wanted to give the impression of being. 'He's tried to buy me and others off too.' She outlined things stopping at the newspaper position he'd lined up for her. 'He'll do anything to silence the story and people like us.'

'People like us? This is still nothing to do with you.'

'He fathered me in a one-night stand.' It was now Yaz's turn to shy away from eye-contact. She couldn't bring herself to say there were doubts over how consensual that had been. 'He's cast a shadow over me since I found out the truth from my mother.' It was such an understatement, she almost wanted to laugh. 'He doesn't get a free pass for anything from me.'

'People like him don't need free passes.' Shaw's voice was low. 'They do what they want.'

'You're maybe right, but fuck that. We don't have to just accept it.' It was obvious Shaw's daughter was having buyer's remorse for taking the path of least resistance. Yaz leaned in and laid it out as best she could. 'I don't know what happened on the night of your father's murder, but I'm getting closer to finding out. There are things that people are trying to keep buried.' Taking out her mobile, she hesitated for a moment before pulling up the image she had of Mikey Birch in the farmhouse. 'He isn't dead.'

'No.' Sarah Shaw recoiled in horror.

'It's true.'

'He murdered my father.'

'I'd like to hear that from him, wouldn't you?' She lowered her arm and placed her mobile down. Sarah Shaw started to cry again, repeating the same words about Mikey Birch and what he'd done like it was a personal comfort blanket. Yaz stood up and started to pace the room. 'The truth of what happened to your father probably isn't what you think it is.'

Shaw shook her head. 'I need to put this behind me and move on.'

'That's what Conrad Knott said to you?'

'It's what I think.'

'No it's not.'

'Who do you think you are?

Yaz came to a stop. It was a good question. She was close to a breakthrough, but not close enough. Shaw reached for the vodka bottle, Yaz moving that bit quicker and grabbing it herself. Fuck her father and his irresponsible choices. He was deliberately trying to fuck the woman up, further insurance for himself. Who would listen to a drunk if they tried to make trouble for him?

Picking her mobile up, Yaz also scooped up the leaflet still on the table for the ReStart charity. Heading into the kitchen, she ignored the shouts coming from the living room. The first thing she did was unscrew the vodka bottle and pour the contents down the sink. Watching it trickle away, it was the right thing to do. Next she looked at the name and mobile number scribbled down on the leaflet, leaving a message when the call wasn't answered.

Heading out of the kitchen, she'd done all she could to help. Sarah Shaw stared at her, eyes burning with anger. Yaz didn't stop, heading for the door and the exit to the stairs and the street. Of all the setbacks she'd faced so far, this was the one which hurt the most.

THIRTY-SEVEN

Angry, Yaz left Sarah Shaw's flat behind, hoping the damage her father had inflicted on his colleague's daughter could be halted and reversed. It made her sick to think of him in there, finding the woman's wound from addiction and feeding it for his own purposes. She wasn't having it.

Finding a home address for Carolyn Seymour wasn't difficult. The house was a period terrace in the heart of the city's bohemian enclave. Many of the generous homes on the long, tree-lined avenues had long been converted into apartments she couldn't afford, the side street terraces equally out of her reach. It wasn't hard to imagine living in the area would be the height of her ambitions if she stuck around. Her sights were set higher. She needed to be away from these people and the city.

A light on downstairs told her the homeowner was still awake. Maybe it was unethical, but principles and decency only got you so far. Doorstepping people at night wasn't how she wanted to conduct herself, but as the door opened, she'd pushed the thought to one side. Carolyn Seymour was surprised to see her. 'I thought it was time we had another chat.'

'This isn't the time or place, Yaz,' Seymour said, starting to close the door.

She reached out and stopped her. 'I don't know about you, but I'm sick of letting Conrad Knott win.'

'It's your choice if you come inside, then. Remember that.' Seymour stared at her for a moment before giving a short nod of the head and disappearing back into the house. Yaz followed, heading through and into the conservatory. Her eyes went straight to pile of paperwork on the desk, the space used for home working.

Yaz glanced at the prints on the wall. 'From the raves?' Stepping closer, she'd seen some the images on Nell Heard's website and in the exhibition. Seymour didn't answer, instead tidying the paperwork into a neat pile. Yaz sat down and waited for Seymour to join her, even though she was tempted to cut straight to the chase. There was a dance to go through first. Rolling the dice again, Yaz placed her mobile down on the desk between and set the voice recorder app going. It would focus Seymour's mind on what they were talking about.

'No chance.' Seymour glanced down and stopped it.

Yaz picked it back up and flicked through her photographs, finding the ones she had of Mikey Birch. Handing it over, she watched Seymour study the image, relaxing further back in her chair. 'Let's start with the fact he's still alive, shall we?' Seymour's face was set, giving nothing away despite the magnitude of the words. The lack of surprise on his former-girlfriend's face told her all she needed to know. 'This isn't news to you. In fact, I'd say you've been waiting for me to tell you.'

'You're cold. You know that, right?' Seymour took out her e-cigarette and started it up. 'It was a long time ago.'

'Even so.' Reading between the lines, Mikey Birch still meant something to the woman, and she wasn't sure how much to reveal. Old wounds were being picked at, but there was more. 'It's a bullshit answer.'

Seymour smiled. 'You don't mess around, do you?'

'And you didn't answer my question.'

'You're right.'

'What happened the night Jake Shaw was murdered?' She wanted to use the detective's name and make it clear what had happened to him, just so there was no romanticising it.

Seymour took her time again before speaking. 'I'd say Mikey was on edge, like something bad was going to happen.'

Yaz interrupted, wanting to be clear. 'You know that, or you think that?'

'Both,' Seymour settled for saying, stalling for time by toying with her e-cigarette. 'There was something bothering Mikey, but he wouldn't say what it was.'

'But you didn't know what it was?'

'Not directly, no.'

Yaz thought about that, trying to put the pieces into place. 'You could have a guess, though?'

'Mikey knew the police were watching him and the raves. It came with the territory, but this was something different. He was on edge about something else altogether.'

Yaz leaned forward. 'You'll feel better for getting it off your chest after all this time.' She was gambling that whatever Seymour knew had been eating away at her for over thirty years, hating herself for being so compliant.

Seymour continued to toy with the e-cigarette. 'I saw him speak to Shaw.'

It wasn't what she expected to hear. 'Why would he be talking to Shaw?'

'He wouldn't say.' The woman was smiling mischievously.

If she believed Seymour, and she did, it meant Shaw and Birch had a relationship of some kind. 'Did he know Shaw was an undercover detective?'

'They had more than one meeting, that's all I know.'

'Fuck.'

'It doesn't necessarily mean anything.'

They both knew it wasn't true. It changed things again. 'You need to tell me what happened on the night of Shaw's murder. From the beginning.'

'All I remember is Mikey went off to meet him and then it all kicked off.'

'You helped him after he disappeared?' The question scored a hit. It was written all over Seymour's face. 'Tell me. I'm not recording.'

Seymour took a deep breath. 'For a while.'

Yaz cocked her head, wanting the woman to continue. Seymour had played her from the start and she hadn't seen it. Misguided loyalty or not, Seymour had even told her people lie. It had happened to her face. Nothing followed from Seymour, both of them growing uncomfortable with the silence between them. Ideally, she wanted the other person to break it, but Yaz also wanted momentum on her side. If you kept asking questions, something would eventually shake free. 'How did you help him?'

'We only briefly spoke via payphones,' Seymour said. 'Maybe once a month at the start. We never actually met.'

Reading between the lines, Seymour had probably been funnelling money to Mikey Birch. Maybe it had been done out of a sense of loyalty.

Another piece of the puzzle fell into place. Conrad Knott had threatened the woman, the suggestion that he'd make sure the place's funding was pulled. The only conclusion was that he'd done it because Carolyn Seymour knew something that could hurt him. He knew all of this too and was scared of what was going to happen next. Shuffling forward in her chair, it made sense. 'You're still in touch with Mikey, aren't you?' Seymour looked away. She wasn't going to make a good poker player.

'Why are you so invested, Yaz?' Seymour regained her composure and stared back. 'What's driving this for you?'

It was Yaz's turn to feel under pressure, calculate what answer she should give. 'It's personal for me,' she eventually offered.

'Personal? You're going to have to do better than that.'

Yaz stood up and walked over to the window, only able to see her own reflection in the night. She turned back to Seymour. 'Conrad Knott's my father.'

Seymour smiled. 'There's a thing.'

'You don't seem surprised.'

'This is your last chance to walk away, Yaz.'

'I'm not prepared to do that.'

'Ask the question you came here to ask.'

Seymour said nothing more about her father. Yaz took her time and composed herself, levelled her gaze on the woman. 'Did Mikey murder Jake Shaw?'

'Are you really sure you want to hear the truth, Yaz?' She held out her mobile. 'Listen to the voicemail.'

Pulling it up, the message was short and direct, the male voice identifying himself as Mikey Birch. Yaz turned away from Seymour and listened to Birch confirm he'd murdered Jake Shaw at the rave. Her first reaction was that it was a con, she was being played. She turned to Seymour, but only received a shrug back. The message continued to play, Birch confirming details about the abandoned farmhouse and what had happened there, proving he was who he claimed to be. Seymour continued to stare at her.

'This is the end of it, Yaz.'

Hearing Mikey Birch say he'd murdered Jake Shaw contradicted everything she'd felt in her bones, a truth she felt so righteously. Yet she'd been so wrong.

THIRTY-EIGHT

Pushing her way into the takeaway, Zach was working the place by himself. He glanced at Yaz for a moment before turning back to the grill, angling himself away from her after placing his mobile back in his pocket, his favourite rap music coming out of the speakers. Orders were piling up on the rack above the grill, several patties cooking away. His mobile sounded again, another order coming in.

Taking her laptop out, Yaz connected to Wi-Fi and turned to the website of the newspaper her father had connected her to. It was a platform in the way *Inform* wasn't. It provided access; their name opened doors and demanded answers. The downside was that newspapers weren't independent. There was always an agenda. Glancing at the business card he'd given her, the question was, could she live with that? Actions always had consequences. Clicking to social media she scrolled aimlessly before turning to her emails, unable to concentrate and wanting a distraction. It wasn't going to work. It wasn't a switch she could hit to stop thinking. 'Are you not talking to me?' she said to Zach's back.

'I'm busy.'

'You could look at me for a moment.' She waited for him to turn to face her. 'I fucked up.' She watched him reach for the bottle of sanitiser and work a blob of liquid into his hands, ignoring her. She held his stare for a moment before pushing the stool out and standing up, heading for the door. 'Fuck's sake.'

Zach shouted after her, offering his own apology. 'What's happened?'

She stopped and took a breath, staring at her own reflection in the window. 'It's gone wrong.'

'Talk to me, Yaz.'

She didn't want to look at herself. Turning away from her reflection, she walked back over and sat down, apologised for her own outburst. 'It's a mess.'

'The podcast?'

'I was wrong.'

'About what?'

'Everything.' She told him about the conversation she'd had with Carolyn Seymour before taking him through the other moves she'd made, including the newspaper her father had offered to set her up with. She watched Zach weigh up what she'd told him, but he didn't respond. 'Say something.'

Zach placed a can of Coke down on the counter next to her. 'You're rethinking the podcast?'

'If I drop things, I get access to his contact book and my dream job.' She told him about the voicemail on Carolyn Seymour's mobile, Mikey Birch's confession to murdering Jake Shaw.

'Do you believe that?'

'I could make a case either way.'

'And the offer of a fancy job depends on which way you jump?'

'I don't know what to believe.'

'You do, Yaz.'

She swallowed a mouthful of the fizzy drink. Zach had a way of seeing straight through her and cutting to the chase. Looking around and smelling the meat that had been grilled earlier in the evening, working in the takeaway was another sign of her own weakness. More hypocrisy. She didn't like much about herself. 'Am I a bad person?'

Zach looked up from cleaning the grill. 'What kind of question is that?'

'One I want you to answer truthfully.'

He shrugged. 'You're not always easy.'

It wasn't a reassuring answer. If she told the world Mikey Birch was still alive via the newspaper, what would people say about her? She drank again from the can before rubbing her face. The question felt more important than she expected it to be. Whether it was the newspaper, or *Inform,* or her own podcast, it was about doing things for the right reasons. She'd followed the thread from the initial photograph she'd been sent, but it had spiralled off in a new direction.

She pulled up the photograph of Mikey Birch and explained what it meant. 'He was never dead.'

Zach cut her off, not wanting to hear anything further. 'You don't want to walk away from this, regardless of the damage you're doing?' He turned back to his work, nothing more to say.

Turning to her contacts list, she called Kerri Lewis, Lewis answering and telling her to wait. She listened as the woman talked to a nurse at the other end of the line. Maybe it was a mistake making the call. Lewis came back on the line with an apology. 'I wish they'd leave me alone.'

Yaz hesitated before talking. 'I'm finding people won't talk to me for the podcast.' What she couldn't shake off was the fact the women were invested. She thought about Pullman's pension and Seymour's charity, tried to see it from their point of view. She couldn't. It didn't make sense to her.

'And you're surprised?'

'They were scared of the consequences of speaking out.'

'It's to be expected.'

'I called Seymour's bluff.'

'What did she do?'

Yaz laughed bitterly. 'She stuck it back on me.' She explained about the message from Mikey Birch.

'And you think that's the truth?'

'It's his words.' She got to the point of why she was really calling. 'My father offered to set me up with a paper in London.' She outlined it for Lewis, spilling the details. 'It's a proper platform.'

Lewis laughed. 'Don't fall for that shit, Yaz. What's the price tag? You have to spike your podcast? He's trying to buy your silence.'

'It doesn't mean I'm buying.' He'd made his threats, no messing about, but she had a plan. The story started on the podcast, and it was going to finish on the podcast, one way or another.

'You think his offer of help makes up for everything, is that it? He's treated you like a piece of shit, Yaz.'

'Maybe a break is the very least he owes me?'

'Don't be naive.'

'I'm not.'

'I fucked up in London,' Lewis said. 'I lost people who were important to me because I didn't think things through. It cost me my girlfriend at the time, friendships I valued.'

'Maybe I'll make wiser decisions?'

'It's easy to end up chasing stories for the wrong reason when you're under pressure. Take it from me and learn from my experience.'

Yaz didn't want to hear it. 'I spoke to Jake Shaw's daughter,' she said, wanting to change the conversation. 'She's been leaned on, offered a cold case investigation if she doesn't talk to me.'

'Par for the course.'

'Knott visited her flat and left a gift – a bottle of vodka.'

'That's how people like him operate. They don't care about the damage they cause. They find a weakness and they seek to exploit it.'

Lewis knew all about Sarah Shaw and her demons. Of course she did. It was also clear they were still talking about the job offer. 'I tried to get her some help, stop it from getting any worse.'

'That's the right thing to do.'

It was partly about her conscience too, she knew that much. 'I brought trouble to her door.'

'Maybe you need to toughen up?'

'Say again?'

'I can lie to you about the reality of your choices, if you want?'

'I don't need your lectures.'

Lewis paused. 'Sounds like you should take the opportunity he's setting up for you, then. Go to London. Go and write for the paper, make a name for yourself. See if it makes you happy. You've made it clear there's nothing here for you.'

'Maybe I will.'

Lewis laughed this time. 'You won't take his offer.'

'Why won't I?' Yaz swore to herself, knowing how she'd been backed into a corner, Lewis effectively controlling the argument. Worse, she'd let herself be led there. 'I'll finish the podcast and then make a decision.'

She rubbed her face, knowing it had been a mistake to call the woman. Standing up and pacing the room, maybe it hadn't been a mistake. Maybe she'd wanted her to put her straight and spell things out. There was no easy answer. Sitting back down on the stool at the counter, the refrigerator behind it hummed quietly but relentlessly, the sizzle of the grill as Zach worked.

'If you don't think Mickey Birch murdered Jake Shaw, there's only one question you need to ask yourself,' Lewis said. 'Who did murder him?'

Yaz came to a stop, knowing it was the bottom line.

'We both know how this ends, Yaz. You wouldn't be able to live with yourself if you let your father help you. You're kidding yourself if you think otherwise.'

PODCAST EXTRACT – EPISODE FOUR

NOT YET UPLOADED

In this fourth podcast in the new 'CrimeTime' series, we'll explore how the contemporary investigation into the murder of Detective Constable Jake Shaw was curtailed and undermined by serving police officers with their own agenda ... it's something that still resonates thirty-five years later for those involved ...

As per procedure, outside detectives were brought in to probe the circumstances around Shaw's murder, the team led by a detective from South Yorkshire Police ... it's clear what was already a difficult job for her was made much harder than it needed to be ... her team's attention initially focused on the fact Jake Shaw had been working undercover at the rave, meaning they had to look to Shaw's colleagues for co-operation ... it wasn't forthcoming ... their investigation was systematically shut down ... pressure was placed on them to ensure that the initial findings of the investigation should be accepted ...all roads led to Mikey Birch and Jake Shaw's corruption, all accepted as fact ... I've tracked the detective down, but I've been unable to persuade her to speak to me on the record ... it's clear she's still too afraid to talk even now, even though she's retired, too scared for her own future ...

We know the undercover team that night consisted of three people; Detective Inspector Conrad Knott was assisted by Detective Constable Jake Shaw, and a third man, Detective Constable Ian Stonegrave ... Stonegrave is still a serving detective, working in a Cold Case unit on a short term contract ... he's refused to speak to the podcast, but it's possible to piece together his story and infer how his career stalled in the aftermath of his colleague's murder ... did his work as an undercover detective unbalance him in some way? It's work that takes an incredible toll on the participant ... it's partly the physical aspect, but more than that, it's the mental aspect ... it's work that sees the participant living on a knife-edge when one false move, or simply dropping their guard for a single moment could result in dangerous consequences ... it's not over dramatic to suggest that despite extensive training, an undercover detective would struggle to not feel fear, maybe even fear for their life at times ... it's an extreme role placing the participant under extreme pressure ...

Do Stonegrave and Knott still have questions to answer about both their conduct during the undercover investigation and their subsequent actions in the aftermath? ... I believe they do ... My first meeting with Stonegrave didn't go well ... he tried to scare me off from talking about the story, but scratch the surface and you find something different ... you find a man scared for his own future, conflicted and a complex mess, worried about the things that worry all of us ... we all have to make our own judgement calls about the protagonists in this podcast, as we follow the evidence and re-examine what we think we know about them ...

THIRTY-NINE

Stonegrave stopped a good distance away from the impromptu security cordon and watched the activity playing out in front of him. Access to the pathway on the Humber Bridge was restricted, members of the public complaining at being directed to the other side. Beyond the cordon, a small media team was at work, Conrad Knott resting against the barrier, hands animatedly gesticulating as he continued to talk to the camera. It was almost dark, and it seemed a ridiculous place for the media to be recording an interview for the evening news.

Stonegrave waited until the camera was lowered, the filming over, before heading closer and telling the security team he was expected. He'd sent a text, saying they had to talk now. Things needed saying and he wasn't going to wait. Approaching Knott, the man acknowledged his presence, both of them waiting for media team around him to finish their work. Stonegrave gazed out across the water at the cluster of petroleum plants which punctuated vast swathes of fields. Next to him, traffic thundered past on the dual carriageway.

'Why they have to use this place, I've no idea.' Knott was talking to himself. 'It's as if there's nothing more to the area than the bloody bridge. No wonder people think we're savages up north.'

'Kerri Lewis's in a bad way.'

Knott didn't answer immediately, turning the thought over. 'I wouldn't class her situation as being remotely important to us.'

'Unfortunate it happened outside of Mason's bar.'

'It's why I encouraged him to look elsewhere for a career, but what can you do?'

'Interesting choice of business partner too?' Knott didn't respond, but he'd made his point. 'No arrests, I believe.'

'Unlikely to be, I'd say. No cameras, no witnesses.'

'I've been thinking on what you said.'

Knott cut in. 'We cleared the air. No need to go over it again. Let's move on from that.'

'We're far from done.'

'You watch your mouth here. Remember who you're talking to. If you've got something to say, say it. Get it out of your system and then we can move on.'

'I don't want to move on.'

Knott smiled and softened his tone. 'Yaz Moy has been dripping poison in your ear, hasn't she?'

'Is that so?'

Knott raised and flexed his hands, examined them before speaking again. 'Moy's finding it's harder to make people talk than she maybe thought. She tracked down Mikey Birch's girlfriend. Remember her back in the day? She runs a charity now called Fresh Juice. Have you heard of them?'

'Can't say I have.'

'She does a lot of good work I want to see it supported, but it does rely on funding and goodwill.'

It was Stonegrave's turn to cut in. 'I get the picture.' He took out a tissue and coughed into it.

'Moy's even got the nerve to be bothering Jake Shaw's daughter to give her false expectations about what's going to happen here.'

It stopped him in his tracks. Shaw's daughter would be well into her thirties despite always appearing as a young girl in his mind. She wasn't a child now and would have questions about her father and what had happened to him. More than that, she deserved answers.

'I've sorted her out,' Knott said, dismissing any further discussion. 'She won't be causing any trouble, either.'

'What did you do?'

'You think Moy's got the credibility to carry a story?' Knott asked, ignoring the question he'd been asked. 'It won't be taken seriously. She's had every opportunity and incentive to do the right thing here, but she made her choice.' Knott looked pained at the turn of circumstances. 'Anyway, don't worry about it. I've sorted her out an opening at a newspaper. She's thinking on it, but she'll do the right thing in the end. This way everyone wins.'

'Not Jake Shaw.' Stonegrave had spent most of the previous evening sitting at the bar in the pub, staring at the mounted bottles of alcohol. It had been a battle, but he'd kept the promise he'd made to Kelly by not touching them. 'I want to know what happened,' he said. 'The truth.'

'You know what happened. We don't need to go over the same old ground again.' Knott laughed and took a step back, hands into his trouser pockets. 'Yaz Moy really has got into your head, hasn't she?'

Stonegrave considered that. Maybe Knott was right, but it was more than that. What was initially a distraction, a young podcaster with no idea what she was doing, was suddenly something far bigger. She'd dredged up old memories and shown him that the past wasn't necessarily the past. Things that he'd deliberately surpressed couldn't stay dormant for ever.

'Don't be naive as she is,' Knott settled for saying. 'You've got a future to think about.'

Stonegrave stared at him. 'You think you get to walk away from this?'

'Is that a threat?' Knott laughed. 'We're friends, surely?'

'We were never friends.'

'You want more money?'

'You think this is about money?'

'Everything's about money in the end.'

'It doesn't have to be.'

Knott leaned over the barrier and looked at the view for a moment before speaking again. 'You're a detective, not a social worker.'

'I don't want your money.'

'You're going to have to enlighten me as to what you do want.'

'It's time for the truth to come out.'

Knott straightened up, held Stonegrave's stare. 'I'd be very careful about what you say, if I was you.'

'She's your daughter.' Knott's face changed, setting. There was a flash of shock, quickly replaced by something harder. Something much more dangerous. It was all the confirmation he needed. Yaz Moy hadn't lied to him.

Knott composed himself. 'Where did you hear that?'

'Does it matter?'

'It does to me.'

'She told me herself.'

'And you believe her?'

'The answer is written all over your face.'

'She was a mistake, it's as simple as that.'

'That's callous.'

'I don't care what you think.'

Stonegrave accepted the point, knowing it was likely to be true. 'It changes things.'

Knott shook his head. 'It changes nothing. She doesn't feature in my life. Never has done, never will do.'

'I feel sorry for you.'

'You feel sorry for me?' Knott laughed. 'I've heard it all now. We've all made mistakes, right? We've all done stupid things when we were young. Things just are what they are sometimes. You can't always change them or put them right.'

'How do you live with yourself?' Stonegrave shook his head. Knott was offering a politician's answer, a politician's way of setting out a case like they were the victim. He'd seen the anger and the way Yaz Moy was living her life. He angled his body away from Knott and looked out at the city again. There was nothing he wanted more than to just fade into the background, become part of its wallpaper. The opposite of what Knott wanted.

'I'm amazed you can sleep at night.'

'I'm doing an important job and making a difference. Yaz Moy doesn't get to stop all of that. No one cares about Jake Shaw, or Mikey Birch, these days. That's the bottom line.'

'Not for everyone.' Stonegrave looked at Knott, seeing him for what he was. 'I've spent too much of my career scared of you, scared of what you could do to me. I've spent my life doing what I'm told to by people like you. I'm done with it.' It all had to come out. He was disgusted with himself for ignoring the truth for so long. 'I don't know what went on that night, but I'm betting Yaz

Moy can help with that. The details might embarrass you when they come out and they won't paint me in a good light, either, but the record needs setting straight for Jake.' All bets were off. What he hadn't appreciated at the time was that it wasn't a drugs deal going down at the rave. It was a murder scene. 'The truth is going to come out.'

Knott closed the gap between them and lowered his voice. 'Make no mistake here. There's only so much I can do to help people. There comes a point when you have to wash your hands of a situation.' Knott continued to stare, a much darker look on his face. 'You want some home truths? Here's one for you. Don't kid yourself about your innocence here, or your skewered sense of morality. You always knew what was going on, even if the words were never spoken. You're as guilty as anyone else.'

There were decisions you made for yourself, and decisions others made for you. Stonegrave's hands had balled into fists without him noticing, turning white. His head was a mess of contradictory thoughts. Whichever way he moved, he was being squeezed, boxed in with any escape routes systematically removed. He was being lied to again. History was repeating itself. Knott thought himself bulletproof, the sense of entitlement too much to swallow down. 'Maybe we deserve what's coming our way?'

'Say that again?'

He didn't need to repeat himself. The words had hit home. 'I've been a coward for too long.'

FORTY

Sitting down on the bed, Yaz booted her laptop up, unsure of her next move. Kerri Lewis had called her out and made her feelings perfectly clear. She's then tried to explain it all to Zach, but he'd been too busy to listen, his eyes glazing over. She regularly spent time in his flat, often for sex, but not this time. Staring at her notes, all the directions her questions pointed to had been shut off. Sitting up more comfortably, there was a link to a replay of the event from Nell Heard's exhibition sitting in her inbox. Setting it going, it was background she was happy to have wash over her. Glancing at the screen again, the event comprised of Nell Heard talking through the exhibits. Heard was standing in front of a more recent image, one Yaz remembered seeing, knowing it had been taken at a Black Lives Matter demonstration in London during the first lockdown. Heard explained the story behind the image, but she wasn't listening all that closely. Staring again at the images on the walls, there was something she wasn't seeing. It was something she'd been thinking about. It was like a slightly out of focus photograph, pieces of the jigsaw that didn't quite fit together.

Glancing back at the screen, Nell Heard was talking more generally about her own life, how it impacted on her work and vice versa. The exhibition made Heard's anti-authority feeling clear. It didn't need reading up on.

It was all there in the photographs. In theory, Yaz should like the woman, feel a kinship with her. But she didn't. Focusing in, Nell Heard moved on to another image to discuss. Yaz leaned in. The image next to it had been taken down, but not replaced. It was odd and didn't make sense. Pausing the event, she pulled up the images she's snapped in the exhibition on her mobile. It was a force of habit to take photographs, but sitting up and looking more closely at the removed image, it was now a lucky break. Lowering her handset, it was all there. She'd missed it previously. 'Fuck.'

Replaying the recording again, wanting to make sure, it only confirmed what she thought. Scrolling through the comments viewers had left as they interacted, one caught her eye. There was one man she wanted to talk to. Lorrie Matthews had a lot of questions to ask and had left several comments. It was a moment of recognition as he'd spoken on camera. She was sure he was also in the photograph that Nell Heard had taken down in the exhibition. Turning to social media, his profiles were easy to find, a heavy user as he promoted his cafe in Leeds. He'd led an interesting life. She left a message for him and smoked a joint as she waited for a response.

The reply came quickly, Matthews only too willing to talk. Turning to Zoom, she found herself facing the man. He was still working in his cafe, the space ramshackle with furniture chaotically arranged behind him, the place closing up for the day. It immediately felt authentic rather than contrived. She could see a poster for a baby group the following morning, another for their suspended coffee scheme and a live acoustic night on later in the week. Lorrie Matthews smiled back at her. In his fifties with long dreadlocks tied back, his tatty band t-shirt said Mega City Four, a name she'd have to Google later.

'I was hoping to speak to you about your days as a New Age Traveller,' she said to kick them off.

He paused. 'There's something I didn't expect to hear when I woke up this morning.'

'I'm working on a podcast about sub-culture.' It wasn't the truth, but it was a lie she could live with. 'I watched Nell Heard's Zoom event last night and thought you'd be a good person to speak to.'

'Once a crusty, always a crusty,' he said with laugh as he pointed to his t-shirt. 'They're my favourite band. I played their tapes to death on my ghetto blaster, back in the day. Good times.'

'You certainly spoke with passion about your days as a New Age Traveller on the Zoom event I saw with Nell Heard.'

He sipped at his coffee, nodding. 'I don't really give those times a label, as I don't feel any different in my head. I live above the cafe now rather than sharing a repurposed bus, but it's a state of mind for me. I always say living on the road changed my life. People thought we were these smelly irritants with no respect for anything, or ourselves, but we cared. We gave a fuck and that was what they didn't like about us.'

'Who didn't like you?'

He laughed. 'The police, the authorities, the local communities. You name them, they hated us.'

'Did they monitor you?'

'Undercover police? To a degree, but we never stayed still for too long. Out of sight, out of mind and someone else's problem if we moved on. Those years changed my life, moulded it for the better. I met likeminded people, and they inspired me to become what I wanted to be.' He gestured around the cafe again. 'I know this is just a coffee shop when all's said and done, but it's a communal space for people to come together and feel supported. We have all sorts of groups using the facilities and it's brilliant. Maybe they buy a coffee, maybe they don't, but we offer a safe escape from the world.' He smiled and tapped his head. 'You might find the odd group who want to get together and plot how to change the world meet here, too.'

Yaz returned the smile. 'Did you feel like you made a difference back then?'

'That's a big question.' He sat back in the chair, hands behind his head, thinking for a minute. 'It was about environmental issues for me. Always was. It scared me how we treated the planet thirty odd years ago, but it terrifies me now.' He rocked the chair back to the floor. 'How do you measure making a difference in life, though? How does anyone do that?'

Yaz stared at the screen. It was a tough question to answer. She was thinking about Mikey Birch and Jake Shaw, how everything cascaded outwards from them and their lives. It was tough to articulate how she felt to the man in front of her. 'You just know, I guess.' It was the best she could offer. Lewis had said as much about when the truth of a story hits you. Mikey Birch and Jake Shaw had taken different paths, but in their own way, they both had wanted a better society. It was a thought that fucked with her head.

'I'm pleased you haven't got an answer for me,' he said. 'It's the people who think they know everything who are dangerous. The ones who ask questions are the ones I trust more. You're doing it right. Why side with the mainstream when you can make something happen on your own terms? They don't deserve your trust. Resist and don't comply has always been my motto. You've got to pick a side and stick to it.'

Yaz knew she was hearing some home truths. The man had something about him and she wanted to continue talking, but there was a purpose to their conversation. Rummaging around in her rucksack, she took out the photograph showing the man as a New Age Traveller. It was the image that Nell Heard had removed from the exhibition. She'd seen it before when talking to Bella, but she'd missed the significance. 'This is you?' she asked holding it up to the screen.

Matthews took some glasses out of his pocket and stared back. 'Haven't seen this for years. Where did you get it?'

'It was in the exhibition.' She suggested Nell Heard had ran out of time to discuss it during the Zoom event, another lie she could live with. 'Do you remember it being taken?'

'Not specifically,' he said, thinking about it, 'though I remember Nell being around with her camera from time to time.'

'She'd just drop in?'

He shrugged. 'It was that kind of scene. People came, people went. No questions asked. No one was interested in people's pasts. It was about what you had to offer at that moment in time.'

It was another interesting response. 'Where was it taken?'

Matthews looked again before shrugging and apologising. 'I can't say for sure.'

It didn't matter. 'What can you tell me about the photo?' She tried to quickly justify the question, remembering her cover story. 'It's an interesting case study, exploring the personal within a larger narrative.'

He didn't question it, instead shaking his head. 'I can't remember a lot, honestly.'

'Good parties back then?'

'The best,' he said with a smile. 'If you remember them, you weren't really there, right?'

'So they say.' It was an opportunity to chance her arm. 'Did you go to the raves that were being put on around that time?'

'Wasn't my scene.' He pointed to his t-shirt. 'I've always preferred guitars to bleeps and beats. That said, I liked them in theory. They were a way of kicking back given the police were clamping down on kids having a good time. The wider picture was just miserable. It was part of the reason I wanted to hit the road. There was nothing for me or people like me.'

Yaz went back to the photograph and the question she wanted answering. 'How about him?' She pointed to the figure in the background, the one who wasn't the focus of the image. 'It'd be nice to speak to him, too.'

'A friend of a friend.' Matthews rubbed his chin, thinking. 'He just appeared one day.' He told her to hold it up again and stared at it intently. 'He was a nice bloke, that was my reading. He fitted in and pulled his weight.'

'Can you remember when he joined you?' She watched him shake his head, perplexed by her line of questioning. She was pushing too hard. 'Doesn't matter.' She lowered the photograph. 'Just curious.'

'He was still around when I left, I remember that much,' he said. 'I'd done all I could by that point. It was the right time for me to find a different outlet for what I wanted to do.' He sat back in his chair again, closed his eyes. 'Yeah, I remember him. He was definitely friendly with Nell.'

'Is that a euphemism?'

He opened his eyes and laughed. 'No judgment. Nell would appear with her kid and stay for a bit. I can't remember the kid's name.'

Yaz leaned in, knowing she had to hear it. 'Bella?'

It took a moment before he nodded, saying she was right. 'Mick would always be playing with her.'

'Mick?'

Matthews told her to hold the photograph up again and pointed to Mikey Birch. 'That was definitely his name.'

Thanking him for his time and ending the call, Yaz scooped up her coat and pocketed her mobile, no longer feeling sorry for herself, ready to move again.

FORTY-ONE

Knowing how Mikey Birch disappeared had to be the start of things moving in Yaz's favour again. She had more knowledge and more facts, rapidly closing in on the truth. Mikey Birch had fathered a child with Nell Heard. It made sense that he would return to the area. People had helped him and would now have to talk. Holding insurance policies was one thing, but she had to mix it up and make things happen on her own terms. More than anything, she needed momentum; momentum to keep the story moving forward.

Yaz edged her way forward, standing close to the small technical crew going about their work against the backdrop of the abandoned dock she'd first spoken to Stonegrave at. Artificial light illuminated the rundown building, Dale Harker posing against it. It felt clunky and clichéd, the wreckage of the city being used as shorthand. Knott was a dead end, but his circle wasn't. Others wouldn't be so keen on the revelations coming to light. It only needed one of them to crack, or step out of line.

Harker hadn't been hard to track down via his social media feeds Yaz was now following via one of her shell accounts. The man's ego couldn't resist explaining he was undertaking a night photo shoot, the location easy enough to recognise. Watching, the woman leading the shoot answered a call on her mobile, telling the crew they should all take five minutes. Yaz grabbed the opportunity, heading straight over to him. Harker was already on his own mobile, scrolling through messages and notifications.

'I thought you might have had more imagination than to choose this place for photographs,' she said to him, waiting for him to look up at her.

Harker lowered his mobile, taking a moment to place her before roaring with laughter. 'You're not a fan?'

'How did you guess?'

'I'll tell you what else you aren't, shall I?' He leaned forward, the smile wiped off his face. 'You're not a journalist for *The Guardian*.'

'It was an embellishment.'

'Less polite people would say it was a lie.'

'You wouldn't have spoken to me otherwise.'

'You never know.'

It was bullshit and they both knew it. 'I wanted to update you with what was going on, give you the chance to talk to me.'

'There's nothing I want to say to you.'

Yaz glanced around. They were still alone. A handful of people milled around, no one paying them any attention, all checking their own mobiles for messages or making small talk as they waited for the shoot to recommence. Harker was going nowhere, the gamble being that he wouldn't want to cause a scene in public. It was an opportunity she wouldn't get again. Holding his stare, she laid it out. 'I want to talk about drugs around the raves.' Yaz set out what she knew, how it painted a picture. She was still reaching, but the picture was forming in her mind. 'The dealers at the raves were tied in with you. It was a partnership. It was too lucrative to not do something.'

Harker scratched at his face, taking his time before replying. 'You should be very careful what you say here. What Mikey got up to was beyond my control.'

Yaz repeated the word *partnership* to herself. 'It wasn't just Mikey.'

'You'll have to make yourself clear.'

She knew she was rolling the dice and playing with fire, but Mikey Birch didn't feel right for what she was talking about. He wasn't a drug dealer. It required a certain hardnosed approach, one she didn't think the man possessed. 'Associating with edgy people hasn't done you any harm.'

'You think I was involved in drug dealing?'

'Why not?'

'You're bang out of order here.'

'Explain it to me, then. Put me straight. Do it officially.'

'You think I'd speak to a poxy podcast after all of this time?' Harker shook his head and looked over her shoulder. 'If you don't mind, I've got work to do. Now fuck off and take your juvenile theories somewhere else.'

Yaz heard someone behind her clear their throat, trying to let her know her time with Harker was up. She spun round and stared at the woman wanting to get back to the shoot, making it clear she was going nowhere yet. The woman glanced at them both before saying they had two minutes before they'd have to restart things.

Harker nodded at her, said he was almost done and waited for her to back off before speaking again. 'Mikey was a loose cannon. I couldn't control him, or what he did.'

'He acted alone that night, is that what you're telling me?' Yaz folded her arms, happy to listen. Harker was making it up as he went along, she was sure of it.

'It was nothing to do with me,' Harker continued. 'So like I said, it's time you fucked off with your fantasies. Go and write your stories that no one's interested in reading.'

'It's a podcast.'

'You don't know anything.'

'Seems there's a lot I don't know?'

'Maybe there's just nothing to learn?' Harker relaxed. 'It is what it is.' He shrugged. 'We'll never know why Mikey acted like he did.'

'Do you remember Kerri Lewis?' She watched Harker make a show of rolling the name around, like he couldn't remember. 'She was the journalist who covered the story at the time. Ringing some bells?'

'I'm not a reader. I prefer to do stuff rather than navel gaze and guess what others are all about.'

She smiled at the insult. 'Kerri Lewis was the victim of an attack outside of your son's bar. The one he owns with Conrad Knott's son.'

'Sounds unpleasant.'

Harker hadn't even flinched. 'It was touch and go whether she'd make it for a while.'

'I can't help you.'

'Pretty amazing that your two sons have ended up such firm friends. Definitely coming from different sides of the track.'

'Funny how life works out sometimes.'

'Sure you can't help me?'

'No.'

'Maybe I should ask Mikey Birch directly?' Yaz enjoyed the silence between them for a moment, knowing Harker was trying to catch up with her train thought, unsure of what she was about to say. She had the power to tear his world down, loving the fact she was in control.

It felt righteous. Pulling up the image she had of Birch on her mobile, she showed it to him and pushed home her advantage. 'Seems Mikey was dossing down in an abandoned farmhouse recently.' Discomfort was written all over Harker's face. 'Cat got your tongue?'

'This is nothing to do with me,' he eventually said, pushing her mobile away.

'It's everything to do with you,' she told him. 'And you need to decide which side you're on. The truth is going to come out and you or Conrad Knott won't be able to stop it.' Yaz took out a piece of paper and scribbled down her number. 'You should call me whilst you can still make decisions. Otherwise you'll just be navel gazing.'

Lewis's words were on her mind. She wasn't buying Birch's confession she'd heard. It didn't sit right. 'Unless you've got something to hide.'

She headed away, not stopping to look back. Once she was out of sight, she came to a stop, gulping in the night air. Looking at her hand, it was shaking slightly, difficult to tell if it was from adrenaline or nerves. It didn't matter.

Taking out her mobile and the business card her father had given her, Yaz looked at it again. Working for the Investigative and Crime Reporting team within a major newspaper was the dream job. The editor's social media feed buzzed with stories and the life she wanted to lead. It was a big opportunity and the platform she wanted for herself.

Hitting call, Yaz took a deep breath, told herself to remain calm. The call answered, she could hear a loud bar in the background. She shouted her name down the line in the hope of being heard. The noise slowly receded, what sounded like a metal door banging against a wall.

'Sorry about that,' Eve Grindell said. 'I was hoping you'd call.'

'Here I am.' She closed her eyes, knowing she had to say it. 'Conrad Knott said you had something for me?'

'You're direct, I like that. He's quite the fan of yours, you know? I've checked out your podcast and website as well. You've got something, Yaz.'

There was no way she was sharing the fact the man was her father. It already made her burn with shame. 'I've got a story for you.'

Grindell laughed. 'He said you're keen.'

'It's a story about him.' The words were out. She opened her eyes again and focused. Grindell fell silent. 'It's an important one.' She knew Grindell was weighing up how much credence to give her words. Whether she was worth taking seriously. 'I want to finish it on the podcast, though.'

'If it's a big story, I could probably work with that, co-ordinate things.'

'It's non-negotiable.'

'I'm going back to the office,' Grindell said. 'Let's talk about it then.'

Yaz killed the call. Things were moving. She was starting to show her hand and increase the stakes.

FORTY-TWO

Drawing her coat in tighter and staring at the alleyway Kerri Lewis had been attacked in, Yaz waited. A piece of crime scene tape had been caught around the drain grill at the entrance, the wind trying to blow it free. The rest of the area had been cleaned up, no sign of what had happened. Stepping back into a nearby doorway, a group of what she guessed were students carrying boxes of beer, passed in the direction of nearby university accommodation.

Glancing at her mobile was a compulsion. Everything came down to finding the right key to unlock things, regardless of how she saw the story being pushed out. There had to be a way to get people to speak to her on the record. The more Yaz thought about it, the more her work had to have some meaning, it had to be important. If it upset some people along the way, she was all for it. The podcast had worked so far because people wanted to talk to her. This was different. Instead, she put her head back and closed her eyes. Exposing the story would be the easy bit, making it stick was something else altogether. It was still her ticket out of the city and had to be done right. But she was serious about the podcast. It was getting finished and it had to be the full story.

Hearing footsteps bounce of the cobbled street and coming to a stop at the face of the alleyway, she stepped forward.

Stonegrave stared back at her. 'We could have done this somewhere else.'

'I wanted to do it here.' They both understood the power of location and setting when talking to people. Sometimes it was pure theatre, sometimes it was more than that. Her message had given him the choice; meet her here or she'd come looking for him at his daughter's pub. She stood her ground, arms folded, wondering if what she was about to do was wise. Conrad Knott needed to be sent a message and Stonegrave was going to be her vehicle for it. Knott was fucking with her and she needed to regain control.

'You think this is how you win friends and influence people, Yaz? Making me come here at this time and trying to call the shots?'

'You're here, though.' She got to the point and told him about the offer Conrad Knott had made, how he was trying to buy her silence. 'Forgive me for not giving a fuck about your beauty sleep.'

Stonegrave held a hand up, told her to slow down. 'You've spoken to Knott again?'

She told him about Kerri Lewis's apartment and what had happened. 'It's a warning shot directed at me.'

'You're paranoid.'

'And you think you know everything?'

He smiled. 'Here's something for you. The older you get, the less you know for certain.'

'Don't patronise me.'

'File it under general advice.'

She took out her mobile and pulled up the selfie she'd taken with Mason Knott, held it out to him.

'That's bold.'

'I sent it to Knott. If he doesn't back off, I'll tell his precious son exactly who I am.'

'Leverage?'

'An insurance policy.'

'You're playing with fire.'

'It's the only way.'

'You've got balls, I'll give you that.'

Pulling up the photograph of Mikey Birch from the spy camera, there was no way Knott would have shared the news with Stonegrave. Bitter experience told her that Knott was a man who guarded secrets closely. She gestured to Stonegrave that he should take it from her. 'Does this change the narrative?' She watched him stare at the image, the fog slowly clearing. Stonegrave manipulated the image, rotated it around, weighing up what it meant. One last look and he passed the handset back without saying a word.

'Do you want to know where I got it from?'

'Where?'

She stepped closer to him. 'An abandoned farmhouse near Driffield.' She looked for a sign that the location had hit home, getting nothing back. 'He's been dossing down there.' She outlined what had happened in the farmhouse, how she'd been sent there, but then attacked. She watched him rub his face as he struggled with what he wanted to say. Instead, she changed the subject, wanting to keep him on the back foot. 'Talk to me about Helen Pullman.' Stonegrave looked puzzled. 'The detective from South Yorkshire who investigated Shaw's murder.' He looked away, which confirmed things. 'You treated her like shit.'

'I didn't have many dealings with her.'

'You didn't speak up, either?'

'It was never that simple.'

'Explain how hard it was for you, then?'

'What do you expect me to say?' He shrugged. 'Orders came down from above and we were told to keep our mouths shut.'

'You were cowards?' The suggestion got no response. 'Did you ever stop to think about the wider impact on people? Mikey Birch's girlfriend is still carrying the trauma of it, and she's got Conrad Knott leaning on her like he's leaning on me. He's threatened to make sure charity's funding is pulled. What kind of person does that?'

'Are you prepared to turn lives upside down again?'

Stonegrave was really asking her if she was a coward too, and she didn't like it. Hard truths had to be faced up to by everyone. 'You're in danger of being thrown under the bus.' Yaz took her mobile back and pulled up another image. She held it out towards him and watched as he looked at the image of himself in the pub with Jake Shaw and Conrad Knott again. He inhaled air and blew it back out again. 'There's only you left to tell the truth now.' She pocketed the phone, sure the message had gotten through and landed.

'What do you want from me?'

'Tell me about Nell Heard. She's in the same village as the farmhouse.' He didn't meet her eye, but definitely knew the name. The look on his face told her she'd scored a hit, despite the way he quickly pulled himself back together.

'Decisions always have a price tag for everyone,' he eventually said.

'What does that mean?'

'Nell Heard was a raver back then too.'

Yaz took it in. 'She was there the night Jake Shaw was murdered?' Of course she was. It was why Stonegrave had mentioned it. Eyes back on him, he was deflating in front of her. She pulled up the other photograph she had on her mobile. 'Mikey Birch disappeared into a network of New Age Travellers.' Stonegrave didn't want to look at the image. 'Nell Heard helped him to disappear.' It had to be what happened. He wouldn't look, so she described it for him. The image showed Birch laughing as he swung a toddler around in his arms in the background of the photograph. The clincher, though, was the hand. She could see where the missing finger should be. It made sense. There was a network he could melt away into, hide in plain sight. Yaz put the phone away.

Stonegrave coughed, bent over slightly, taking his time before speaking again. 'The question is, Yaz, can I trust you?'

She looked at him. 'I'm the only one who wants to get involved.' There was one card still left to play. 'You haven't stayed in touch with Shaw's daughter?' The question caught Stonegrave off balance. Telling him what Conrad Knott had done in an attempt to silence the woman hit home.

'Jake was a good man.' Stonegrave glanced around before lowering his voice, eyes hardening. 'The truth needs to come out, whatever it costs.'

'I know I'm going to unleash a storm.' If she'd learned one thing, it was that sometimes you had to follow through, whatever the reservations. Things were never black or white, always shades of grey. 'We're all collateral damage to a man like Conrad Knott,' she said. She'd done what she could. 'It's time you picked a side.' She watched him pace in a small circle, both ignoring the cold wind seeping in, the rain starting to fall.

'I told Knott I was out.'

There it was. He'd said the words and committed.
'What did he say?'

'He said I'd regret it.' He told her about the implied job offer via financing the Cold Case unit. 'It comes with strings attached. Money solves any problem in his world.'

'You're doing the right thing.'

'Better late than never.'

'Did you ever speak to Kerri Lewis about what happened?'

Stonegrave shook his head. 'She tried to make contact with me, but I was never going to talk to her. The timing was never right.'

'You spoke to her recently, right?'

Stonegrave took a moment before a slight nod. 'Fair to say she wasn't receptive.'

It was hard not to judge the man. Things were eating away at him and he couldn't disguise it. The discomfort from the memories being dredged up was written all over his face.

'You want the world.'

The words took her by surprise. 'I need this story or I'll be stuck here forever.' It wasn't the full story. 'I want the truth.'

'I'm being used,' Stonegrave said to her quietly, 'and I don't like it.'

'It's the way of the world.'

He nodded his agreement. 'I didn't have you down as a cynic.'

'I'm learning all the time.'

'Try not to fall into the trap.'

'My mum was a cleaner and Conrad Knott took advantage of her.' She made sure he was listening. 'He took advantage because of his position and because she didn't have a voice. No one believed what he did to her.'

'You want to talk about it?'

'It's so fucking hard to talk about. The man's toxic,' she said. 'My mum had fuck all, but he held what she did have over her as a threat to keep her in line. If she spoke out to anyone, we'd have lost our flat. He controlled her life, even though he didn't want any part of it.' She turned back to face him. 'I bet your relationship to him wasn't all that different?'

Stonegrave leaned against the railings, not meeting her eye. 'I'm dying.'

Moy laughed before freezing. It was a reaction to news she didn't have the first clue how to deal with. She apologised. 'I didn't mean to laugh.'

'You'd think it gets easier saying that, but believe me, it doesn't.' Stonegrave kicked out again at a stone underfoot as he explained how his consultant had broken the news with little sugar coating. 'I've dealt with enough death in my field of work. It just becomes another bump in the road. It focuses the mind, believe me. I want my daughter to be proud of me and she can't be that if I'm complicit with someone like Conrad Knott.'

'That's heavy.'

'She deserves better than me.'

'It's not too late.'

Stonegrave looked away for a moment before meeting her eye again. 'You want revenge? Is that it? Is that what you're about?'

She shook her head. 'I want the truth, but what you really want to know is if you can trust me with your life?'

It was the question he really needed an answer to.

Stonegrave smiled. 'My life's not very valuable these days.' He had another question for her. 'So who sent you the photograph of Mikey Birch at the farmhouse?'

'It was sent anonymously.' She shrugged like she didn't care if he believed her or not. 'That's the truth.'

'Everyone wanted Birch to be dead back then. It was a useful full stop.'

'No one kicked back?'

'Case was closed, end of story.'

'Until now.'

'I found Jake dying,' he said quietly. 'I held him as everyone else ran away.'

Yaz processed what he was saying, knowing he'd suppressed events from that night, ignoring the damage it had done to him over the decades. He wanted her to understand. 'It must have been unbearable.'

'He was my friend.'

'You need to start acting like one, then.'

'You don't pull any punches, do you?'

'We're past bullshitting each other.'

'Ever had anyone die in your arms?'

'My mother.'

'It's not something you're prepared for when you're young.' He corrected himself. 'It doesn't matter how old you are. Jake's death was a painful death.'

'It must have been a comfort that you were there?'

'You think?' He shook his head. 'You said we were past bullshitting each other?'

Yaz nodded. 'We are.' She searched his face. There was something there, something he wanted to say. 'Did you look at Dale Harker for Jake Shaw's murder?' She laid it out for him. 'He was about the money, right? He was the one with something to lose, certainly more than Mikey.'

'I've got something for you.'
'What?'
'I want something in return.'
'Name it.'
'I need you to promise that you won't accept the easy answers and give up on this.'

FORTY-THREE

Knott collected up the bottle of whisky and headed towards the door. Stonegrave followed. The sound of vacuuming and empty bottles being tidied drifted up the stairs, the team working quickly to lock the bar down for the night. Catching Knott up, they walked in silence to the edge of the rooftop terrace. Stonegrave leaned over the edge, looking at the city stretching out. Other than Kelly, the place wouldn't miss him when he was gone. It would still throb and hum, his own existence meaning nothing. Nothing he'd done would count for anything. Straightening up, he was on Knott's territory, but it was the way it had to be.

'Do you want a drink?' Conrad Knott waved the bottle of whisky at him. 'What harm is it going to do you now?'

Stonegrave swallowed back the urge to say something, instead taking the bottle and swallowing the fiery liquid back. It tasted good. He slammed the bottle down and coughed, eyes watering. Letting his chest resettle, he wiped his face down, ignoring Knott's smile. He'd festered in the pub, not able to settle, or want to go downstairs and talk to Kelly. There were things she didn't need to know about her father. Leaning against the wall, he battled to control his breathing. Looking out, he could see the outline of the giant Tidal Barrier, a structure designed to stop the city from another devastating flood. He'd always thought his job was to do the same. His job was to hold the bad stuff back, act for the right side of things and for the right reasons. Now he wasn't so sure about that. He felt the cold of the night starting to crush his insides. It had to be the truth. 'You had a meeting here with Dale Harker.' Knott didn't respond. 'I was at the door.'

'That sounds like bad manners to me. You should have joined us if you were that interested.'

'He made his money from drugs. He might be a big man now, but he's scum.'

'That sounds like a wild accusation to make.'

'Did you take money from him back then?'

'That's definitely a wild accusation and you should think very carefully about what you're saying.'

'You used me.'

Knott laughed. 'You'll have to explain that to me.' He nudged the whisky closer to Stonegrave, encouraging him to have another mouthful. 'I've done nothing but look after you.'

It was a lie. He'd thought about it, played it through in his mind. 'You groomed me from the start.' He could see how it had happened now. Knott had bent others to his will. Initially it had been cards and bonding over pints of lager sunk during pub lock-ins. Knott had picked off the weaker ones, those who chose to go home to wives and families. He'd created a gang for himself, those willing to walk on the wild side. It made Stonegrave burn with shame to realise he'd fallen for it, even if it hadn't taken long for it to sour. It was all so obvious with hindsight.

Knott fixed his stare on him. 'You were looked after.'

'By bullying and controlling? You're toxic.'

'Everyone made their own choices.'

'Including Jake?'

'He was corrupt.'

Stonegrave grabbed the whisky and drank another mouthful, the burn as it slipped down turning his guts inside out. It was what he deserved, his head starting to swim from the alcohol and bad memories.

'You play with fire, you get burned,' Knott said. 'He wasn't the first and he won't be the last.'

'Is this some kind of joke to you?'

'Far from it.'

He watched Knott pace around the empty VIP area they were standing in, knowing he was looking at a man with everything to lose. The power was in his hands.

Knott came to a stop. 'Talk to me about Yaz Moy.'

'What about her?'

'You're working with her?'

Of course Knott knew. He always did. 'She doesn't need my help to put the story together.' He left it at that and picked up the bottle, drew back a mouthful of whisky and smiled after swallowing it down. It wasn't just Moy's couldn't give a fuck attitude, it was her edge. It was how she drew her power. She had all the bravado and expectation of youth, like life hadn't really touched her yet, but she had a way of looking at a situation and seeing the truth. 'You're scared,' he said pointing to Knott, a statement that seemed so obvious, yet one that had taken so long to see. 'You're scared of her.'

'I'm not scared of anything.'

'The truth is long overdue.' He wasn't paying attention as Knott stepped forward quickly, a punch to his stomach. He doubled over, pain spreading through his body. Falling to the ground and looking up at the sky, he struggled to breathe.

'I'll ask again, but this time less politely,' Knott said, towering over him. 'What have you told the daft bitch?'

'You're a coward.' He managed to get out as a response, the words an effort, as he shuffled to prop himself up against the brick wall. Knott lashed out again, a kick to his chest. Stonegrave threw his head back, staring at the night sky, a painful laugh. 'Beat me all you like, it's not going to change what's done.' He was struggling to get his words out and sit back up right. They stared at each other, two old men fighting. He put his hand out for the whisky bottle, Knott throwing it to him, watching as he spluttered through another mouthful.

Knott bent down, taking the drink back. 'You think you're morally superior to me? Is that it?'

'I know what I did and what I didn't do.' Stonegrave used the wall to slowly pull himself back to his feet, mirroring Knott, before asking the question that needed an answer. The only question that counted. 'Tell me what happened that night at the rave.'

Knott made a show of looking pained. 'You know exactly what happened. Mikey Birch murdered Jake Shaw. Birch knew the net was closing in on him and he lost control.' He threw back a mouthful of whisky. 'Shaw only had himself to blame. We all knew the risks we were taking on, right? You go undercover, you run the risks. It's the way it is. It's why you do the work for a short period and get out before it fucks you up. Come on, you're not that stupid? We saw the signs and got out in time. Shaw took another road.'

'I know Mikey Birch is alive.' He looked at Knott's face, wanting to see surprise and shock. There was nothing. 'I've seen the photograph,' he repeated. 'You've played me like I'm an idiot.'

'What does the photograph really show?'

'It shows Mikey Birch, still alive and out there.'

'And you've spoken to him yourself?' Knott held a hand up to stop an answer. 'Of course you haven't. It could be anyone in that photograph, and that's assuming it's genuine. Moy knows all about computers and technology, we have no idea about where that photograph came from. We know ourselves that Birch is dead, so it's fake news. If she tries to put it out in the public domain, she'll find herself in a legal minefield that's well beyond her comprehension.'

Stonegrave smiled. The suggestion of fake news. It was an easy catch-all phrase, a way of trying to deflect when confronted with news you didn't like the sound of. It was bullshit from top to bottom. 'I've seen another photograph of Birch. He disappeared into a network of New Age Travellers. He wasn't murdered.'

Knott took his time responding, staring at his own fist as he flexed it. 'I suggest you tread very carefully here.'

Stonegrave stepped forward, unsteady on his feet from the alcohol and the beating. 'It's time for the truth to come out. Things need making right.'

'That kind of thing comes with a price attached.' Knott shrugged, like it was nothing. 'Are you sure it's really one that's worth paying?'

'I've always known what happened that night and I should have spoken up.'

'You know nothing, and you'd do well to keep it that way.'

'Kerri Lewis knew.'

'A grown woman of her age still shouting and crying about the police and protesting? I'd say it's about time she grew up, but that ship has probably sailed.' Knott threw another mouthful of whisky back.

Stonegrave knew he'd never recovered from the trauma of that night at the rave, professionally or personally. He'd buried it in the hope it would stay locked away, but it was important that what happened next was done on his terms. Leaning against the wall, Stonegrave coughed hard, eyes watering. Taking out a tissue, he spat out mucus into it. Knott watched him, a smile on his face, enjoying his discomfort. 'I haven't got much time left, but I can still put things right.'

'Don't be so melodramatic.'

'I got my test results back.'

'What's the verdict?'

'It's not good news.' Dragging himself back into the moment. His affairs needed putting in order, but he would be the one who'd decide when it would all happen. He replayed the meeting with the consultant in the bland room in the hospital, thought again about his choice of words and the implications. 'I've got a few months, if I'm lucky. I certainly won't see another Christmas.' It surprised him how dispassionate he could be as he laid it out, like it was someone else's life and diagnosis they were talking about.

Hearing the door to the rooftop bar open, he turned and watched Dale Harker walk over and join them. Behind Harker, two men. Both were muscular and dressed in black.

Knott told Harker they were nearly done. 'I'm talking to him.' The inference was that they should leave him to it. Stonegrave watched them retreat.

'He's not happy with you,' Knott said, once they were alone again.

'You think you can threaten me?' There was still one card still left to play. 'Didn't you ever wonder what happened to Jake's notepad, with all his notes and records of the operation?'

'What does it matter now?'

'I've got it,' he said with a crooked smile.

'I picked it up in Birch's flat after seeing you put it there.' It was supposed to be evidence of Birch's guilt waiting to be found. He couldn't explain why he hadn't done something with it, but it was another lie he told himself. He knew exactly why he hadn't done anything with it. He'd been too scared to. The narrative had been locked in early. Silence had suited them both.

'Where's the notepad now?' Knott asked.

The words were out before he could stop them. 'It's somewhere safe.'

FORTY-FOUR

The takeaway door was locked for the night, but lights were still on in the back. Yaz knocked again, seeing Zach tidying away in the kitchen area. There was every chance he had ear buds in, listening to music as he worked. It meant he wouldn't hear his mobile, either. She slumped to the floor, her back against the door and sent a text message knowing he'd see it eventually.

She was tired, her head spinning with what was happening around her. Stonegrave had clammed up after say he had something for her and hurried away. Her first instinct had been to follow him, but she'd watched the night swallow him up. Patience would be the key. He would have to make a move and she would be ready. Sometimes you could push too hard, not least when he'd told her he'd been given a death sentence. How did you deal with that level of heaviness? She'd brushed up closely to death via her mother, but it felt different viewing it from a more detached perspective.

The door behind unlocked and opened, meaning she fell backwards into the takeaway. Straightening herself back up, she looked at Zach. He didn't speak. She followed him inside and locked the door behind them. He went back to scraping the grill that had been turned off.

'I need to talk to someone,' she said. 'A second opinion.' Pulling up the image of Mikey Birch as a New

Age Traveller, what still didn't make immediate sense was Heard had displayed it so publicly. Maybe she wanted to make a point, maybe it made her feel like she was getting one over on the authorities. It didn't really matter. She understood the implications all too well.

Zach put the cloth in his hand down. 'What's up?'

Slowly and deliberately, she laid out her theory to Zach, ignoring the incredulous look on his face. Saying it aloud was a means of making sense of what she was thinking. She explained what the photograph meant.

'Sounds like you're making assumptions.'

'Theories, not assumptions.'

'There's a difference?'

'Of course there is.'

'You'll have to explain that one to me.'

She hadn't told him about the job offers on the table, not wanting to get into the necessity of moving away. It was maybe cowardly, when things were meant to be casual and uncomplicated between them, but it was a conversation for another day.

Zach held his hands up, told her to slow down. 'You need to think this through, Yaz.'

'What is there to think through?'

'You'd really do it?'

'Tell the story?' She was puzzled. 'Why wouldn't I?'

'You'd ruin lives for a story?'

'I'd be telling the truth.' The theoretical was smashing headfirst into reality, and she had a choice to make. 'We can't all have our fathers bankroll us.' The words were out before she could stop them. She knew all too well how it had hurt him to allow his father to guarantee the lease on the takeaway. It had been the only way to get the unit, kept him in the man's debt, despite his disapproval. The success of the place wasn't enough to bring them back together.

'You really mean that, Yaz?' He turned to look at her. 'You're well cold.'

Standing up and pacing the room, maybe sharing with him had been a mistake. Maybe they were just too different. He pushed through the door and stomped up the stairs to his flat without looking back. Sitting back down on the stool at the counter, the refrigerator behind it hummed quietly but relentlessly, the takeaway in darkness. Her mobile lit up, an incoming call from DC Oberman.

'Have you seen the news?'

'What news?'

'Have a look online.'

Yaz did as she was told and turned to social media. The story was already being covered by the local media, a short video clip embedded within the tweet she was reading. Watching it, blue flashing lights lit up the waterfront, illuminating the walls covered in graffiti. The area was essentially abandoned, no need for anyone to be there. The voiceover described the scene; a large emergency services presence and she could see a uniformed officer standing guard. Officials buzzed around the scene, a uniformed officer keeping the small crowd of curious onlookers at a safe distance. A witness said a man was seen being pulled from the water.

'What's going?' she asked the detective.

'I was hoping you could enlighten me.'

'Why would I able to do that?' She was trying put things together as well as focus on what the detective was asking from her. 'What's going on?' she repeated, this time more forcefully.

'Talk to me about the new bar you've been frequenting, Yaz?'

'What?'

'The one you went to with Kerri Lewis.'

'You obviously know plenty.'

Oberman spoke to someone else for a moment before coming back on the line. 'Now's the time to tell me, Yaz. I've let you take some liberties, but it ends now.'

If it was a game of poker, Yaz knew she was holding a low-scoring pair against someone with royal flush. But she wasn't going to back down, weighing up what she should give to the detective.

'I know the bar owner,' she offered, wanting to see if it would provoke a reaction.

'Of course you do. He's Conrad Knott's son.' Oberman was getting pissed off. 'Do you know him personally?'

Yaz hesitated. 'Not really.'

'Let's cut the shit, shall we? Why did you interview him by pretending you're from the local paper?'

'You and Stonegrave have been busy.'

'Not as busy as you.'

Yaz weighed it up, deciding to just hit Oberman with the truth. 'We share a father.'

The detective paused, chewing the words over. 'You'll have to explain that one to me.'

'We don't have a relationship.'

'Fucking hell.'

'Does that change things?' She was trying to read between the lines, trying to work out if she was supposed to be making a connection to what had happened. Her brain was working overtime in different directions.

'When did you last speak to him?'

'Why?'

'It's important.'

'It's also none of your business.'

'I'm trying to piece together his movements tonight.'

'Why?'

'Hold on.' Oberman said she had another call to take, the line temporarily going dead.

If her father, estranged or not, was the victim, she wasn't sure how she'd feel about it. She wanted to be cool about it, knowing he didn't care for her, but it was complicated. Sliding off the stool and standing up, she was starting to lose control. Yaz paced the takeaway. Her feelings made no sense. She cared nothing for her father, but it was complicated.

Oberman came back on the line. 'You need to tell me what's going on. I've answered your questions. You need to answer mine,' Yaz said.

'I've just had word he's died.'

Yaz felt her mouth go dry, finding herself leaning against the takeaway counter, no idea what she was feeling.

'The early suggestion is that Stonegrave had been drinking in the bar and fell into the water.' Oberman's voice trailed off.

Yaz focused. 'Stonegrave?' She asked Oberman to repeat what she'd just said. They weren't talking about her father. She couldn't hold it back. Everything was falling to pieces. She turned away and vomited on the floor.

FORTY-FIVE

Yaz ran up to the door, hammered repeatedly on the buzzer. 'Bastard,' she shouted up at Conrad Knott's apartment, the lights still on. There was no way Stonegrave had simply fallen into the water after drinking in the bar. She wasn't having it. It was the same as the message Mikey Birch had passed on via Carolyn Seymour's voicemail. His confession didn't add up, or feel right. There was a reason Birch and others wanted her to stop digging any deeper, but it wasn't going to work.

A group of teenagers appeared, laughing and pointing at her. She told them to fuck off, staring them down until they shuffled away into the night. Turning back to the buzzer and hitting it again, this time she kicked out at the door. If it set an alarm off, all the better. 'Let me in,' she shouted, holding the buzzer down. Stepping back again, she heard the soft hiss of the door releasing its locks.

Pushing her way through, Yaz headed straight into the lift and up to the top. Stepping out and still raging, Conrad Knott was waiting for her at the door with a drink in his hand, a smirk on his face. She launched herself at him, sending the glass to the floor, shattering in pieces at their feet. Knott grabbed her by the wrists, pinned her up against his doorframe, his smile gone.

'I suggest you calm yourself down.'

Yaz struggled, kicking out, but she was overpowered. Instead she settled for hissing in his face. 'What did you do to Stonegrave?'

'I suggest you think very carefully about what you're about to say.' He let her go, taking a step backwards away from her. 'We've all had a shock tonight.'

'Nothing more to say?' She wasn't in the mood to be ignored. Knott turned his back on her, and ignoring the comment, walked into his apartment. He poured them both drinks, tempting her with a glass. She took it from him and threw it back, wiped her mouth with the back of her hand.

'I thought you didn't drink?' he said.

The brandy tasted foul at the back of her throat, but it did the job, instantly making her feel calmer and in control. If it was what her father wanted, he was mistaken. Feeling calmer didn't lessen her anger.

'Stonegrave called me, said he wanted to speak to me urgently. I can't say I particularly wanted to talk to him, but he was insistent and distressed.' He shrugged. 'I told him to come to the bar.'

'Is that so?'

'He got some things off his chest and then he left.' Knott shrugged. 'Accidents happen.'

'You don't sound too upset by that?'

'Maybe the shock will hit me later?'

'Maybe it will.' Yaz glanced around his apartment, everything in its place – the high-end electrical goods, the minimalist furnishings. The framed photographs of her brother. The man with everything.

When Knott spoke, it was quiet but firm. 'I didn't do anything, Yaz. He came at me, drunk and making wild accusations. Then he left. That's it.'

'Bullshit.' She didn't recognise Stonegrave from that behaviour. The opposite, in fact. He was lost, someone trying to find answers in his own way. It meant he was another name on the list she was now acting on behalf of.

Knott folded his arms and perched on the edge of the nearest chair. 'You weren't there, were you? You have no idea what happened.'

'Enlighten me.'

'I'll tell you what's going to happen, shall I? Stories have a natural cycle, and these days, you don't even become tomorrow's chip paper unless you're really unlucky. You can throw as much shit as you like at the wall, but it isn't going to stick. The narrative is the narrative – Jake Shaw was a rogue bad apple and it doesn't matter who killed him. Stonegrave is dead, no one cares. It's ancient history.'

'Finished?' Yaz walked over to the framed photographs arranged on a shelf underneath the flatscreen television. The one of Knott with her brother on a golf course caught her eye. It had been taken somewhere abroad, maybe Spain or Portugal. Both looked tanned with big smiles on their faces. She knew Knott was watching her. Turning back to face him, she went back to the reason she was there. 'Stonegrave told me what happened that night at the rave and afterwards.' It was an exaggeration, but she wanted to see his reaction. 'Jake Shaw died in his arms. And I know what you did to his daughter.'

He considered the words, taking his time before answering. 'An official re-investigation is the only way she'll get closure, even if she doesn't like the fact it'll come to the same conclusion.'

'You know it won't happen, certainly not if she's drinking again? Who'll listen to an addict making demands? You're a piece of shit.'

Knott smiled and took out a packet of cigarettes, lit one up before tossing them across the room to her. 'You like a smoke, right? I should stop, really.'

'Not good for the public image?' Yaz fumbled around for a lighter and mirrored Knott, taking a long drag on her cigarette. 'I don't usually bother with the legal stuff,' she said. 'You wanted to know how I make ends meet? I sell small amounts of cannabis to friends and people I know. I'm not ashamed of that.'

'You expect me to be shocked? You think I haven't done things that I regret?'

'I know that's the case.' She wanted him to feel uncomfortable at the direction things were heading. 'You'd be surprised at what I've been learning.'

'You want to be careful. It could get you into serious trouble.'

'Is that a threat?'

Knott gave a small shrug. 'What are you going to do about it?' He cut her off from talking, pointing a finger in her direction. 'I'll tell you what you're going to do about it, you're going to do fuck all, and I'll tell you why, shall I? It's because it's not in your best interests to make a noise about the situation. Who knows where it might lead? It would be like opening a Pandora's box. You'll only make a bad situation worse.'

'Is that so?'

'I know you. I know what makes you tick, and more importantly, I know what you are. You're a woke warrior, Yaz, and who likes that these days? It puts people's backs up straightaway.'

'You think I care about that?'

'You care too much and that's your problem.' Knott smiled and shook his head. 'I wouldn't place too much stock in what Stonegrave has told you.'

She watched him take another deep drag on the cigarette, reading him like a book. Stonegrave had spoken to him, maybe even threatened him with what he knew. Taking a last drag on the cigarette, not wanting it, she snuffed it out in an empty mug, daring him to say something.

Knott remained passive. 'I'm afraid when you try to stand any of his claims up, they'll fall apart all too easily.'

'Sure about that?'

'Very much so.'

'What makes you think people want to listen to your fantasies about a corrupt detective?' He walked into the kitchen and put the remains of his cigarette out in an ashtray. 'I just don't see it. It's old-fashioned news. People don't want those stories anymore.'

'People want to hear the truth. They don't forget about stories like this.' She told him about the photograph she had of Birch embedded within a group of New Age Travellers. 'He didn't die all those years ago.'

Knott walked past her without saying a word, heading out onto the apartment's balcony.

Yaz followed him, angry. 'Did you hear what I said?' He quickly reached over her and closed the balcony doors behind them. It was just them, outside of the apartment, the occasional headlights of vehicles down on the city centre loop.

'We need to straighten some things out, don't we?' He shuffled around, his back against the railings. 'I've played nicely so far, even offering you the work opportunity you seem determined to throw back in my face, but you're running out of road fast.'

She didn't see him move. His hands reached out and grabbed her by the shoulders. Dragging her to the edge of the balcony, he roughly shoved her up against it, kicking her legs apart so she couldn't move. She tried to resist, buck back at him, getting nowhere. Staring down, she was unable to see the pavement in the dark. 'Fuck you,' she hissed. She breathed hard. 'Fuck you.' He pushed her harder against the edge. Fear ran through her, but she couldn't stop probing. 'Is this how it ended for Stonegrave? Your face was the last thing he saw?'

'Watch your mouth.'

'Maybe I'm the story?' she said. 'Maybe my story is the one I should be telling. How the unsolved murder of an undercover detective thirty-five years ago led to my door and a father who didn't want to know me because it'd harm his political career?'

Knott pushed her further towards the edge. 'You think that's a story? I'll spin it so fast, you won't know which way you're facing. If asked, I'll say you were the product of a one-night stand, something I deeply regret as I wasn't able to support you or your mother when you needed it. That's the story the media will report. I'll be a man who has learned a tough lesson in life but is determined to do better, be better. If anything, I'll come out with sympathy.'

What really grated was that he wasn't wrong. There was no doubt her father could engineer whatever outcome he wanted.

'Your problem is you see the world in black and white, Yaz, not all the shades of grey adults know it is. It's childlike in its naivety.'

The words were designed to deflate her, but they charged through her, giving her more power and more determination to bring him down. She screamed out, bucked her legs again and aimed a kick, but he saw it coming and spread his weight behind her to cancel it out. 'I've got the photographs of Mikey Birch,' she said, continuing to buck in an attempt to free herself of his grip.

'Maybe you came here and got emotional?' Knott suggested, ignoring what she'd said. 'Maybe a leak of your medical records after your death will show you were unstable? Who knows what made you jump out of this window?' he hissed into her ear.

'Fuck you.'

'We're finishing this right now, Yaz. You were given your chance. You were told to leave things alone, not play with fire. You weren't clever enough to make sure you didn't get burned. Your story's dead. It's over for you.' He leaned in, his hand on the back of her head, shifting his weight ready to lift her up and over the balcony wall. 'I want Shaw's notepad back.' His hands went to her pockets. 'You own this mess, Yaz. You whipped Stonegrave up and brought back all the bad memories. His death should be on your conscience.'

She kept moving, finding a bit of purchase as her feet planted down, managing to get her back arched out. It was a small window of opportunity, and she brought her foot up and hammered it into his shin. Knowing she'd hurt him, his grip weakened slightly, and she drove home her advantage. Steadying herself with one leg, she aimed a blow into his knee. As he screamed and let go, she quickly turned and drove a shot into his balls. Knott slowly folded, falling to the floor in front of her. Helping him on his way, she kicked him as hard as she could in the stomach. Scrambling over his prone body and opening the door, she tripped, quickly picking herself up as she fell back into the apartment. Without looking back, she ran for the exit and the stairs.

FORTY-SIX

Hurrying across the city centre, the imposing municipal halls and landmarks outlined by LED lights guided the way. The city had had never felt smaller or more claustrophobic, all the worse for its dark corners and hidden secrets. Yaz closed in on the pub, slowing as she looked at the single light on in the bar. It was past closing time, but peering through the window, she could see a small group huddled around a table in the corner.

Yaz drew a breath in and tried to slow down, think. The thought of going over her father's balcony, her death written off as a suicide and put down to her unstable personality, chilled her to the bone. Outside of his apartment, she'd continued to run without stopping, not looking back. She'd gone from thinking the podcast was dead, no story to tell, to seeing the truth and understanding the price she'd have to pay in telling it. Stonegrave was dead and she was next in the firing line. There was no way she was buying the suggestion his death was a tragic accident.

It needed more. If she pushed the podcast out, Conrad Knott would have to admit to being her father, but so what? He was right; no one would care. There was no traction there. She could see how it would play out. In his alternative universe, he'd say she had aggressively confronted him inside his apartment and needed help, nothing more than an attempt to serve revenge up on him. He'd be the victim, she'd be a footnote as he moved onwards and upwards. But there was still a card to play. Knott had let something slip as they'd fought. He thought she had Jake Shaw's notepad. Stonegrave had something tangible to share. Something that would move the dial. He'd said as much to her. The fact she was in danger was all the proof she needed.

The pub door was locked. Knocking loudly on it, it eventually opened. Heading inside, Kelly was sitting with a man she didn't recognise. Kelly's eyes were red from crying, a pile of scrunched up tissues on the table in front of her. Taking a breath, she made her way over, stopping just short of the table. 'I'm sorry to hear about your dad.' There was nothing more to say, nothing that made any sense.

'How do people like you live with yourself?'

Yaz held her ground. 'People like me?'

'My dad was getting his life back together until you appeared with your podcast.'

It wasn't true, but she had to be the punch bag and let Kelly get the bile out.

'Things were getting better for him until you came along. He had a job offer and something to look forward to at last.'

'A job offer from Conrad Knott?' Yaz couldn't keep the incredulity out of her voice. She glanced around the pub, the smell of the night's lager in her nose, before focusing back on Kelly. 'You know it wasn't really a job offer. It was a bribe for his silence.'

'It doesn't matter now.' Kelly stood up and walked behind the bar. Pouring herself a neat vodka, she swallowed it straight back, continuing to stare unflinchingly.

'Your dad wanted the truth to come out. Jake Shaw was murdered and it still meant something to him.' The man at the table also stared silently at her.

'You think you can leech all this for your podcast?' Kelly looked appalled. 'Forgive me for not giving a shit.'

'I don't blame you for feeling that way, but this is something bigger than just me now.'

'Spare me the sanctimonious bullshit you're justifying your actions with.' Kelly poured herself another drink. 'You and your sort would do anything for a story, wouldn't you? You don't care who you hurt, or whose life you ruin.'

'That's not true.'

'You keep telling yourself that.' The drink was thrown back, the glass slammed down on the bar. 'I've got the real media trying to talk to me and the police.' Kelly turned away. 'I just want to be left alone.'

Yaz stayed rooted to the spot, trying to not let her anger show at the suggestion of *real media*. Kelly walked back towards the man at the table. He stood up and put his arm around her, guided her through the door in the corner which led to the place's smaller bar. Standing alone, she looked at the stairs leading up to the living space. Knott would be knocking on the same door soon enough. She didn't hesitate.

Into the main living space, she spotted a sleeping bag bunched up in the corner of the sofa. The room was functionally decorated, little more than a place to crash down and watch television in. It didn't take long to find Stonegrave's rucksack. Sitting down with it on her lap, it wasn't much to show for a life. Fumbling around for the zip, she opened it up, quickly deciding it would make more sense to empty out the contents for easier sifting through. Most of the items were clothing, a few personal momentos. She pulled out a number of letters, flicked through them. They were from debt agencies, chasing money with increasing threats about court action.

Rummaging around at the bottom of the bag, she pulled out an old-style dictaphone. Toying with it, it was something analogue in a digital world, something out of place. Being careful, she figured out how to access what was on it. Hitting play, Stonegrave's voice slowly started to talk, confirming the date and what he was about to say was freely given to whoever wanted to use it. Pressing stop, Yaz stuffed both items into her pocket.

A notepad on the floor caught her eye. The cover had faded, curled up around the corners. It looked well used. Yaz picked it up, instinctively knowing what it was. Flicking through, she was looking at Jake Shaw's missing notepad. Scanning the details, she could see dates noted along with explanations of what he'd observed during the raves, as well as references to various names she recognised. Steadying herself, she paced the room before reading again what Jake Shaw had written. She knew exactly what it meant and what it told her. The ground underneath her had shifted again.

Heading back outside, she rounded the corner and leaned against the pub's wall. She made two phone calls, laying out what was going to happen next, not allowing either of them to talk. She was calling the shots now. Pulling up the image of Mikey Birch taken via the spy camera at the farmhouse, she uploaded it to her website and typed out a brief explanation. Setting the post to live would change everything and spread like wildfire. Hitting the publish button, it appeared on her website before automatically feeding through to her social media accounts. There was no turning back now.

PODCAST EXTRACT – EPISODE FIVE

NOT YET UPLOADED

In this fifth podcast in the new 'CrimeTime' series, the focus is much personal ... what I haven't said so far is that Conrad Knott is my estranged father ... I wasn't expecting this story to lead to his door when I first started investigating it ... what I need to say is that he's never acknowledged me in his life ... my mother was denied confirmation and financial support when it was needed ... although he's my father, it's nothing more than a biological fact ... more than that, he has tried to buy my silence, dangling the promise of a job opening with a prestigious media outlet ... the price? This podcast had to be deleted, the story of Jake Shaw's murder left untold ... but the conclusion I've arrived at is that this podcast is not to be bought in exchange for compliant silence ...

I've thought long and hard about what I should do ... as I've said before, I don't have all the answers ... I put my faith in the story being told by Stonegrave, the detective working undercover with Knott and Shaw, and have worked tirelessly to obtain new evidence that supports this ... I've spent time with his story and asked him questions and probed what he's told me ... I've spoken to other parties in an attempt to verify things, attempting to separate truth from lies ... I've listened and observed ... Stonegrave was a man crippled with guilt at how his life and career had played out, someone looking to rebuild lost relationships with his daughter ... he handed me a recording that has become his last testament following his recent death... but more than that, I believed him when he told me his story ...

My website and social media channels feature a photograph I want you all to see ... it concerns the missing link in the entire story, the glue that binds it together ... I debated with myself when to share such a specific piece of information with a wider audience, as once it's revealed, it's in the public domain and can spiral out of my control ... I received an anonymous email, sending me to an abandoned farmhouse in rural East Yorkshire ... setting up spy cameras, I captured the image of Mikey Birch, the suspected murderer of Jake Show ... he's very much alive and didn't die that night at the rave ...

Circumstances forced my hand ... what I couldn't foresee were the consequences of doing so, both for me personally and in respect of the story the podcast is telling ...

FORTY-SEVEN

Setting Stonegrave's dictaphone to play and letting his words fill the car, Yaz drove directly to the farmhouse. Gripping the wheel more tightly, this was the end game. Sifting information into piles in her head, she tried to slow her thinking down. Jake Shaw's notepad changed everything. The emotion in Stonegrave's voice told her it had been a difficult thing for him to do, but equally it was clear the recording was aimed at her. He wanted her to hear what he had to say. It started with the build-up to Jake Shaw's murder before moving on to what happened on the night and then the aftermath. It was the truth as he saw it. It was her job to prove it.

Parking up and killing the car's engine, Yaz stared out at the village hall before glancing up to the farmhouse at the top of the hill. It was where Mikey Birch had chosen to resurface at. Ignoring both places, she instead headed for Nell Heard's cottage, a light in the front room was on. Checking online, the story was trending on social media. Generic pieces on his murder were starting to resurface after being dusted down by media websites, all showing the image of Jake Shaw she recognised. The genie was out of the bottle, and she couldn't put it back in. Even though it was spiralling out of control and social media notifications were blowing up on her phone, it needed to be harnessed before it slipped through her fingers. It needed acting upon while people were listening to her.

The door to the cottage was opened before she had to knock. Heading inside, she followed the light through to where Nell Heard was waiting. Heard didn't acknowledge her presence, staying still in her chair. Yaz took the opportunity to look around. The room was cluttered with books and canvases, the overflow of the exhibition. A pile of photographs took up half of the space on the settee, other artefacts from Heard's travels around the world on every other available surface space.

Heard picked up her packet of cigarettes and lit one up, taking a long drag before speaking. 'What have you done, Yaz?'

It was a rhetorical question that didn't require answer.

'There's no going back now, is there?' Heard said taking another drag.

'No.'

'I sent Bella out to walk the dog.'

'At this time?'

'What choice did I have when I knew you were coming?'

'You've seen what I posted on social media?'

'We both have. You might think I'm a daft old hippie, but I like to keep up. It keeps me young.' Heard took a drag on her cigarette, picked up an empty mug to use as an ashtray. 'Like you, I wanted to change the world once upon time.'

'Let's not start with the meaningless platitudes.'

Heard shrugged the comment off, saying she was picking the battles she could win. 'Sounds like you're going to have to learn that lesson the hard way.'

'Don't patronise me.'

'I'll do as I please.'

'Stonegrave's dead.' She had Heard's attention. 'I've got his testimony. He left it for me to find.' Yaz paused, knowing they were getting close to discussing the reason they were talking to each other. 'I know.'

'You know nothing, you stupid girl.'

'Conrad Knott is my father.' Yaz watched, seeing her words hit home. 'It's the truth.'

Nell Heard couldn't meet her eye, but cut her off her from speaking further. 'Don't say it.'

'It's why I need the truth.'

Heard's eyes burned into her as she spoke. 'You're delighted with your little bit of exclusive news, aren't you?'

Ignoring the comment, Yaz turned back to Stonegrave's death, how its timing wasn't a coincidence. 'He didn't just fall into the water.'

'You're reaching again, Yaz.'

She shook her head, knowing she wasn't. 'I'm finishing things.'

'Leave me and Bella out of it.'

'It's too late for that.' She thought back to the image of New Age Travellers which showed Mikey Birch in the background. 'You invited this in.'

Heard shook her head and took a last drag on the cigarette before angrily stubbing it out in the mug. 'You'll have to explain your thinking on that one, as I didn't invite anything in.'

'It was a stupid decision to put that image in your exhibition.' Heard didn't respond. 'Why did you do it?'

'Because it's a strong image.'

Yaz laughed and shook her head. 'We're past playing games, surely?'

Heard accepted the point. 'You're like a dog with a bone.'

'What other way is there to be?'

'Sometimes you bite off more than you can chew. Ever thought about that?'

Yaz noted the frosty edge to the comment, but didn't care for it. 'You helped Mikey Birch disappear when he was staring at a murder charge?'

'You make it sound more than it was. It was hardly some kind of grand conspiracy we had going on.'

'That's it? That's all you've got to say?'

'What do you want from me?'

It was a good question. 'You were lovers back then.' She presented it as a statement, not a question, wanting to see the reaction it would bring.

Nell Heard batted it away with a poker face. 'Sounds like you're making assumptions about me?'

'You were lovers,' she repeated.

'I didn't have you down as a prude, Yaz.'

'I'm not, but you didn't tell me.'

'You didn't ask.' Heard sipped at her drink again. 'You're supposed to be a journalist. You didn't ask the right questions.'

Yaz decided to let her have that one. Maybe she was right, but you only knew what the right questions were with hindsight. 'Tell me about your relationship with Mikey,' she said, wanting to change the direction of the conversation. 'How close were you?'

'He had a girlfriend.'

'That doesn't answer my question.'

'I think it does.'

'I've spoken to her.' She thought about Carolyn Seymour, how she hadn't really known everything about Birch. 'Was Mikey worried about the police?'

Nell Heard smiled and shook her head. 'Mikey wasn't worried about anything. That wasn't his style.'

'He was under pressure. Drugs means money. It wasn't all hippy shit.'

'Hippy shit?' Heard rolled the words around. 'You're better than that, Yaz.'

'Am I?' She stepped forward. 'Jake Shaw was murdered, and Mikey was the only suspect the police looked at.' She followed Heard through to her kitchen and watched as she washed the mug out under the tap before speaking again. 'What was it, then? A favour for old time's sake?'

'Mikey was a free spirit. He was never still for very long. He knew a lot of different people.'

'That's still not much of an answer.'

'Mikey would always talk about just disappearing.' She took in a deep breath, composing herself. 'He was always going to do it at some point.'

'New Age Travellers were just too handy?'

'It was easy to disappear back then if you wanted to. Different times, maybe. All you had to do was shave your head or leave it longer, dye it, or whatever. Grow a beard if you wanted to. It's not hard to change your appearance quickly and there was no social media or cameras on phones. People didn't ask questions.'

It tied in with what she'd knew. It was a fluid scene, people coming and going. It would be easy to blend in and make a new life for yourself. At least for a while.

'I was there for a good time, like everyone else. The business side of things never interested me.'

'But Mikey just turns up in an abandoned farmhouse in the same village as you, thirty-five years down the line? I don't believe in coincidences.'

'That's a very cynical outlook.'

'Why did you display the image of Mikey as a New Age Traveller?'

'I didn't expect him to see it.'

It was as simple as that, a mistake. 'Shall we cut the shit?' Turning to the image, she pulled it up on her mobile and held it out to Nell Heard. 'What's he doing?' There was no answer. She asked again, more forcefully. 'What's he doing?'

'He's playing with a child.'

'I've done the maths.' There was nothing more to say, so she closed the image down. 'It's Bella.'

'You think you know everything, don't you?'

'I know you were at the rave.' Yaz looked at the woman. Stonegrave had told her. 'But what about the day after?' She watched Heard scratch at her shoulder, clearly uncomfortable with the conversation. 'Mikey was dead so far as the world knew.' Heard still needed prompting. 'What happened?'

'Fate happened.'

'You'll have to explain that for me.'

'We both knew people, New Age Travellers, crusties, whatever you want to call them. Mikey used old friends to disappear and we met up at various gatherings. It was as simple as that, but he wasn't Mikey anymore. If anyone knew who he was, they didn't care. Why would they? Who was going to care about the murder of a corrupt police officer in that scene? He had no choice but to run.'

'And you kept his secret?'

Heard nodded. 'We travelled about together and it was good whilst it lasted. We got involved with different types of activism and then it ended. I'm a photographer. I needed to keep moving and see different things, get involved in the world again. That's my work. Mikey stayed where he was, happy with things. It suited him.'

'But now he's reappeared?'

'It would appear so.'

Yaz could see how it happened. The world had changed, everyone connected at the push of a button. It wasn't a stretch to imagine Birch getting word of the exhibition, or tracking Heard's career from a distance. Maybe learning of Bella's pregnancy changed something for him. It was enough for him to doss down in the abandoned farmhouse, catch a glimpse of what he thought was his flesh and blood, the next generation on the way.

She took out Jake Shaw's notepad and held it up for a moment before handing it over. 'Jake Shaw wasn't corrupt,' she said. 'He was undercover.'

'Is that so?'

'You don't believe me?'

'I'm cynical enough to believe it. Plenty of snide coppers about in those days.'

Yaz started to frame a question, but decided to leave it there. Heard had confirmed enough. It needed something more to move the dial in her favour. It had to be the truth. It was as simple as that. 'Have a look.' Nell Heard glanced at it, but remained impassive. Her body language couldn't mask the discomfort with what she was reading.

'I told you I'm not a prude,' Yaz said, 'but you were busy with the boys back then. It's all detailed in the notes.'

'That's none of your business.'

Yaz agreed. 'It's not, but it changes things.' It was all there in the notepad. Nell Heard had been sleeping with Conrad Knott too. Jake Shaw had detailed it.

Heard closed the notepad and tossed it back to her. 'Why have you come here, Yaz?'

'What does that mean?'

'It's a simple question.'

It wasn't one with a simple answer. Too much had happened to her. 'I want the truth,' she settled for saying, even if she was scared of it.

'What do you do when the truth is just too damaging? What do you do if the truth might hurt the wrong people? Or if it hurts yourself more?'

'It still remains the truth, doesn't it?'

'You really want to do this, Yaz?' Heard was defiant. 'Are you sure?'

'It's the deal I signed up for, right? I'm going to tell the story and tell the truth. If you won't speak to me, I'll have to speak to Bella.'

'Why don't you talk to your mate, Kerri Lewis?'

'My mate?'

'She was at the raves. Did she tell you that? I know she's pulling your strings.'

They both turned as they heard the front door open. Bella walked into the room. If Bella had heard what they'd been talking about, she didn't acknowledge it.

'The farmhouse is on fire,' Bella said, out of breath. She looked from her mother to Yaz, trying to work out what was going on. 'I saw two men go inside,' she said.

'They went in together?' Yaz asked. She was on her feet, ready to move. She'd set things in motion. It was on her.

Bella shook her head and said not. 'Only one of them came back out.'

FORTY-EIGHT

Yaz dumped her mobile and ran for the stairs at the foot of the hill as quickly as she could, not stopping to look behind. *Two men went in, only one came out.* Mikey Birch and Conrad Knott. One of the two men was Bella's father. Jake Shaw's notepad confirmed as much. Shaw had seen Knott and Heard having sex, Knott abusing his position as an undercover police officer. He hadn't just crossed the line, he'd trampled so far past it, it was out sight. It was a career-killer in its own right, something he wouldn't be able to shrug off. There'd be no political promotion for him now, or ever. There was every chance he'd find himself involved in a court case.

It was personal, though. If Conrad Knott had fathered Bella, it meant Yaz had another sibling. It was a thought that made her stop for a moment, grab for the railing at the bottom of the steps leading up to the farmhouse. The alternative was that Mikey Birch was Bella's father, coming back because he thought he was about to become a grandfather. Yaz had no idea how much of the conversation Bella had heard in her mother's cottage. All kinds of things needed to be said, but events were overtaking them. Yaz knew it was on her; she'd set it up and made it happen. Actions always had consequences. Starting to climb the steps, only Nell Heard knew the truth. It had to be finished, even if no one wanted her to do it. Everyone was sitting on murky secrets.

Reaching the top of the steps, Yaz leaned over, gulping in the cold air. Staring across at the farmhouse, she could see smoke spiralling into the night sky. The fire in the farmhouse was starting to take hold, flames dancing behind the front windows, the smoke wafting through the air forcing her to cough.

Trying to keep her distance, Yaz headed to the rear of the property and the door she'd used before. Pulling the sheet metal back, the heat from inside immediately hit her, the roar of the fire forcing her to take a step backwards. It was tempting to leave and wait for the emergency services to arrive, but Birch and Knott had gone inside because of decisions she'd made. Walking away wasn't an option.

Regrouping and stepping inside, she lifted her arm to her face, trying to acclimatise to the environment. There was no immediate danger in the kitchen area, but the fire was starting to spread fast. Lowering her arm and squinting, she assessed what she was looking at. The kitchen was empty. Moving further into the farmhouse, it became darker and more difficult to navigate. It was putting herself into more danger, knowing it would be all too easy to become disorientated, even though she knew the layout from previous visits. Coughing again, Yaz started to back out in the direction of the door, knowing she had to get out of the place before it overwhelmed her too.

But she couldn't leave. Closing her eyes, she moved forward again through the kitchen, inching her way into the front room. Trying to shelter against the worst of the smoke, she opened her eyes and glanced down to see the body on the floor. Lying on their front and in dark clothes, it was too dark to see who it was. It was instinct to bend down and search for a pulse. Trying to focus and not panic, the fire roared louder in her ears, closing in. It wouldn't be long before it consumed the rest of the farmhouse. Coughing again and with her eyes stinging, Yaz found a faint pulse. The man moaned, a flick of his leg confirming he wasn't unconscious as she had first thought. She blinked and opened her eyes again, wanting to see who it was, but the smoke was too strong to see through. Birch or Knott, it didn't matter. The truth wasn't dying on her in the farmhouse.

Grabbing at the man's feet, she pulled him along the floor and out of the room. Grunting, it was hard work, falling backwards as she made her way to the kitchen. Reaching the room, Yaz fell onto the floor before rolling onto her front, gasping for air. Pulling herself back up and taking a deep breath, she knew they needed to be clear of the building before it was too late. Concentrating on the job in hand and steeling herself for another big effort, Yaz closed her eyes and dragged the body by the feet again, manoeuvring around the corner of the kitchen units.

Eyes closed and focused, one last effort and they were at the rear door of the farmhouse, the effort making her cry. Feeling around the edge of the door, she shoved it open, the cold night air thumping around her face. She smiled, drawing it in. Hearing the roar of the fire behind her, it wasn't over. Dragging the prone figure clear of the farmhouse, the terrain became rougher and wet. Clear of the house, Yaz fell backwards onto the grass. Her eyes watered, her mouth tasted of smoke and the smell of the fire was lodged in her nose. Letting her breathing settle, she wanted to scream. Instead, she drew herself back up and stared at the sky for a moment, still greedily drawing the air in, no sight or sound of the emergency services. The man next to her on the grass coughed and started to shuffle and moan, alive, but in pain. *Two men went in, one came out.* As carefully as she could, she grabbed at the man's jacket and rolled him over onto his side. The man's face was cut and marked, dried blood congealing. His clothes were damaged and ripped, probably more damage she couldn't see. His hair fell down over one eye. She was staring at Mikey Birch.

FORTY-NINE

Pushing herself up, Yaz didn't know where to start. When she'd started recording the podcast, Mikey Birch was supposed to be long dead and buried. She watched him roll over onto his back and stare up at the sky in serious discomfort, his breathing uneven and ragged. 'You best start talking.'

'Who are you?' he asked.

'Your fairy godmother.' She put him in the picture. 'Your former girlfriend is a mutual friend.'

Birch looked at her before closing his eyes. 'Carolyn told me about you.'

'I listened to your voicemail.' He didn't respond. They both knew. She changed the subject. 'Why did you attack me in the farmhouse a few nights ago?'

'I had no idea who you were, or what you wanted.'

'Doesn't matter now,' Yaz said. Pointing back at the building, she had a more pressing question that required an answer. 'I want to know what happened in there.' When he didn't respond, she gave him a prompt. 'I just saved your life. I'd say you owe me.'

He grimaced before speaking, accepting the point. 'We had a disagreement.'

'Who?' She leaned in, wanting to hear it properly. 'Say his name.'

'Conrad Knott.' He shifted his gaze, settling on her. 'But you know that already. You set it up.'

She'd called Carolyn Seymour and insisted she pass the message along to Birch that they were going to meet. She'd also called Knott and made similar demands. She'd given them both the location of the farmhouse.

Blood started to spread around Birch's leg, leaking through his jeans. Yaz shuffled up on the grass. Looking around, there was nothing she could use as a makeshift bandage, nothing to stop the flow with. Taking her jacket off and trying to ignore the cold, she turned her back on him and removed her t-shirt. It was all she had. Forcing his hand to hold the folded-up t-shirt, it would maybe absorb the worst of it. He screamed as she tried to help. 'Shut the fuck up,' she shouted back. 'I'm doing what I can.' Listening, she could hear the faint sound of sirens beyond the sound of the farmhouse burning. She put her jacket back on, trying to stay as warm as she could.

'The confession on the voicemail is bullshit, isn't it? You didn't murder Jake Shaw. You were hoping it would stop me in my tracks and that I'd back off.' She looked at him, knowing it was the truth. It had never rung true or made sense once she'd thought about it properly.

'I've already died once. I can die again.' His smile turned to a grimace as the pain hit. 'Ask your questions.'

'You saw the photograph of yourself online? The one Nell Heard had up in her exhibition?' The one showing him playing with Bella, she held back from saying.

Birch nodded his agreement. 'I came back.'

'You were hanging around the village, living in the farmhouse? You watched Bella at work in the pub?'

'I couldn't stop myself, but Nell paid me a visit, told me I wasn't welcome.'

'Maybe you should have taken the advice and left?'
'Not this time.'

'Why did you run back then?'

'Why do you think?'

She glanced at her t-shirt he was pressing against his wound, more blood.

'I wasn't going down for it.' He shuffled around on the grass, trying to find a comfortable position.

'You disappeared into a network of New Age Travellers?'

Birch nodded his agreement. 'We knew a lot of people, good people. There were always raves going on and I managed to join in.'

'It must have been tough?'

'At first, maybe. I left everything behind, but what was the alternative? I wasn't going to let them fit me up for it. Killing a cop? I wouldn't have seen the outside world again.' He shook his head. 'It was easy enough to disappear back then before cameras and the Internet.'

'Probably helped that no one really wanted to find you?'

'Out of sight, out of mind.'

'Letting them find your finger was a nice touch.'

Birch managed a smile. 'That was impulsive of me, but it boxed off the story nicely for them, gave them something to find. I knew the flat they'd find it in was linked to people I knew. Be easy enough for the police to add it all up and get the answer they wanted.'

'Did Carolyn help with that?'

He shook his head. 'That was me. I had a friend who patched it up for me afterwards. It was a small price to pay if they were happy to think I was dead.'

'The murder weapon was found in your flat, though.'

Birch managed a laugh. 'You'll be telling me you still believe in Father Christmas next.'

She looked up at the sky knowing she believed his explanation of events. 'Carolyn was a better friend to you than you were to her.' She let her words hang there.

Birch shuffled again, anger evident in his eyes. 'You think you know it all?'

'I don't know as much as I thought. Maybe you were onto something back then.'

He understood what she was saying and calmed back down. 'I hope you were out at the lockdown raves? I liked reading about them. Say what you like, but it shows some defiance and spirit. Why should the young constantly pay for the mistakes of their elders?'

Yaz nodded and let him talk. Glancing at the blood pooling on the t-shirt he was holding, it was important to keep him engaged and talking. 'Conrad Knott did this to you?'

'Because of you and your podcast.'

'What did he tell you?'

'What do you mean?'

'About me.'

'You?' Birch looked genuinely surprised by the question. 'Why would he tell me anything about you?'

'Because he's my father.'

Birch chewed the revelation over before speaking. 'There's a thing,' he eventually said.

They fell silent for a moment lost in their own thoughts, watching the fire spread in the farmhouse, the heat in the air increasing. The structure continued to groan, slowly turning in on itself and moving closer to collapsing. 'Tell me about Dale Harker and the drugs at the raves? You two set up *Bliss* together.'

Birch shuffled around again finding a more comfortable position. 'You don't believe all that? Drugs were a part of the raves, obviously, and things got a bit heavy, but they weren't key. Not to me. I was there to have a good time.'

'But they were part of it all?'

'You should speak to Dale Harker about that shit.' He winced as he looked down at the t-shirt.

'He's done well for himself.'

Birch managed a smile. 'You can say that again.' He shuffled again looking to find a more comfortable spot. 'He got involved with some bad people, though he did make some serious money and used it wisely to reinvent himself. I don't care. His life and choices are of no interest to me.'

Yaz thought about that, knowing it was the truth. Harker didn't want this story back in front of people for his own selfish reasons. He didn't want Mikey Birch telling the truth. But for all that, the man wasn't a murderer. Jake Shaw's notepad had made it clear she'd been wrong about that. Glancing at him again, he needed to go to hospital. The sirens she could hear were growing louder. Standing up, there was no sign of any vehicles in the distance. There was still a little bit of time left. She looked back down at him. 'Talk to me about Jake Shaw.'

Birch smiled. 'We all knew what he was. For a start, the undercover police were a few years older than we were and they always dressed like your grandad. They stood out like sore thumbs at the raves. It was a nonsense. They were doing their jobs, I guess, but it was only because the media whipped it up into something it wasn't. They didn't want to be there anymore than we wanted them watching us.'

'You spoke with him, though?' The look on his face confirmed what his girlfriend had told her, what she'd read in Shaw's notepad. Things were becoming clearer. 'You cooked something up together, didn't you? You were both going to make a move against Conrad Knott.' Yaz slowed her thinking down, angled herself away from Birch and processed what she knew. How it all fitted together. It was about holding an insurance policy. Birch had wanted his freedom, nothing more. Drugs and money had always been a red herring. 'You knew about Knott and Nell.' It had always been about something else entirely.

'I had to know.'

She sat back down on the grass. 'About Bella?'

'That might be my grandchild she's carrying.' Birch screamed out in pain, squeezed tighter on the makeshift bandage.

'I need to know the truth,' he said.

'That makes two of us.'

The sirens were closing in on the farmhouse. Fumbling around in her coat pocket, she took out the keys to Kerri Lewis's BMW and held them out to him, explained where he'd find the vehicle parked up. She pulled them back as he reached. 'If you take them, we're not finished, right? You have to talk to me for my podcast. *We* finish this.'

FIFTY

Hurrying back down the hill, Yaz knew she'd just made a big call. Her story depended on Mikey Birch, yet she'd let him disappear again. He'd done it once and there was nothing to say he wouldn't do it again. It was an instinctive decision, one she'd live or die by. Catching her breath at the bottom of the steps, she collected her mobile and made the call.

'I've seen social media,' Knott said, answering. 'You've just made the biggest mistake of your life.'

'I'm giving you one last chance to tell me the truth for the podcast.'

Knott laughed. 'Your podcast? You're well past you making demands. You're a little girl playing with the grown-ups. What do you think is going to happen here?'

'You'll have to resign by the time I've finished with you. That's for a start.'

'No one resigns these days, do they? This is why you'll always be small time. You can't control yourself and you've let it become personal.'

'Fuck you.'

'You've lost the plot, Yaz. Calm yourself down and think rationally. Take the job in London and go.'

'Fuck you,' she repeated, this time with more force. 'And fuck your threats.' He was trying to needle her, make her lose her cool, but it wasn't going to happen. 'We need to finish this, me and you. Where are you?'

Knott paused before answering. 'I'm at the exhibition.'

Yaz killed the call and pocketed her mobile. Staring at the outline of the hall as it stood in darkness, she drew in the cold air before making her way closer towards it, no sign of any activity inside. The hall stood well away from the village's cottages and handful of shops, it's only pub. Not even the sirens were enough to get people out of their cottages. She fired off a quick text message to the one person who might be willing to help her. Kerri Lewis had told her you had to decide who you trusted. It was an essential part of the job. She was taking a gamble on top of another gamble.

Heading down the side of the hall, Yaz looked for a hiding place and emptied her pockets of what she didn't need before moving back toward the front. It was the best plan she had. Approaching slowly, she nudged at the village hall door with her foot and opened it just enough to create a gap to slip through. Setting the voice recording app going on her mobile before placing it into her pocket, she stepped inside.

The floorboards squeaked underfoot as she walked the perimeter of the hall, her back to the wall, alert and on edge. The door behind her locked, the lights powered on, forcing her to momentarily shield her eyes. Quickly lowering her arm again, Yaz looked at the body on the floor in the middle of the room. *Another body.* This time the body was definitely dead, blood around the head slowly trickling outwards. No movement, no sign of breathing.

'Good of you to join the party, Yaz. Seems we're getting everything off our chests tonight.'

Yaz turned to look at Conrad Knott before her eyes went back to Nell Heard on the floor. 'You killed her.' He'd gone one better than with Mikey Birch. She felt sick, her head spinning. She reached out for the wall behind her to regain some balance, swallowing down her disgust and fear.

'Why the surprise, Yaz? It was always going to end this way after you brought things back up again.'

'It's my fault?' She couldn't look at the man. 'You piece of shit.' Words weren't enough.

'You should direct your anger at Mikey Birch.'

'Is that so?'

'He did this.'

She laughed at his lies, unable to stop herself. It also couldn't be true, given she'd dragged the man out of the burning farmhouse after leaving Nell Heard behind in her house. The timeline didn't work. Instead of laying it out, she kept quiet. She was in danger and had to be careful. She kept her voice calm, controlling her emotions. 'You abused your position as an undercover detective. You ruined lives.'

'We all ruin lives, Yaz. It's the natural order of things. Sometimes we don't mean to, but in my case, it was my job to do that back then to people who deserved it.'

She couldn't hold the anger back, spitting the words out. 'Nell Heard deserved this, did she?'

'You think you know it all.'

'I know enough.' The arrogance of the man took her breath away, ashamed they shared the same genes.

'In that case, I'd say you should tread very carefully here in case you say something you regret.'

'I don't regret anything.'

'That's a bold statement made with the benefit of youth. Life hasn't tested you, Yaz, it hasn't forced you to make a difficult decision yet. Sometimes, though, decisions are made for the greater good.'

'Sounds like you're trying to justify something to yourself.' She stepped forward, knowing she had to check Nell Heard for a pulse if nothing else. A desperate long shot.

Conrad Knott mirrored her move, blocking off access and pushing her back with a warning. 'Tread carefully here.'

'Or what? I'll end up like her? Like Mikey Birch?' she said, holding his stare, daring him to do something. 'Is that it? Is that what will happen to me?'

'Your words not mine.'

Yaz took a step back as she quickly scanned the space. If he came for her, she was as ready as she could be. She focused back on him, wanting him to talk. 'Mikey Birch reappearing must have been a nightmare for you?' He remained still, staring at her. 'All those years clambering up the slippery pole towards the top of government and it all gets taken away from you.'

'It should have stayed in the past where it belonged,' Knott eventually said.

'What about the future? What does it look like for you? Shall I sketch it out?'

He cut in, laughing. 'You're worried about my future?' He shook his head. 'Mikey Birch did this. That's going to be the official line. Like you, I just happen to find myself here.'

'No one is going to buy your bullshit.' Feeling the mood change, Yaz looked for something that she could use as a weapon, a piece of wood or some kind of tool that a photography exhibition would make use of. She made sure she had his attention again before speaking.

'You think anyone's going to buy the suggestion Mikey Birch did this before finding himself in an abandoned farmhouse that's on fire? You're going to have to come up with a better story.'

'The story is whatever I want it to be,' Knott said. 'Haven't you accepted that fact yet? I have the power and the ability to shape events to fit my narrative. In some ways, it's perfect. Maybe Mikey Birch was trying to blackmail me? Maybe Nell Heard was going to expose him? The simple explanations are often the right ones. Hardly matters if he's dead.'

'Mikey Birch is still alive,' she said, watching Knott process the information.

'He won't get far,' he said, trying to brush it off.

'I gave him my car keys.' She hoped he was in the wind by now, far away. It gave her a fighting chance. They both turned towards the door, hearing someone trying to open it.

'I've just picked up your message,' Bella shouted out through the letterbox. 'Mum?'

Yaz moved for the door, Knott striking out with an arm across her body. He twisted her other arm behind her back before covering her mouth to stop her shouting out. 'Stop there,' he hissed.

She felt her stomach lurch. He'd lured Nell Heard to the hall and then done the same with Bella.

'Your choice, Yaz.' Knott released the hand on her mouth. 'Make the right one.'

'This isn't Bella's fault,' she said, pushing him away, thinking fast. She had to do something. Rummaging around in her pocket, she took out her mobile. 'I dragged Mikey Birch out of the farmhouse and recorded his story.' Yaz held the device out towards him. 'His story can disappear.'

A smile grew on Knott's face when he understood what he was being offered. She knew she would have to stay, but it would spare Bella having to see her mother's body. 'Let her go,' she told him, 'and then wipe it.'

Knott grabbed the mobile and pocketed it, nodded towards the door. 'Get rid of her.'

FIFTY-ONE

Closing the door after sending Bella away, Yaz locked it as Conrad Knott instructed her to do. Walking back into the hall, she stared at her father.

'You murdered Jake Shaw.' The words were out, but he didn't respond, the silence between them sucking the air out of the room. There was no going back, but it was the truth. Knott stared hard at her before picking up a metal bar from the windowsill. She could see blood and worse on it. Her eyes went to Nell Heard's body, making the connection.

'You talk an awful lot, Yaz.'

'You saw a chance to get Jake Shaw off your back and you took it,' she said, looking for confirmation of her theory. 'He was going to blow the whistle on you. An undercover detective making one of the ravers pregnant? Game over.' She laid it out for him. 'Stonegrave was appalled by your behaviour. He'd taken significant risks to go undercover, and you were in danger of blowing it for your own self-preservation.'

'Nature of the beast.'

It was desperate stuff. 'Mikey Birch was worried about the direction the raves were taking, the way Dale Harker was getting into bed with serious organised criminals to sell drugs. Birch and Shaw weren't natural bedfellows, but they both knew which way the wind was blowing and wanted out for their own reasons.'

'You're making it up as you go along.'
'Jake Shaw wasn't corrupt.'
'That's not what the record shows.'
'The record can be changed.'
'Not in the real world.'

'Stonegrave has Shaw's notepad.' She was dangling bait, wanting to see if Knott would bite. There was no need to tell him she now had it.

'It doesn't change anything.'

'Sure about that?'

'You need to ask yourself why he's kept hold of it for so long.'

'He was a coward.' It was the truth, but he wasn't the worst or only one. It was difficult to accept he'd simply retained it over the years and done nothing. It was a lesson in being better herself. The day she turned a blind eye was the day she stopped what she was doing. 'You manipulated the situation and made a cover for yourself.' Yaz took a breath, watched Knott move the iron bar from hand to hand, knowing she was scoring hits. 'You're a piece of shit.' It was all coming out. Her eyes flitted around the room, looking for something she could grab hold of. 'How am I doing so far?'

'You think this is news to me, Yaz? I wasn't the only person Nell Heard was fucking.'

'It was more than fucking. You abused your position.' It didn't need spelling out. An undercover operation that went wrong was one thing. Exploiting a young woman and potentially fathering a child? There'd be no coming back from that for him. It was also nothing to do with any undercover work. They both knew it struck much closer to home than that.

Yaz looked again for something to defend herself with as Knott stepped forward. She took a step away, hoping to make her way towards the table in the corner, seeing a piece of rock being used as a paperweight to hold down a pie of leaflets. It was nearest thing to a weapon that was available. Straightening herself up, ready, she threw another statement out, wanting to keep him off balance. 'You planted the knife that killed Jake Shaw in Mikey Birch's flat. You intended to plant Shaw's notepad, but Stonegrave found it. You didn't see him remove it.' It was a logical conclusion and what Stonegrave had confirmed on the recording he'd left for her. 'You didn't speak about it for so long because it would be mutual destruction if either of you acted.'

She'd heard Stonegrave's voice break up on the recording, his guilt at not doing anything. It still made him a coward, but he'd belatedly done the right thing. It counted for something. She'd already concluded that if you stripped away the rhetoric and the wildly inaccurate contemporary reporting of the rave scene, Mikey Birch hadn't been a businessman. He'd gone into things for the right reasons and rapidly found himself out of his depth. The man had never fitted the profile of a murderer.

Knott pointed the metal bar at her, a grim smile on his face. 'Maybe you should be a detective.'

'Maybe you pushed Stonegrave into the water.' It was another reach, but also another self-evident truth.

'He made his choice.'

It was all the confirmation she needed. It only added to her resolve that he'd account for his sins. 'You made sure the investigation into Shaw's murder went nowhere.' Yaz was thinking about her conversations with Pullman, the retired detective from South

Yorkshire. How she'd backed away when the truth was close to being told.

'You think you know it all.' He jabbed out the metal bar in her direction again. 'What made you so fucking virtuous?'

'It's about the truth.'

'For a shitty podcast no one is going to listen to?'

'For Jake Shaw,' she said, angry. 'For the other people you've murdered.'

'You should have taken my offer when it was on the table, but you didn't stop to think like an adult.'

'I'll take my chances.' It was how he operated. He found weak spots and squeezed. It was how he'd tried to deal with her; carrot and stick from job opportunities to outright threats.

'I've done a lot of good in my life,' Knott said. 'You don't get to judge me.'

'It's over now.'

'It's far from over.'

She watched as Knott processed what she'd said. She was in deep trouble. Her father only saw a threat, nothing else.

Knott stepped towards her. 'You haven't proved anything.'

'You think you get to walk away from this if you kill me?' She'd edged closer to the table and the heavy-looking paperweight. It was far from ideal, but it gave her a chance. Maybe it would only be one shot, but she'd make it count. She would have the element of surprise on her side.

'No one is going to take your word over mine. I'll win.'

That's what it came down to for him; winning. Yaz was edging closer to where Nell Heard's body was on the floor. 'You've deprived a baby of its grandmother.' A thought struck her. Nell Heard had taken confirmation of who the father of Bella was to her grave. The thought slayed her. Knott didn't respond. 'What about its grandfather?'

'That's nothing to do with me.'

'Could be, though. It's you or Mikey Birch.' She locked eyes with him. 'Could be my family too.'

'We're not family, Yaz. Never were, never will be.'

'Not what the DNA will say.'

'That doesn't mean anything, not really. What is it you really want from me? You want money? That's the only kind of relationship we can have.'

'I don't want your money.'

'Your mother took it, though.' He stepped forward, this time with purpose. 'I gave her money to get rid of you, but she lied to me and here we are.'

There was no way she was giving him the satisfaction of knowing the words hurt and felt like a knife being twisted inside her. 'You bastard.' It couldn't stay inside. Yaz leaned towards the table and grabbed at the paperweight, Knott closing the gap between them quickly. He lashed out with the metal bar, striking her in the stomach before she could land the first blow. Falling to the ground, Yaz screamed as the pain spread through her body, reaching every corner and pressure point. Another blow landed, her back feeling like it was folding in on itself. The room swirled as she started to lose any sense of where she was, or what was happening.

Loud sirens stopped the attack, blue lights reflecting off the hall's windows. Oberman had responded to the message and done as she'd asked. She's seen a kindred spirit and rolled the dice, calling it correctly.

The arrival of the local police was enough to buy her a few seconds to roll away and drag herself back into the moment. The pain didn't matter. With Conrad Knott frozen to the spot, momentum was swinging in her direction at last. Her eyes watered, a huge effort needed to pull herself up to her knees.

'It's over for you,' she managed to spit out. They stared at each other, breathing hard. Politician and podcaster. Father and daughter. Knott remained rooted to the spot. The game was up and he knew it. The door to the hall was tried with increasing force, more noise and shouting, the police close to forcing their way inside.

'Fuck you.' Yaz shuffled back against the wall, trying to ignore the pain. 'There's nothing on the mobile I gave you.' She managed a smile, a small victory. 'I always carry two.' The one with Mikey Birch's words on was hidden away safely outside of the hall. 'The one you've got is the one I use for recording interviews with.' Knott froze, the truth dawning on him. Her vision started to swim. 'It's backed up online already and Kerri Lewis knows what to do with it.' Forcing herself to focus, she wanted to remember his face at this moment in time. It was also a lie. Things had moved so fast, she hadn't spoken to Lewis, or anyone else. 'Doesn't matter what happens to me now, what you choose to do. It's all going to come crashing down around you. I promise you that.' She smiled, daring him to do his worst. Everything was on a knife edge. The hate for her in his eyes, father and daughter, couldn't have been any clearer. 'You thought you could threaten me and I'd shut up? You thought you could use my mother as a weapon? You're disgusting.' She smiled. 'You're also naive.'

Watching him head for the door, she forced herself up, steadying herself for a moment before following.

Hitting a worktop unit as she crashed through the kitchen, the door in the far corner was open. Heading towards it, the cold outdoor air hit her in the face. Forcing her to stop, she took a breath. It was pitch black, dense trees and woodland behind the hall. There was no way of knowing which direction Knott had taken off in.

Turning back to the hall, he could run, but his race was over. Hearing noise coming from the front, her first instinct was that the howl had come from an animal. Starting to run, she knew it was human. A young police officer was trying to restrain Bella, stop her from entering the hall. She'd managed to get sight of her mother. Yaz pulled at her, edging them to a safe distance away. They both collapsed against the wall, slipping down it to the floor.

'I know,' Yaz managed to say, fighting another wave of pain. 'But it's going to be ok.' It had to be enough for now.

FIFTY-TWO

Yaz looked out of the hospital window, dawn starting to break through the clouds. The city sprawled out in front of her, still asleep and not yet ready to face the day. She was tired, the adrenaline that had propelled her through the night all but gone, leaving her with little to give. She turned away from the view and watched as Kerri Lewis pulled herself up the bed, trying to make herself comfortable. 'It should have been me.'

'Probably best it wasn't.'

Yaz chewed the suggestion over. It hardly seemed fair or reasonable. 'Conrad Knott attacked you?'

'Probably.'

The situation had weighed on her mind, a puzzle she hadn't been able to initially unlock. Knott had become increasingly desperate to shut her podcast down, taking larger gambles. He couldn't afford to be exposed. Once she'd put the pieces together, the conclusion felt obvious. Once Knott knew Mikey Birch was still alive, he'd made moves to make sure any blame was laid at the man's door, calculating that he'd be driven further underground. It would be taking her story and twisting it for his own ends. It wasn't going to happen now. 'It's all fucked.' It felt like the best summary she could offer.

'You've shaken more loose than I've ever managed.'

'It's not that simple.' Yaz shuffled her chin further down into her coat. Looking away, she took in the drab watercolour prints on the wall, the pile of tatty magazines on the table next to Lewis's bed.

Lewis shuffled up again in her bed, still in physical discomfort. 'The bottom line, though, is you know the truth. You've done good work. It's some effort to keep pushing the story out when you're in here.'

'They insisted I was checked out.' The social media posts she'd pumped out were a holding position, a base camp ahead of the podcast. It was also a coping mechanism. If she continued to work, she wouldn't have to stop and think about what she'd seen and learned. Oberman had taken charge of her, making sure she was treated as a witness, nothing more. It was clear her podcast wasn't going to be welcomed, but she'd made the point that if they couldn't stop a newspaper printing a story, they weren't going to stop her. Deep down, she knew Oberman was on her side, even if she couldn't say as much. It was down to the detective to run with it, get her own career back. Lewis had been right. You had to choose who you worked with.

Yaz walked back over to the window and glanced down. Lights were on in the pharmacy, the same in the newsagent next door. One or two people walked towards the town centre, heads bowed, their body language easy enough to read. The city was dead to her.

'You've done brilliant work, Yaz.'

Dismissing the comment, there were still things that needed saying. 'You were at the rave the night Jake Shaw was murdered.' Pulling up a plastic chair, she wanted to see what response it got. 'Nell Heard told me.' She hadn't time to think about it until now, but she didn't doubt it was the truth.

Lewis nodded. 'I was at the rave.' A pause. 'I was young, enjoying myself.'

'You didn't think that was important information to share with me?'

'I would have lost my job if I'd come clean back then.'

'You lied to me.' Yaz couldn't keep the disgust off her face.

'Not really.'

'Sounds like you were a coward?'

'I agree with you.'

'Good.' The confession was a surprise.

'Truth is, I didn't really see anything, but I carry the guilt of not doing more.'

'What does that mean? You either saw something or you didn't?'

'I saw Mikey Birch with Nell Heard just before it all blew up.'

It left her momentarily speechless, trying to map out the timeline in her head. 'You knew he didn't murder Jake Shaw?'

'I'm not proud of staying silent. I made a promise to myself I wouldn't do it again.'

'Spare me the self-pity.'

'Different times back then. You have to understand it was a battle getting a foot in the door back then. Times weren't changing as quickly as I wanted. If I'd rocked the boat, I would have been finished.'

'My heart bleeds for you.'

'You don't think I've tried to make amends with my work?'

'You could have changed the story if you'd done the right thing.'

'You're better than me. That's the truth. I saw it from the first moment I heard your podcast. You've proved it by not taking the offer from your father, even though it would have given you what you wanted.'

Yaz shook her head, trying to think clearly. Lewis might have a thirty-five year overview of the situation, but she had a fresh viewpoint. She'd looked Stonegrave in the eye and listened to his story, knowing his imminent death had happened sooner than it should have. 'You manipulated me.'

'You're making it sound like something it wasn't.'

'I'm not your puppet.'

Lewis signalled her agreement with the point. 'Just make sure you win here. There'll be plenty of people looking to take credit for your work, so welcome to the real world. Just don't make the same mistakes I did. Take control. It's your story and truth to tell.'

Yaz went to her pocket and took out Jake Shaw's notepad, showing it to Lewis. 'I've photographed it all and backed it up online.'

'You haven't spoken to the police?'

'Not about this.' She'd been thinking about Pullman, the retired detective who'd led the investigation into Shaw's murder, and how she'd refused to help. She'd chosen to look after herself first and foremost. It was a reminder of how the world made you invest up to the point you couldn't do the right thing out of fear. 'I will when I'm ready.'

'How did you get it?'

'I used my initiative.' Back to the window again, she had her own confession to make. 'Like I did with your things.'

'My things?'

'I needed to borrow to them.' She explained how she'd given the BMW to Mikey Birch. Birch had been good to his word, texting the location of where he'd left it, the keys hidden out of sight on top of a tyre. 'It felt like the right thing to do.'

'Quick thinking.'

'He wasn't keen on making his presence known to the police.'

'Not surprising. How was he?'

That was a big question to grapple with, she thought, weighing it up. 'He seems to be at peace with himself.'

Lewis picked up her mobile, checked it again before placing it back down. 'I take it you've seen the news?'

Yaz nodded, knowing Lewis was deliberately not looking at her. Conrad Knott had been found dead in nearby woods. Official news hadn't broken yet, but social media was buzzing with speculation.

'He's your father.'

'Not really.' She'd pushed him and made it clear to him that he was finished. It had been the truth as she'd seen it, no sugar-coating. No regrets. It didn't mean she wasn't suppressing trauma, though. It was Bella she felt all the sympathy in the world for. She was heavily pregnant and now alone. The woman might be her sister. Her father had created a lifetime's worth of chaos and damage for them to deal with. She was thinking about DNA tests, what could be proved that way and via her own story. The truth would come out. It opened up the possibility of the family she'd never had.

She'd been denied a relationship with her brother, unsure if she'd really liked him after they had spoken his bar. The decisions she was making now would have an effect on what there was to salvage. It was too much to think about, too draining. She wanted to think about something else.

'What happens next?' Lewis asked.

'I've got some conversations to have.' There were calls that had to be made, explanations owed to Stonegrave's daughter and Zach. She also had to speak to Jake Shaw's daughter. None of them were going to be easy.

'You've spoken with *Inform*?'

She nodded. There was no way the woman wasn't in the picture. Maneesh Kapoor had been in touch as soon as she'd posted on social media. All she knew was that she wasn't prepared to take the position her father had opened up for her. It was the dream job, but it wasn't one she could accept in good faith. More than that, she'd come to realise that as she'd faced him down, the truth was everything to her. Being able to look herself in the eye and follow her own narrative was what truly counted and what was worth fighting for.

'It's a chance to write important stories, widen your scope,' Lewis said. 'You can make it about anything you want to. It doesn't have to be about cold cases and settling old scores. Make this time count as a positive.'

'It's a big step.' It was easy to dream about when it was such an abstract notion, but it felt different now. It was a big move and an even bigger gamble, but the alternative felt like cowardice. Following the story and uncovering the truth had taught her at least one thing. Working within the mainstream media wasn't going to be a good fit for her. It wasn't going to offer the freedom to satisfy her curiosity. Answering to people wasn't going to happen, clocking in and clocking out, just wasn't going to work.

'You've earned this, Yaz, don't forget that. No one can take this away from you. Others can and will write up the story, but you've got the version that counts. You're being offered the platform to do it.'

Yaz looked Lewis in the eye, one last thing to resolve. 'I was tempted to ignore the email with the photograph of the farmhouse, just delete it.' Lewis wasn't meeting her eye. 'I know you sent it.' It had been something she'd mulled over as she'd waited to be seen by a doctor. It had been a case of reversing the logic of story writing. Instead of asking who wanted a story suppressing, she asked herself who wanted it out there. Who benefitted? It always came back to Kerri Lewis. Maybe it would be a book or a documentary, but she needed something to jumpstart her career. Maybe she also needed redemption after not doing enough all those years ago. Maybe Lewis had kept an eye on the story over the years, and learning Bella was pregnant, figured Mikey Birch may choose to resurface. It was the best guess Yaz had, and it made some kind of twisted sense. 'I should have put it together sooner.'

'What would you have done if I hadn't? Carried on as you were? I'm not going to apologise. I did it because I knew you'd get it and understand.'

It was another thing to be angry about, if she wanted to let it happen. 'Men do bad stuff and people like us clear it up?'

'Don't waste the opportunity this gives you, Yaz.'

There was no chance of that, but before she could crash and sleep, she needed to get the conclusion to the podcast recorded and uploaded before others told the story. The irony of becoming the story wasn't lost on her. Her father had been right about that, if nothing else.

PODCAST EXTRACT – EPISODE SIX

NOT YET UPLOADED

Most of you will have read about what happened at the farmhouse I was sent to via an anonymous email ... you maybe think you know the story via what the mainstream media are saying and what's buzzing on social media ... this, though, is my truth ... I'm recording this as the city wakes up for the day and more of the story emerges ...

It's a difficult thing to talk about ... I've seen things that I previously thought I'd never have to confront head-on ... my father, someone I'm not sure I can even call estranged, really, as we've never had a relationship is dead ... how do I feel about that? The truth is, I don't know ... it wasn't something I remotely expected to have to deal with when I started this story ...

Conrad Knott was about to become a Minister of State, a position of real political power, and putting this podcast together saw things start to unravel for him ... the more I asked questions, the more the truth started to emerge ... Knott is a dangerous man ... the record now shows he murdered to protect his own name and ambitions ... he crossed the line as an undercover detective, engaging in sexual behaviour with a member of the public, something Jake Shaw was set to whistle blow on ... something that would cost him his life ...

But what about Mikey Birch, the man who stood guilty in relation to Shaw's murder for the last thirty-five years? ... I've spoken to him and listened to his story, learned why he ran when the finger of blame pointed in his direction ... Birch was a man with a network to disappear into, the New Age Travellers, and spent many years moving around the country ... he made a decision and stuck to it, something you have to admire ... This was never a story about drugs. The raves Mikey Birch put on in the fields of East Yorkshire were about a young man trying to make something happen and do something positive ... he provided something that shined brightly for a brief period and changed lives ... will he come back now he can assert his innocence? ... part of me hopes he does, but it's not my decision to make ...

Recording this podcast has been a journey about understanding who I am in every sense ... the answer is that I still don't know ... I have a future, though, for what feels like the first time ... I started telling the story not knowing my own capabilities, but they've now been properly tested ... I also need to deal with the fallout that comes from Conrad Knott being my father, both in terms of my relationships with others and my own mental health ... I know it won't be easy ...

All these things mean I have to ask myself if I regret following the story of Jake Shaw, the murdered undercover detective? ... The simple answer is I don't regret anything and this story needed telling ... I'll never regret doing that ...

This is my truth ...

ACKNOWLEDGEMENTS

Luca and all the team at Black Spring Crime Series, as we set out on a new adventure together.

Matthew at Exprimez Literacy Agency for the show of faith when it was really needed.

Nick Triplow and Nikki East, my Hull Noir co-conspirators, for their help and friendship, and for the team effort in keeping the show on the road.

The teams at Hull Libraries and East Riding Libraries for all the ongoing support and help, as well as the brilliant booksellers in region: Julie at JE Books, Nick and Mel at The Rabbit Hole, and Chris at Waterstones Hull.

Alexandra Sokoloff for her brilliant book 'Stealing Hollywood', which made me think harder than ever about the craft of writing. I ripped up a lot of words, but I'm pleased I found it at exactly the right moment.

When searching for the spark that would bring Yaz Moy to life in my mind, I found two. The fearless reporting of Lyra McKee (rest in power) quickly became an inspiration, as did the enduring image of Saffiyah Khan facing down hate during an anti-Muslim demonstration in Birmingham. Thanks and respect.

And last, but obviously not least, my family. Cathy for everything (as always), Alice for almost managing to be quiet for long enough to let me write, my mother and father-in-law too. I'm very lucky.

The Black Spring Crime Series

Curated and edited by the best-selling author Luca Veste, and endorsed by the likes of Lee Child, Mark Billingham, Ian Rankin, and Val McDermid, the Black Spring Crime Series is filled with fantastic reads, waiting to be discovered. From psychological thrillers to historical crime novels, to classic noir, we have something for everyone, with many more to come! Some of our selection are listed below!

A Crime in the Land of 7,000 Islands,
Zephaniah Sole

This psychological literary fiction tells the tale of Ikigai Johnson, a Special Agent working out of the FBI's Portland, Oregon field office, who pledges to bring justice to children abused by a monstrous American in the Philippines. Amidst an expertly accurate police procedural, Ikigai recounts her tale to her eleven-year-old daughter through fantastical allegory.

This is a powerhouse crime thriller written by a serving FBI agent fused with folk tales and the influence of anime. Described by bestselling author Stuart Neville as 'an extraordinary feat of storytelling'.

Jasper's Brood, J.K. Nottingham

It Takes a Killer, To Raise a Killer, To Raise a Killer ... Jasper is a killer. Raised by a man who is not his father, but a serial killer to become just like him. Only, he is different. He wants to help people. The only way he knows how. To be just like him.

Cormac McCarthy meets North-East England in this unforgettable novel, with a fresh and exciting voice from a debut author.

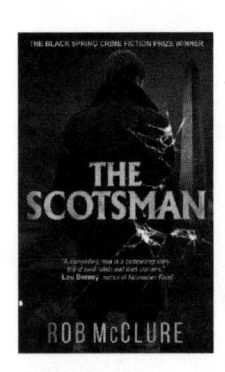

The Scotsman, Rob McClure

Chic Cowan will do anything to find his daughter's killer. Six months ago, Glasgow Detective Chic Cowan received a call that his daughter had been murdered, 4,000 miles away from their home in Scotland. Across the Atlantic Ocean in a United States riven by protests and riots. He is determined to find out the truth.

The Scotsman is the blistering debut from a new Tartan Noir talent. This is Rebus meets *Taken*.

The Salt Cutter, C.J. Howell

Bolivia. 1991. A soldier arrives in the small town of Uyuni. A place people endure rather than enjoy. The soldier knows they're coming for him. Hunting him down so they can deal their own brand of justice. He needs to get out. To make it to the border and escape what is waiting for him. He's prepared to do anything to survive. Even kill.

This is noir fiction at its finest. With characters that you will root for, heartbreak, and breathtaking writing, this is a story that will linger in reader's minds long after you've turned the final page.

Winter of Shadows, Clare Grant

In the midwinter of 1862 in York, a young woman is found dead by the river, her body marked by a sinister act of mutilation. The mysterious death spreads fear, for this is not the first corpse to be discovered. Speculation grows there is a killer stalking the city's medieval streets.

This glorious historical crime thriller, described by Ambrose Parry as, 'hugely atmospheric', introduces the character of Ada Fawkes, the country's only crime scene photographer, who you won't forget in a hurry.